DEVIL'S BARGAIN

A Cass Leary Legal Thriller

ROBIN JAMES

Devil's Bargain

A Cass Leary Legal Thriller

By

Robin James

For all the latest on my new releases and exclusive content, sign up for my
newsletter at:

http://www.robinjamesbooks.com/newsletter/

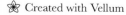 Created with Vellum

Chapter 1

DELPHI, Michigan

"Well, I'd say you've got a winner. Except for the bird poop," Jeanie said.

I stood with my arms tightly folded around me. Mid-march and the brutal Michigan winter we'd had wasn't quite ready to loosen its grip for spring, much to the consternation of some pesky robins who had jumped the gun and crapped all over my brand-new office sign.

Jeanie wasn't wrong. The bold blue paint had barely dried on the sign. The Leary Law Group, P.C. was newly minted and newly moved. A few weeks ago, I'd gotten a lead on a soon-to-be new listing at the coveted corner of Main and Clancy Streets, directly across from the Woodbridge County Courthouse. It hadn't come cheap, but my billings were finally up. It seemed like a good omen. I took the leap.

"I'd like it more if it said Leary and Mills." I bumped her shoulder with mine. Jeanie Mills was the entire reason I went to law school in the first place. She was practically a Michigan institution in and of herself. One of the first and toughest female lawyers in the county, she'd taken me under

1

her wing when my family name and white trash birthright might have dragged me down. But Jeanie was seventy-one now and less than a year from a cancer scare. She'd earned the right to work when and how she wanted. I had to settle for her *of counsel* status on my letterhead instead of a full partnership. She took the office just below mine though. There was still time to convince her.

"I'm proud of you, kid," she said, beaming up at me. By the looks of her, you might not peg her as the bulldog of the family court system. Jeanie was inches shorter than my five foot three. Her hair was still dark, but for a few streaks of pure white at the front.

"I'm proud of you too," I said. "Now let's get the hell inside. It's freezing out here."

I put an arm around Jeanie. A year ago, that simple act would have broken my heart. She had steel in her back, but her cancer treatments had taken more out of her than she wanted to let on. Now Jeanie felt strong, hearty, vibrant again. I got a little choked up and turned my face away from her. She wouldn't like the fuss and hated when I got sappy.

Unfortunately, the lobby wasn't quite as bright and shiny as the sign out front yet. I needed new flooring and a wall for my secretary, Miranda. I wanted her to have her own office for the first time in her life. She was another godsend and victory. I'd poached her out of retirement just like Jeanie. Miranda knew more about legal procedure than most young lawyers and she was sick to death of working for them. I let her run the office how she saw fit and knew her ideas were always right. My next step was finding more support staff to take some of the load of my growing practice off Miranda's shoulders.

"Got anything scheduled today?" Jeanie asked.

"Nope," I said. "Just a few discovery motions to finalize. Then I'll run them over to file."

Jeanie shook her head. "You need a paralegal, Cass. High time you stopped doing that crap yourself."

"I like doing that crap myself," I said.

"You're a control freak. Trust me. I was like you thirty-some years ago. It takes years off your life."

I sighed. We had this argument a lot lately. Over the last year, since leaving my high-powered, big-firm job in Chicago, I'd become a one-man band back here in Delphi. My love for it surprised me most of all.

"I'll think about it," I said. "But it has to be the right person. I'm not in the mood to redo someone else's work. Sometimes it's just easier to do the stuff myself instead of taking the time to teach somebody else what I like."

"Well," Jeanie said. "That's some short-sighted thinking."

I raised a hand to ward her off. We had that particular argument a few times before too.

"Cass," Miranda called out. She was on the stairs. For the time being, my office took up half the second floor of the building. We cleared a conference room in the other half. There was a utility room next to mine that Jeanie wanted to put said mystery paralegal in.

"The sign looks great, Miranda," I said.

Her smile was tight as she came down. I tilted my head. Something was up.

She folded her hands in front of herself in a distinctly formal gesture. It dawned on me we may not be alone. Instinct flared. I crossed the lobby and peered out the window into the back lot. My heart dropped as I spotted the shiny black Lincoln Town Car parked right next to mine. It bore Illinois plates.

"I'm sorry," Miranda said. "He didn't have an appointment. He just kind of barged in when you and Jeanie were outside."

"Mr. Thorne?" I asked. My throat ran dry. What was he doing here?

A year ago, I'd left my job at the Thorne Law Group in Chicago. They hired me just out of law school. I thought it was my dream job at the time. My ticket out of Delphi and a way to escape my past. But the dream turned into a nightmare. I was a mob lawyer. It took me ten years to fully understand the nature of the people I worked for. I had been so close to becoming one of them. Sometimes I worried part of me had.

"Do you want me to call someone?" Miranda asked. She had a look of fear in her eyes. I knew what she was thinking. Exactly who could we call with enough power to get rid of a member of the Thorne family?

"No," I said. "I don't have anything else on the books today. I'll take the meeting. Then I'll get rid of him."

Miranda and Jeanie passed a series of wary looks between them. I gestured to silence Jeanie. Whatever waited for me at the top of those stairs, it was better if I faced it alone.

I took a breath and started up the stairs. Son of a bitch. It was casual Friday. I wasn't expected in court. I was planning to move boxes around in the conference room after lunch so I dressed for it. I wore my hair in a messy bun, no makeup, a big cable-knit sweater that actually belonged to my brother, and jeans. I wanted the armor of a power suit for this meeting.

I stood at the door to my office. My heart thundered as I saw the man sitting in front of my desk in profile. That strong jaw. Straight nose. Broad shoulders beneath an impeccably tailored suit and shoes shined to a gleam. He didn't yet see me. He straightened his sleeve, revealing a gold cufflink.

My brain short-circuited. He looked so much like his brother. For that brief instant, old feelings bubbled to the

4

surface. My palms started to sweat. Then he turned his head and stared at me with cold eyes that were nothing like his brother's at all.

"Liam," I said.

Liam Thorne gave me a devilish smile and rose from the chair. He looked me up and down, not even bothering to hide his scorn. I straightened my back. This was *my* turf, dammit. If I didn't have the power suit, I'd match him with attitude.

"Cass," he said. "Glad to see things are looking up for you."

It was pure sarcasm. I wouldn't rise to the bait.

The man was calm, cold, always calculating. As senior partner for one of the most powerful law firms in Chicago, Liam Thorne was used to dominating every room he entered. His tactics stopped working with me years ago. Until one fateful night when I knew my life was in his hands.

"I told you never to come here," I said. "I'm sorry you wasted a trip."

"Sit down, Cass," he said, his demeanor shifting, becoming more relaxed. Whatever he wanted to talk to me about, I sensed he'd prepared for it for a while. I forgot to ask Miranda how long he'd been sitting here. Jeanie and I had been gone most of the morning and came through the front door. I never heard his car pull up. Liam might very well have been here a long time. There was an empty cup of coffee sitting on the desk in front of him.

I slid into the chair behind my desk, grateful for the relative protection it provided.

Liam was pure alpha dog. I knew he could smell fear. He settled back in his chair as I took mine.

"You've done well for yourself," he said. I couldn't figure if it was a question or a statement.

"I have," I said.

"Your name keeps popping up in the local papers," he said.

I raised a brow. "Since when have you started reading Michigan news?"

He smiled. "I like to keep tabs on my associates."

"I'm not one of them anymore, Liam."

I wanted to tell him we had to cut this short. What I wouldn't give for the excuse of a court hearing to draw me away. But as Liam sat across from my desk giving me that piercing, chilly stare, I knew damn well he'd done that homework too. He likely knew my schedule as well as Miranda did before he came.

He reached down. I noticed for the first time that he had his briefcase on the floor next to his left leg. He pulled two thin files out of the side pocket and placed one on the desk. I looked at it, but didn't touch it.

"I have a client for you," he said.

My heart stopped. Blood made a rushing sound in my ears. I kept my cool, folding my hands on the desk.

"Liam, I don't work for you anymore, remember?"

His eyes went even colder. I swear, the guy was part vampire. I couldn't even see him breathe.

I went just as cold. I'd misjudged this man one too many times. The Thorne Law Group had provided legal cover for his family business for decades. Up until a year ago, I was an integral part of that cover. On the surface, the Thorne family ran one of the most lucrative exporting businesses in the country. But even that was a front for some of their more shady endeavors as one of the most influential families in the Irish mob. While Liam ran the law firm, his brother Killian ran the main business.

Sometimes I forgot how much they looked alike. As I looked at Liam, that familiar set of his jaw, the way he sat rod straight and kept that laser focus on me reminded me so

much of Killian. And I hated that it still stirred a part
of me.

"We didn't leave things on the best terms," Liam said.
"I'll admit that. But loyalty, Cass. That's all I ever asked of
you."

Best terms. If I'd been drinking my own coffee, I might
have spit it right out at that. I still had nightmares about the
last time I saw Liam. He'd driven me to the docks and had
me board the Thorne family yacht. With each step I took, I
believed in my heart I would never see shore again.

"What do you want, Liam?" I said. "I'm not interested in
rehashing old stories. I said I don't work for you. And it's not
loyalty you want from me. It's silence. I've kept up my end.
Your end is you walk out of here and stay the hell out of
Delphi."

He smirked. "Aren't you even a little bit curious?"

"No," I lied.

"Well, let me start over. You seem to be under the
impression I'm making you an offer. The terms of your separation were as clear as I could make them. You get your little
life here, Cass. You get to be the hick lawyer you were born
and bred to be. In exchange, yes, you keep your mouth shut.
But from time to time, it's in my interest to make sure I can
still trust you. This is one of those times. And that's your new
client. I suggest you get yourself up to speed quickly."

"Go to hell, Liam," I said, hating that I let myself lose
that much control. I made a mistake allowing even a second
of the memory from that night at the docks seep in. Liam
wanted me dead that night. He caught wind of the fact that
I'd had a conversation with the FBI about some of the darker
aspects of the Thorne family dealings. They wanted me to
violate my oath and testify against my own colleagues and
clients.

It had gotten too much for me. I'd sold too much of my

soul. There was no way in hell I was walking any of it back. I'd lived through the most frightening moment of my life on the deck of Liam's yacht. Bound and gagged, only a phone call from Killian had saved me. I'd lived through something just as frightening in recent months, but that was different. Liam knew me. His vendetta was personal. And now I knew he wasn't planning to let it go.

"Go home, Liam," I said. "Whatever it is you need, I can't help you. You've wasted your time."

He let out a weary sigh. "Fine," he said. "So I'll explain it. It's what you're good at now anyway. Hopeless cases. Murder trials."

The sound of waves crashing against the side of a boat filled my head. I resisted the urge to rub my wrists. Sometimes, in the quiet, I could still feel the hard plastic zip ties digging into my skin.

Damn it all to hell. I looked. I flipped open the file.

Liam was nothing if not dramatic. The top document in the stack was an 8 x 10 color photo of the murder victim. White male. Thick dark hair. Big brown eyes frozen open in a death stare. His neck was slashed open, cut straight through. He'd been garroted.

"Jesus," I said, flipping the file shut.

"Maybe it's you who should pay more attention to the local news," Liam said. "This one's practically in your backyard."

"What's your angle, Liam?"

"Your client is Theodore Richards. He's been charged with first degree. Like I said, your specialty. This should be a cakewalk for you."

"I'm not interested," I said, sliding the file back to him.

"That's not what I asked you. In fact, I didn't ask at all. I'm telling you. You'll do this. You'll see that Theodore Richards walks."

"It's not happening. Find someone else."

Liam's face changed. It was barely perceptible. But his cheeks flamed a little red. I knew this man. His temper was volatile. I leaned back in my chair. I kept a letter opener in my top drawer. Today I should have brought a gun.

"Don't make me be inelegant about this, Cass," he said. "You know I don't like it."

"Ask me the number of fucks I give," I said.

His eyes flashed. "And I like vulgarity even less."

He pulled his cell phone from his pocket. He pressed one button and set the phone down. Sighing, he put a second thin file on my desk on top of the other.

A tremor went through me. If the first file was some type of carrot, this one was going to be the stick.

"Take a look," he said.

This was another nightmare. I wanted to be anywhere but here at that moment. Somehow, I managed to keep my fingers from trembling as I leaned forward and opened the second file.

My breath caught. It was a picture of another man. This one as familiar to me as my own face. My younger brother Matty was walking to his car at one of the construction sites where he worked. He was unaware of the photographer.

I flipped the picture over. Beneath it was another picture of Matty. It was taken from a greater distance as he sat at a diner just a few blocks from here. He was with his wife, Tina. Even in the still photo, I could tell they were arguing as Matty gestured with his hands and Tina had a scowl on her face.

I turned the next picture and felt sick. It was Matty again. He was in bed, sleeping. Tina slept beside him. It was taken right outside his bedroom window.

"You can't ..."

"Keep looking," Liam said. He sat back and crossed his legs.

I turned the next picture over and the next after that. He had pictures of my older brother Joe in much the same scenarios. One at work as he painted an office building. Another taken from inside Joe's bedroom as he slept, just like the one of Matty. The third took the breath right from my lungs. Joe was waiting in the parking lot, picking my seventeen-year-old niece Emma up from school.

I kept going, knowing what I'd find, but praying I wouldn't. The final photograph was of Emma. It was another shot from across the street as Emma lay on a couch in the arms of a teenage boy I didn't recognize.

I slammed the folder shut.

"I'll kill you. I'll fucking kill you," I whispered, fighting to keep tears of rage from falling. My whole body shook. "If you dare touch my family ... that wasn't our deal."

"Our deal is what I say it is," Liam said. "Circumstances have changed. And you needed a little reminder."

"I've done *nothing* to you. I've kept your secrets. This isn't necessary."

"I think it is," Liam said.

"Killian will never stand for this," I said. The moment the words were out, new terror sparked in my heart. Did Killian know Liam was here? Had he sanctioned this invasion of my family's privacy and bold new threat?

Liam leaned far forward. "Killian isn't the savior you think he is, honey. And you can't keep running to him every time you need something. Not without paying the price. This is your price. You'll take this case. And you'll win it."

"Fuck you," I said. "You've made your point."

He put a hand up. "You have a sister, I believe. And I believe you used my family services to locate her recently. You didn't think that debt would go uncollected, did you? So it's up to you. If you defend Theodore Richards, then you and your family have nothing to worry about. You have twenty-four hours to decide."

Liam rose from his seat and straightened his jacket. "Oh, you should know. Mr. Richards has had some bad luck with his previous lawyer. The man died last week. Your trial is a month away. I look forward to hearing from you by tomorrow night. Don't keep me waiting."

"Get out," I said, my voice lowering to an octave I didn't know I had in me.

He turned and headed for the door. My head was spinning. I didn't want to show it. I knew Liam had the power to do all the things he said and more. The echo of the waves lapping against his family yacht still haunted me.

I thought it was over. I thought we were done. But the cold gleam in Liam Thorne's eyes just before he turned and walked out of my office pierced through me and nearly stopped my heart.

Chapter 2

"YOU WANT to tell us what the hell that was all about?"

Jeanie stood in my office doorway with Miranda just behind her. They'd waited just long enough for Liam Thorne to drive away before pouncing on me. I was still shaking.

"Can you just give me a couple of minutes?" I asked. "I need to make a call."

"I know who that was," Jeanie said. "You planning on expanding the business without telling me?"

"Jeanie, please. Just ... let me deal with something. Then we can talk."

She let out a noise not unlike a growling bulldog. Miranda had a cooler head and pulled Jeanie away. They closed the door behind them and I reached for my cell phone.

It took four rings for Joe to answer. Each one felt like a hammer blow inside my head.

"What's up, little sis?" he asked. I started breathing again.

"Where are you?" I asked.

"What? I'm driving. Heading out to a new job site in Tecumseh. What's going on? You sound weird."

Liam's thin file with the intrusive pictures of my brothers and niece was still on my desk. I resisted the urge to open it again. Once I heard Matty's voice after this call, I planned to shred the damn thing. Of course, Liam had the JPEGSThe one picture of Emma was bad enough. I hoped to God there was nothing more compromising. Though Liam hadn't voiced that particular threat, I knew he could blast pictures of her all over the internet with one click.

"I just ... I don't know. I had a weird dream. Just wanted to hear your voice. You're good? Emma's good?"

"Uh ... yeah. She's at school. Her car's got an oil leak. Matty and I are going to figure it out later this afternoon. I dropped her off."

I squeezed my eyes shut. One of Liam's pictures might have been from this morning. I didn't know what to tell him. Did Liam have someone tailing my family members as we spoke? Or was this just his way of making sure I knew how easily he could get to them? Instinct and my past dealings with Liam told me it was the latter. It was a bargaining chip. If I did what he asked, he'd stand down.

I ran my hand over the second file folder with the crime scene photos in them. More than likely, Liam had already left a copy of the main case file with Miranda. He didn't want me to waste a second getting into the case. If I decided to take it, that was.

"Good," I said. "That's good. I mean that Emma's got you guys to help her out."

I knew I wasn't fooling my brother. I tried to feign a more breezy tone. But there was nothing I could do to mask the oddness of my call in the first place. We never really called each other just to check in. Joe and Matty mostly just treated my house as theirs and more often than not, I'd find them camped out on my couch or raiding my fridge just about every other day. I liked it that way.

"Okay," Joe said. "You sure there's not something …"

"I've got to go," I said. "Why don't you guys come over for dinner tonight? I'll make potato soup or something. We haven't had it in a while and the weather's perfect for it."

"Tonight's a no go. It's my anniversary."

"What? Oh. Right. You remembered? Gold star, brother."

"Yeah. I'm taking Katy to this Glenn Close movie she wants to see. But you might want to call Emma. I don't know what she's got going on but I bet she wouldn't turn down your soup. I kind of like the idea of her spending time with you tonight anyway. She's got this new boyfriend I'm not all that crazy about."

I winced, envisioning the pictures in the file on my desk. Emma was just seventeen. I knew Joe wasn't naive enough to think she couldn't be sexually active. He didn't need photographic proof to worry more than he already did.

"I'll call her," I said. "Or tell Katy to pass along the invite when you talk to her. Happy Anniversary."

"Yeah," he said. "Why don't you call Emma and pretty much don't take no for an answer? She's at her mother's this week. That's part of the problem. Her mother is too worried about trying to be Emma's best friend. She lets her get away with murder. I'd appreciate it if you could maybe talk to her about this new guy. His name is Wade something or other."

I let out a sigh. "I don't know, Joe."

"She doesn't listen to Katy. The whole stepmother thing … I just …"

"Okay," I said. "I'll text her this afternoon. Just, take care of yourself, okay? Are you picking Matty up after work?"

"Uh. That's the plan."

"Great," I said. I heard movement downstairs. Jeanie had

to be ready to tear her hair out waiting for me. I'd put her off for a few minutes, but I knew that was the only grace I'd get. Joe was okay. Emma and Matty were okay. Now it was up to me to make sure they stayed that way.

"I'll talk to you later, Cass. I gotta run."

"Okay ... but promise ..."

Joe had already clicked off. Liam's men were good. The best at what they did. Joe would have zero clue that anyone had been watching him. It sent a chill down my spine.

I put the phone down and slid the other file in front of me. There were only two things in it. The 8x10 photo of the dead man, and a two-page charging document.

Just like Liam had said, the accused, Theodore Richards, had been charged with first-degree murder. As I read the information, my blood ran cold.

The victim's name was Mark Channing. It was familiar. There wasn't much detail in the charging document. The victim's body was found almost six months ago on a new home construction site in Gross Pointe Farms. Just like the photograph showed, he'd been garroted with a piano wire. The police couldn't determine if he'd been killed or merely dumped there so they had no choice but to indict in Wayne County.

I couldn't tell much from the sparse details listed, but it looked like they tied Richards to the crime with carpet fibers found on the body and the testimony of a confidential informant who'd seen him in the area of the victim's home the night before he went missing.

"God, that's thin," I said. Already my lawyer's brain was churning with all the ways I could raise reasonable doubt.

"Channing," I whispered. "Why do I know that name?"

And what was so damn important about the accused that Liam Thorne wanted to make sure he got off? None of it could be good. Liam said Richards's previous lawyer was dead. Why? How?

A soft knock on the door pulled me out of my head. Jeanie stepped inside. "We need to talk," she said. "I'm done waiting."

I gave her a nod and pointed to the chair where Liam had been sitting. "Sit down," I said.

"Are you okay?" she asked me. Of all the people in my life, I'd confided the deepest parts of my past to Jeanie. But I hadn't told her everything. Much of it was still protected by attorney-client privilege. She could guess at most of it though. The Thorne Law Group had been in the business of laundering money for the Thorne family enterprises. They had risen to prominence in the Irish mafia two generations ago. Killian and Liam had expanded the business and brought it to Chicago twenty years ago. Their reach was long. Their associates deadly. And I had direct knowledge of their financial infrastructure. The bitch of it was, for the last decade, Killian had been trying to turn the business entirely legitimate. It was Liam who resisted.

"So, what does he want from you?" Jeanie asked. I couldn't lie to her. I couldn't so much as evade the question. Last year, in a custody trial over my niece, the whole town got to hear about my relationship with the Thornes.

I slid the one file across the desk and put the other in a drawer. Jeanie didn't miss it. Her lips pressed into a grim line. She took the file and opened it. Her eyes darted back and forth as she looked at the crime scene photo. She tilted her head and turned the picture. Recognition came into her expression. Her eyes widened and she looked up at me.

"Holy shit. Is that Mark Channing?" She leafed through the charging document.

"Why do I know that name?" I asked her.

Jeanie let out a low whistle. "Well, I'll be damned. How the hell is he connected to the Chicago mob?"

I picked up my phone and opened a search browser.

"Mark Channing," Jeanie repeated. "His murder made the national news last fall, Cass. He worked for the U.S. Attorney's office out of Detroit, I think."

She was right. The first news article had the details of his murder. The picture staring back at me from my phone screen was a stark contrast to the grisly death photo Jeanie held. In life, Mark Channing had movie-star good looks with thick black hair, piercing eyes, and a thousand-watt smile. And I was just looking at his stiff government ID photo.

"Shit," I said. "I sort of remember. Yes. He was a federal prosecutor."

"He was more than that," Jeanie said. "I heard he was being groomed for higher office. He was on a short list for a congressional appointment. They were looking at him to fill Bob Delaney's seat. He died of colon cancer last year."

"Dammit," I said. "This wasn't just a murder, it was an assassination."

"Right," Jeanie said. "So what the hell is Liam Thorne doing with this file? And why is he giving it to you?"

"He wants me to take the case," I said. "The accused is somebody by the name of Theodore Richards. I have no idea what his connection is to Thorne. That's the God's honest truth. I don't remember his name popping up in anything I did for them."

"Say no," Jeanie said, abruptly closing the file. "Don't touch this, Cass. Mark Channing has pretty much been deified since his murder. I'm surprised you didn't recognize the name right away."

"He was murdered last October," I said. "I was kind of in the middle of another major murder trial at the time."

Jeanie raised a brow and nodded. "Fair point. Still. This can't be worth it to get involved in."

I didn't answer right away. I tried to keep my face neutral, but Jeanie knew me too damn well. The color drained from her face and her shoulders dropped.

"He's not really asking, is he?"

"Jeanie …"

She slammed a fist against the desk. "Dammit. What's he got on you? Did he threaten you?"

I wasn't sure what to do. I couldn't outright lie to Jeanie. She'd see right through it. At the same time, I didn't want her going off half-cocked. She didn't understand Liam's nature the way I did. She'd only put herself in his crosshairs too.

"He's calling in a favor," I said, sticking to as much of the truth as I dared for now.

She shook her head. "Vangie," she said. "He expects you to pony up for using Thorne resources to find your sister last year. Is that it?"

Jeanie Mills really didn't miss a trick. "Something like that, yes."

"So what? Vangie's back where she belongs. She's okay. He can't expect to drag you back into that firm over something like this. Tell him to go to hell. What's the worst he can do?"

The moment she said it, Jeanie's eyes narrowed with understanding. She sat back hard in her seat. "Shee-it."

"Precisely," I said, grateful she understood my dilemma without me having to pull out the threatening photos of my family.

"What are you going to do?" she asked.

"I don't know. I honest to God don't know. I need to see the full case file. Liam says the trial's scheduled for next month."

"What? No way. Even if you consider this, we get it adjourned so you can get up to speed."

"Something tells me I won't get a whole lot of cooperation from opposing counsel on this."

"It's in Wayne County?" she asked. "What judge? Who caught it for the prosecution?"

"I don't even know that yet. I don't think it'll matter much. Even though he was federal, the Wayne County prosecutors are going to feel like he was on their team. Nobody's going to do me any favors."

Jeanie let out a bitter laugh. "Shit, Cass. You do have a rare talent for picking cases that make most of the world hate you."

"Thanks. I'll get a tee shirt made."

"So, worst-case scenario, you gear up for a murder trial you don't want to take. Representing a client who, considering who's backing him, is probably guilty as hell. And if you say no, what happens?"

"Jeanie, I gotta take this one step at a time."

"What happens, Cass? Don't bullshit me."

I dropped my shoulders. There was no putting her off. I reached into my desk drawer and pulled out the other file. Jeanie grabbed it from me. I couldn't watch her as she looked at the photos of Matty, Joe, and Emma. Guilt washed over me. I did this. My past associations put all of us in this fix. I'd give anything to undo it.

Jeanie's face turned red. She slammed the file shut and tossed it on the desk. She chewed her bottom lip and kicked the leg of her chair with her heel.

"Say something," I said, not realizing until that moment how badly I needed her counsel. And I hated that my actions could put her at risk too.

"If you take this case, does it end? Are you paid in full with Thorne?"

"I hope so," I said.

"Dammit," she said.

"What? Tell me what you're thinking."

Jeanie made me wait a full minute before she finally rose from her chair and leaned over the desk. "As much as I hate everything about this, I think you've got no choice. I don't know these people like you do, but I know enough."

"You're saying I should take the case?"

Jeanie's eyes flashed. "God help us both, but yeah. And I'm saying you damn well better win!"

Chapter 3

LATER THAT AFTERNOON, I did the one thing I swore I would never try to do again. I called Killian Thorne.

There's a saying that when you find yourself in a hole, the first thing to do is stop digging. As the phone rang, I knew it was the equivalent of picking up the biggest shovel I could find. But Killian wasn't Liam. No matter how much Liam postured, Killian was the real power behind the Thorne family.

I made the call as soon as I left the office for the day, sitting behind the wheel with the engine running. If Jeanie knew what I was about to do, she might find a literal shovel and beat me over the head with it.

The call went to voicemail and my heart sank. This was Killian's private number. As far as I knew, only a handful of people even had it. And he would know if I was the one calling, something had to be wrong.

"Killian," I said. "It's Cass. We need to talk. I ... you know I wouldn't be calling you if it wasn't important. You just ... you need to call me back as soon as you get this."

I clicked off the call. Shit. If I was going to defeat the

monster that was Liam Thorne, I'd need to bring in the devil himself. No matter what it cost me, I would protect my family.

I waited a full minute, but Killian didn't call back. That was strange. In the history of our relationship, I couldn't remember ever even having to leave a voicemail for him. He always answered. Always. God. Had something changed? I couldn't let myself believe that Killian endorsed Liam's actions. Killian was different. He was ...

A blaring car horn snapped me out of my head. I pulled up to the parking lot exit. Another car behind me waited for me to make my turn. I waved a hand and headed for the intersection.

Joe had left me two messages since we last spoke. He wanted me to go straight to his ex Josie's to pick Emma up. I wasn't looking forward to it. Josie more or less blamed my brother for everything that had ever gone wrong in her life. She came from the *good* side of town, from a well-to-do family. When she started seeing my brother their senior year in high school, it had been the town scandal. Joe Leary was trash as far as everyone who mattered was concerned. When Josie got pregnant on prom night, they pretty much tried to run my brother out of town on a rail.

He'd tried to make a go of it with their daughter, Emma. Joe worked two and three jobs making sure Emma never wanted for anything. But he and Josie were just too different. She cared too much what other people thought and it poisoned their relationship. Even through all of that, Emma was an amazing kid. Everything Josie put him through was worth it because of Emma.

I pulled into Josie's driveway. She lived in a blue-and-white two-story on Beach Street. It was a nice part of town. Joe paid her mortgage most months even though he wasn't legally required to. I knew it caused tension between him and his current wife, Katy. But Katy was a good, solid influence on my brother. And she loved Emma as if she were her own.

Josie, on the other hand ...

I heard glass break as I killed my engine. Shouts and a scream came from inside the house. My heart raced as I scanned the street. But there was no one around. Not even a single car parked in the street in front of Josie's house.

I slammed the car door shut and made my way up the walk.

"You're out of your mind!" It was Emma's voice.

"You ungrateful little brat!" Josie screamed back at her. Her voice sounded ragged. She was slurring her words.

I didn't bother to knock. I let myself in the front door. The foyer opened to the living room and what I saw inside made my heart sink. Josie was a lot of things, but she had always been neat and meticulous about her person and her surroundings. The house was in shambles. She had mail piled up on the floor. I stepped through empty potato chip bags and pop cans on the way to the kitchen. The whole place had a sour smell to it. She had dirty dishes piled up in the sink and stacked high on the counters.

"Emma?" I called out.

"Oh fine!" Josie screamed when she saw me. She and Emma squared off in the living room. Josie herself was a shock. She wore a dingy tee shirt and sweat pants. Her hair, normally styled in a chic bob, stuck out in peaks. Her eyes were bloodshot and slightly out of focus.

She was on something. I didn't need to get any closer to see it.

"Josie," I said. "Is everything all right?"

"Everything is not all right," she answered. She was out of breath. Her face flamed red. "This little brat thinks she knows everything. She thinks she can just come and go as she pleases. She thinks she can back talk. I see you, Emma. I'm not an idiot. I know what you're doing behind my back."

Emma threw her hands up. My niece had her backpack slung over her shoulder. Her blonde hair whipped around her as she paced in front of her mother. Emma had been crying.

"Look at her!" Emma said. "You're not fooling anyone, Mom. I'm done. You're crazy."

Josie's eyes widened. God. I knew that look. She raised a hand and took a faltering step toward Emma. I acted on instinct and got between them. Josie's nostrils flared. She was sweating.

"You're no better," she said to me. "You storm in here and you think you can judge me!"

"Josie, I'm not judging you. I'm just here to get Emma. We talked about this, remember? I texted you. Emma's going to come over tonight for dinner."

"Did he put you up to this?" Josie yelled. "That piece-of-shit brother of yours has been trying to cheat me for months. I will *not* stand here and take this. You tell him. I will sue his ass for everything he's worth."

Emma rolled her eyes and made a "crazy" gesture, circling her index finger around her ear. I put a hand up to silence her. Antagonizing Josie wasn't going to do either of us any good.

"Joe isn't why I'm here," I said. "And whatever you've got going on with my brother, that's between the two of you. I'm taking my niece to dinner. You were fine with it a couple of hours ago. Take some time to yourself, Josie. It looks like it'll do you both some good. Emma's going to spend the night at my place tonight."

I was probably throwing lighter fluid onto the situation by suggesting it. But I'd be damned if I was going to let

Emma stay in this house tonight. Whatever the root of their problem, they were both in need of a cooling-off period.

"Take her!" Josie screamed. "Get her out of my damn sight!"

Emma played it tough, but I knew her mother's words hurt. God. Seventeen was hard. Just standing here in the middle of this brought back memories I didn't like to think about. It was one of the reasons I'd run as far away as I could from Delphi when the time came.

"Come on," I said to Emma. "Just get your coat."

"You think it's so easy!" Josie was screaming at the top of her lungs and pretty much snorting. I was worried about her. She had her issues with my brother, but I knew deep down, she had a good heart. She was just one of those people whose parents had told her how amazing she was her whole life. Which is a good thing, unless it's all you believe. Now she had a tendency to blame everything that didn't go her way on other people. Still, it wasn't for me to judge how she lived her life. I only cared about how it affected Emma.

"Just go," I whispered to Emma. I saw her stiffen. She was about to turn around and go another round with her mother. She caught my eye and her shoulders dropped. Good. I could only work on defusing one bomb at a time.

Josie was still yelling as we walked out the front door. My whole body clenched as I waited for her to bring it out to the front lawn. The neighbors would come out to stare. They would judge. It reminded me of a scene from my own teenage years, only then it was my drunken father chasing me down the driveway with a beer bottle in hand.

I scanned the street again. If Liam's men were out there, they were hiding well. Had they been watching me too? The trouble was, Liam already knew exactly where to find me. For now, he needed me. I just had to figure out why the Channing murder case was so important to him. The

Thorne Law Group rarely got involved with state court cases. I'd spent most of my time with them defending white-collar crime in federal court. Something didn't track.

Emma leaned forward and buried her face in her hands. As soon as I'd cleared the stop sign at the end of her street, she let out a primal yell. "I just can't *take* it with her anymore!"

"Just try to calm down," I said. "You're both at the end of your ropes. Give each other some breathing room. You'll help me make the soup. You'll stay with me tonight. Maybe through the weekend. Let's just wait and see."

Emma sniffled. I put a hand on her back and rubbed up and down. She reminded me a little of me at her age. But lately, she'd been so angry.

It was only a ten-minute drive to my house on Finn Lake. I'd inherited it from my grandparents. At first, my younger brother Matty resented me for that because I'd spent so many years away from Delphi. I hadn't even been there when Grandpa Leary finally passed away. Matty had. He'd also struggled so much with his own demons. Grandpa hadn't trusted him to keep the place in the family after he'd gone.

Now I made the little yellow house on the tiny peninsula in the southern corner of Finn Lake my own. My brothers, sister, and now Emma knew they were welcome here any time. My name was on the deed, but this was a Leary family house.

A few slabs of ice still floated near the shore. Matty wanted to put the dock in by the end of the month but I wasn't sure Mother Nature would allow it. He was still a little miffed that I'd committed the cardinal sin of selling Grandpa's old pontoon boat. I bought a bigger and better one this year.

"Shoo!" I yelled as we got out of the car. One of the

neighbors on this side of the lake had taken to giving bread to a family of geese. They were currently camped out on my shoreline.

"Dammit," I muttered. "They'll shit all over the place."

I clapped my hands loudly, waving my arms. The geese honked and waddled back into the water. We'd had a warm spell two weeks ago and it fooled half the birds in southern Michigan into flying back home too soon.

"Grandpa used to shoot at 'em with a BB gun," Emma said. "He kept it in the shed."

"I'm not planning to shoot them," I said. "Yet!" I yelled the last part. Mrs. Steiner lived three doors down. It was her husband who'd been drawing the birds here with the bread.

"Thanks for letting me come over," Emma said. She calmed down considerably. The lake air worked its magic on her. This place had always been a sanctuary for my brothers and me when we were younger too. Whatever family drama unfolded, we could leave it behind as soon as we got to the lake.

We walked inside together. Emma plopped down on the couch. I grabbed an Afghan out of the basket I kept near the door and pulled it over her. She smiled up at me. God. I'd been her twenty years ago. Grandma Leary did the exact same thing when I came here to escape my dad's house.

"You know you're welcome here anytime," I said, echoing my grandmother's words too. "But sooner or later you're going to have to deal with everything going on. You mind telling me?"

Emma sighed. "She's been drinking too much. And there's pills too ... I think. Ones she's not supposed to have. I don't know. She's been dating this new guy. He's a total douche. You know, her usual."

"Hey," I said.

"I don't mean like Dad. You know he's different. Even if

Mom can't see it. God. Whatever. He dumped her. She's been impossible ever since. Josie's just not happy unless she's got some guy in her life treating her like shit. And she's been on me constantly about Wade."

Wade. I assumed that was the boy Emma'd been seeing. I hated that I already knew this private aspect of her life. And it made me want to kill Liam Thorne all over again. As Emma spoke, I discreetly checked my phone again. Still no message back from Killian.

"Wade," I said. "That's your new boyfriend?"

"Sort of," she said. "We've just been hanging out. He's a good guy. He's a sophomore at Michigan State. That's why Josie's freaked. She says it's cuz she thinks he's too old for me. It's not that. Really, she's jealous. In another year, I'm going to graduate. I'm going to do like you did and get the hell out of here. Go to college. She blames me for getting the chance to do what she couldn't. How messed up is that?"

"I'm worried about her, Emma," I said. "I know your mother has her issues, but that might be the worst I've ever seen her."

I decided to stop there. This was a conversation I might need to have with Joe. In her current state, he might want to think about having Emma stay with him on a more permanent basis. At least until Josie could get a handle on it. The custody arrangement between them had gone mostly smooth over the years, except for a few hiccups. Joe had bent over backward to keep things out of court with Josie. Now, at seventeen, Emma was on the cusp of being able to make a few decisions for herself.

"She's her own worst enemy," Emma said.

"Aren't we all." I leaned in and kissed her forehead. Emma smiled.

"I wish I could just stay here. If I'm at my dad's, Mom

freaks. If I'm at my mom's, Dad worries. I'm so sick of both of their bullshit."

I didn't know if that was a direct question. I decided not to answer. Not until I talked to Joe. Plus, with everything swirling around, having Emma stay here long term was a terrible idea.

"I'm sorry," she said. "I'm not trying to put you on the spot. Promise. I'm just ... I'm just tired. I like the quiet. You know?"

"I do," I said. "More than you know."

I sat at the end of the couch with her for a few more minutes. As soon as Emma quit talking, she started to drift off to sleep. Just like that, she looked like a little girl to me again. I hated that she had to live with even a shade of what I had growing up. It was apples and oranges of course. Joe was nothing like our dad. He was good. He was stable. And he'd jump in front of a train to protect Emma.

So would I.

I went to the kitchen to start putting dinner together. Emma came here wanting to help, but I decided to let her sleep. When she finally did wake, she was calmer, quieter, happier. It was good to see. I made up the guest room for her. In the morning, I'd try and help her figure out what to do about Josie. I answered three texts from Joe, assuring him that Emma was just fine. It was enough for now.

I fell asleep beside her late that night as we watched a new crime drama on Netflix. Something startled me awake. I found myself curled up on the chair beside her. It was the damn geese again, honking and strutting along the shore. They were angry about something.

Emma was gone. I rubbed my eyes. She'd put the same Afghan over me. More than likely, she'd just gone up to the guest room. Still, my heart raced as I went upstairs to check.

Sure enough, I found her sleeping like the dead with her earbuds in. I let out a yawn and went into my room.

My phone vibrated on the charger. The number popped up and I caught my breath. It was Killian Thorne. Finally.

Shaking, I picked up the phone and answered. "Hi," I said.

"Good morning," he said. "I didn't mean to wake you."

Wake me? How did he know? I could hear the geese honking again. They were outside, but I heard them through the phone as well. I went to the balcony window.

Killian stood on the shore, looking out at the water. He cut a tall, imposing figure. His black wool coat lifted in the breeze and flapped behind him, almost like a cape. He turned and faced the house. His eyes went up and up until he spotted me standing in the window. A slow smile spread across his face and even from here, I could see his ice-blue eyes spark.

Chapter 4

I GRABBED a pair of jeans off the floor, threw them on and twisted my hair up. Emma was still mercifully asleep and snoring in the guest bedroom. It was just past nine in the morning. I don't know how I let myself sleep that late. Grabbing a coat from the hook on the way out the door, I went out to meet Killian.

It was cold enough that his breath frosted as he turned and gave me that slow smile.

"Good morning," he said. He stood with his hands in his pockets, dressed as he always was. Even on a Saturday morning, he had on a suit and tie beneath his wool coat.

"You should have called me," I said. "I didn't mean for you to come all the way out here."

Killian tilted his head slightly to the side. His eyes were the thing people noticed about him first. Palest blue that made his pupils more prominent than normal people's. He wore his hair cropped close, in almost a buzz cut but thicker on top.

He spoke with a thick Irish brogue. Liam had worked to cover his, but Killian didn't. It was but one more thing that made them different as night and day. But anyone would be a fool to think Killian wasn't every bit as ruthless as his brother. He was more so because he could wrap it in devastating charm.

"You didn't sound like yourself," he said. "And I know you wouldn't have called if it wasn't something important."

"So you what, got in your car and just drove for five hours to get here?"

His lips curved in a little smirk. No. Of course he hadn't driven. He'd taken the family plane.

"What's wrong?" he asked. "Don't try and pretend it's nothing. I know you."

I looked back at the house, hoping our voices hadn't carried and woke Emma. I wasn't sure how I'd explain Killian's presence to her. I suppose the polite thing to do would have been to invite him inside. At the moment, social etiquette was the last thing on my mind.

"I need to know something," I said. "And I need it to be the truth."

Killian's eyes narrowed. He took a step toward me. My breath caught. He put a leather-gloved hand on my arm.

"Have you stopped trusting me already?"

Trust. There was a word. In his own way, Killian had been the one man in my life who had never lied to me. Even my brothers kept things from me, as family does. But Killian had always been brutally honest when I asked him something point blank. I was counting on that now.

"Liam came to see me," I said.

I kept my eyes locked with Killian's, watching for some sign into his thoughts. It was just a tiny thing. His mouth went slightly slack. He let go of my arm. I'd taken him off guard.

"When?" he asked.

"Yesterday morning," I said. "He came to my office with

a proposition. No, that's not the right word for it. It was a direct threat."

A muscle jumped in Killian's jaw. The leather creaked on one of his gloves as he curled his hand into a fist. It didn't mean Killian wasn't a part of this, but I knew he was angry.

"What do you mean, he threatened you?" He raised his voice enough that I worried either Emma or one of my busybody neighbors would hear.

I decided to lay it all out. It was a risk. But I wasn't sure I had any other option. Killian was the only person I knew who could rein Liam in when he crossed a line. In the past, it had saved my life.

"He's got men on my family," I said. "They got close, Killian. Close enough to take pictures of my seventeen-year-old niece while she was sleeping with her boyfriend. You made me a promise when I left last year. I expect you to honor it."

Killian's face had gone whiter. I could almost feel the rage bubbling inside of him.

"He wants me to represent someone named Theodore Richards," I said. Again, I studied Killian's face. He could wear a stone mask for everyone but me. I knew him too well. A nerve twitched near his eye and my heart sank.

"Jesus," I said. "You knew?"

Killian touched my arm again. I jerked away.

"No," he said, his voice dropping an octave. "I swear I had no idea my brother was planning to approach you in person. And I promise you, I didn't endorse any method of persuasion other than paying you what I know you're worth."

I took a step back. "But everything else was a family decision?"

Killian looked toward the house. If he was expecting me to invite him in, I wouldn't.

"Not exactly," he said. "But yes ... it's in the interests of the family for Mr. Richards to have a skilled advocate in his corner. It'll be good for you. And you can name your price."

"I'm not interested in any more Thorne family money, Killian. When I left, it was for good."

"Are you sure about that?"

My own rage simmered. "Don't."

"It's my turn to call in a favor, Cass. When you asked me to find your sister for you last year, you knew what that meant."

My heart thundered. I hated the truth of his words. Without Killian, another young girl might be rotting in prison for a murder she didn't commit. My sister had been the key witness to help exonerate my client. And I'd turned to Killian to help me find her when she didn't want to be found.

"What's Richards to you?"

"You know better than to ask me that."

Nothing had changed. I spent ten years learning not to ask too many questions of my clients when I worked for the Thorne Law Group. I'd turned a blind eye for years until I finally couldn't anymore. I got out before I lost too much of myself. But as Killian stood before me, I wondered if I was really out at all.

"It's a weak case," Killian said. "Entirely circumstantial."

"People always say that like it's a thing," I said. "Circumstantial evidence is what convicts ninety percent of the time, Killian."

"I'll handle my brother," he said. "You're not at risk."

"You've said that before."

"And do I need to remind you how well I've delivered on that promise before?"

If I closed my eyes, I could still see the fathomless water of Lake Michigan lapping against the hull of the *Crown of*

Thorne. Old habits and old nightmares came roaring to the surface. I turned toward the lake and rubbed my right wrist where the zip ties they bound me with had once cut through.

"So you're the carrot then. Liam was the stick? Is that what this is?"

"Cass, look at me." I wouldn't. "I swear on my life I didn't put Liam up to this. Liam has no *men* that don't answer to me when it comes down to it. I'll make sure you and your family are safe. That's a promise. *I've* never broken a promise to you."

His tone wasn't lost on me. The way Killian saw it, I was the one who had betrayed him. I'd taken a meeting with an FBI agent during a racketeering trial for one of the family's most dangerous associates. In the end, I'd breached no confidentiality. I made no deals. The secrets I knew about the Thorne family stayed buried.

"Did he do it?" I asked. "The victim was a federal prosecutor. Was he coming after you? Is that what this is all about?"

Killian turned to stone.

"Killian?"

"I've never met Theodore Richards. I've never had anything to do with him."

"That's not an answer."

"Cass, I need your help. I wouldn't be here if I didn't. You're the only one I trust with this. I'll deal with Liam. You have my word on that. You've got nothing to fear from the family or me regarding yours. I'll send some men to keep an eye on all of them if that's what you want."

"No!" I shouted. The geese finally lifted off from the shore two doors down. "No. I don't want your men or Liam's men anywhere near us. This is *my* home, Killian. You don't own me anymore."

He let out a hard breath. "I've never tried to own you. That's never what we were about."

"If I do this ..." I said, finally turning to him. "If I even *consider* doing this you need to know it's not about Liam. I don't answer to him or his threats."

"And you'll never have to. I meant what I said last year. You're untouchable. You have no idea what that promise has cost me."

A shudder went through him. I knew he was the reason I got out of Chicago with my life. When I called him for help, he'd been there. I walked away with nothing. I gave up my old life, my bank account, everything. When I came back to Delphi, I had barely more than the clothes on my back and the deed to Grandpa Leary's lake house. It had been the hardest decision of my life. Now I was faced with another one.

"I'd die for you," Killian said. "You've always known that. It's still true."

"Don't," I said.

"I used family resources to find your sister. You knew I would."

I knew what he was getting at. Killian may be the head of the Thorne family in Chicago, but he had powerful and volatile allies and adversaries. If he'd used family "resources," as he said, those allies and adversaries had to know about it. They would expect reciprocity. And the bitch of it was I knew all of that going in. At the time, I felt it was worth it. My sister was worth it. The future of my client, Aubrey Ames, was worth it. Now Killian meant to collect the debt.

"This is insane," I said.

"It's a simple legal case," he said.

I crossed my arms. "And why do I think there isn't going

to be anything simple about it? What happened to Richards's last lawyer? Did Liam have him killed?"

"What? No. You can look into it yourself. The lawyer's name was Alan Fitzgerald. He had a massive stroke or something. Natural causes. The guy smoked like a chimney and was about seventy pounds overweight. There's no mystery there, Cass. Nothing nefarious."

I took a few steps away from him. Something made me look toward the house. Emma was awake. I saw her watching us from the upstairs window. The bedroom curtain snapped shut as soon as my eyes found hers.

Dammit. Killian was right. Liam was right. I knew exactly what I was getting into when I called Killian for help again last year. He could do what he promised and keep us all safe. But if word got out I ignored him in return, Killian's ability to keep that promise would weaken. I was damned if I did and damned if I didn't.

"What happens if I can't?" I said. "I haven't looked at the full case file yet. I don't know anything about what the prosecution has or what kind of witness Richards would make if I chose to call him to the stand. All I know is that you've got a sympathetic victim. The judges, the prosecutors, hell, half the jury will probably think of Channing as playing for their team. This might be a no-win case, Killian. What then?"

I turned back to him. Killian's mouth had curved into a smile. "I have faith in you. I know how good you are. You're the best. That's all I want."

"Shit," I said.

Killian's smile widened. "It'll be good for you too. For your business. The Channing trial will make national news. You'll make a name for yourself."

"Great. As somebody I care about just pointed out, I'm becoming famous for taking cases that make most people hate me. That's not really the brand I want to develop, Killian."

"And you know every accused deserves a fair trial and a robust defense. That's what you're providing. I'm not asking you to go against your moral compass, Cass. I'm just asking you to do what you're good at. That's all."

"That's all," I said.

"Aunt Cass?" Emma had come to the back door. She had a weak smile on her face as she waited for me to introduce Killian. He waited too, giving me that trademark head tilt.

"Fine," I said. "I'll review the case and meet with the guy. For now, that's all I'm promising. And that's only *if* I have your word you'll do what you said. You deal with Liam. If I see so much as a hint of his presence around town ..."

Killian lifted a hand. "You have my word. And you know exactly what that's worth."

I did. God help me. God help us all. I did.

Killian gave a friendly nod to Emma, then headed off toward the side street where his driver waited.

Chapter 5

JUST NORTH OF Greektown in downtown Detroit, the Frank Murphy Hall of Justice took up almost an entire city block. It was also one of the ugliest buildings downtown, in my opinion. Tall, gray, and oddly narrow, the upper floors didn't match the rest of the structure's architecture. From a distance, the top third of the building almost looked like someone had slapped a massive cement, double-wide trailer on the top. The interior wasn't much to look at either.

Judge Francisco Benitez had one of the oldest courtrooms in the building. Every courtroom in Detroit had the same floor-to-ceiling brown paneling. It made everything dark, dingy, and depressing. And I didn't belong. There were no polite smiles for me as I worked my way through security and checked in with the clerk. I was an outsider. It's like that in just about every county and Wayne was no exception. Even as the largest jurisdiction in the state, out-of-county lawyers can always feel the chill.

I was lucky to get this hearing so quickly. But I knew going in that was probably an ominous sign. The judge may just be placating me. Give me a fast hearing, swiftly denied, and on we went. As it was, I'd only received the full case file from the office of Theodore Richards's recently deceased lawyer last night. The trial was scheduled for five weeks out.

"Ms. Leary?" A deep voice drew me away from the clerk's desk. Its owner wore a tailored navy-blue suit and red tie. Very patriotic. I recognized him from my google search last night. This was Tony Abbato, assistant prosecuting attorney for the county, my opposing counsel.

"Mr. Abbato," I said, smiling. I extended my hand to shake his. Tony was handsome, mid-thirties, like I was. Medium height with an athletic build, Tony had a thick head of black hair slicked back to a shine. His grip was strong and he flashed white teeth as he put a hand on my back and gently ushered me to an empty jury room across the hall.

"Judge Benitez runs the most efficient docket in the building," Abbato said. "We've only got about two minutes before we need to get in there."

"Understood," I said. "I was really hoping I could have your cooperation and professional courtesy on my request for relief. I'm not asking for a huge extension. Even just a few more weeks so that I can get fully up to speed on the case."

Abbato's smile didn't leave his face as he twisted the knife with his answer. "I appreciate that. But I hope you can understand the position I'm in. The public wants this case tried."

"And I'm not in the habit of trying cases in the public. I'm more concerned with protecting my client's constitutional rights."

"Well, like it or not, this *is* a matter of public concern. Your predecessor was mounting a vigorous defense. I was looking forward to doing battle with him. Alan Fitzgerald is a bit of a legend in these halls ... was ... I mean. I'm sure he's done the lion's share of your work for you."

"Be that as it may, I'm asking for two or three months at

most. My client is, I'm sure, just as interested in putting this matter behind him as you and the public are."

Abbato raised a brow. "Have you even met your client yet?"

I bit my lip. I hadn't. I was on my way to the Wayne County Jail straight from here.

"You better get in there." Benitez's clerk poked her head into the jury room.

Abbato threw me a wink and tried to put his hand on my back again. I found it condescending. He probably fancied himself a charmer. Maybe to juries he was. But I seriously doubted he'd get winky and handsy if I were a man.

"Let's go," Abbato said. "Best of luck."

I shot him my own fake smile as we walked into Benitez's courtroom together.

Francisco Benitez was every lawyer's worst nightmare of a judge. He was shrewd and smart, but he harbored contempt for trial lawyers that made it difficult to practice in front of him. The rumor was, he rarely read any briefs in advance of his hearings. He liked to rule from the cuff. I hadn't had the pleasure of appearing in front of him personally yet, but his reputation was already well known to me by the time I graduated from law school a decade ago.

"All rise!" The clerk read off the case number for the State versus Richards matter.

I took my place at the defense counsel's table as Benitez rounded the corner and stepped up to the bench. Criminal motion day was in full swing. Benitez probably had two dozen or more hearings in front of him today. He would want things swift and to the point.

Benitez was short and stocky with a head of tightly curled gray hair. He had bushy black eyebrows that lent him an almost Groucho Marx-esque appearance. He adjusted his necktie and scanned the documents in front of him.

"Proceed, counsel," he said to me, without looking up from his papers.

"Thank you, Your Honor," I said. "I've just filed an appearance on behalf of the defendant, Theodore Richards. As the court is aware, Mr. Richards's prior counsel, Mr. Fitzgerald, passed away unexpectedly three weeks ago. I was just given the case file late last night. Under those circumstances and in the interest of serving my client's right to effective assistance of counsel, I respectfully request an adjournment of trial for a minimum of ninety days."

Benitez still hadn't looked up from his notes. "You two couldn't work that out amongst yourselves?"

"The State's attorney was unwilling to stipulate, Your Honor," I said.

Benitez cracked his knuckles. "We're set for trial the first week May?"

"Yes, Your Honor," Abbato chimed in. "And for the record, the State feels nearly six weeks is more than ample time for the defense to prepare. Mr. Fitzgerald has already completed his discovery."

"Your Honor," I said. "With all due respect to Mr. Abbato, I haven't even had a chance to meet with my client yet. The substitution of attorney was handled through his previous lawyer's office."

Benitez finally looked up. "How is that the Court's problem? Or Mr. Abbato's problem, for that matter? I assume Mr. Richards had met extensively with Mr. Fitzgerald, did he not?"

Great. I already knew how this was going to shake out.

"I believe so," I answered. "And I have not asked the Court for an indefinite extension. This is a first-degree murder case, Your Honor. Mr. Richards is looking at a mandatory life sentence if convicted. I believe it's in the

Court's interest as well to afford Mr. Richards this consideration."

"You think I'm worried about the Court of Appeals, Ms ... uh ... Lorry?"

"Leary," I said. "Cassiopeia Leary. I won't belabor the points in my brief or waste the Court's time with ..."

"You're here," Benitez said. "You're standing right in front of me talking. You're using up the Court's time already, Ms. Leary. This murder was committed months ago. You expect me to discount the consideration of the victim's family?"

Oh jeez. There was press in the gallery, of course. Benitez meant to put on a show before he drove the spike in. He'd just delivered the sound bite that would drive clicks on social media by this evening.

"Your Honor—" I said.

"Your motion is denied," he cut me off. "The trial date stands. If you need directions to find your client, walk out to Gratiot and turn left, Ms. Leary."

And ... there was the second click-bait sound bite. I knew well enough to quit while I was behind.

"Thank you, Your Honor," Abbato said. "You can be certain that my office will cooperate with Ms. Leary in any way we can."

He was smirking. The guy was literally smirking. Benitez banged his gavel and made a dismissive wave of his hand. Behind me, I heard a sob. I let out a breath and squeezed my eyes shut.

I hadn't gotten that far in my internet searches, but I'd bet my license Mark Channing's family was sitting directly behind me. I gathered my files and shoved them into my messenger bag.

"Sorry about that, kiddo," Abbato whispered beside me. White heat flared through me. Kiddo? Good Christ.

"I'll be in touch," I said. I slipped the strap of my bag over my shoulder, gave Abbato a painted-on smile and stared straight ahead as I made my way out of the courtroom. Abbato was shaking hands with Channing's supporters. To them, I knew I was the devil incarnate, second only to Theodore Richards himself.

I made it as far as the elevators before another voice stopped me cold. "Cass!"

I turned as the man ran toward me, his blue necktie flying behind him. I pushed the elevator button three more times. It never helps, but we do it anyway.

"Cass, wait," he said. He was also roughly my age, athletic with a deep tan and blond hair he wore in a crew cut.

Special Agent Lee Cannon caught my elbow just as the elevator doors opened. This was a disaster. No. It was the apocalypse. I looked left and right, trying to see if anyone else was watching. But the fourth floor of the Murphy Hall of Justice was a merciful bustle of activity. No one seemed to care one bit about what was happening in front of the elevator. I only prayed no one saw Cannon step into it with me.

I hadn't spoken to Cannon in over a year. He was the one who had reached out to me about the Thorne Law Group's dealings. He had made me a deal and offered me witness protection if I agreed to testify against my own clients. Someone tipped Liam Thorne off about the single face-to-face meeting I'd had with Cannon. I had almost died because of it. Now here he was standing shoulder to shoulder with me as the elevator doors closed.

I turned to him. "Are you out of your mind?"

Lee actually looked shocked by my words. "I was about to ask you the same question. I thought ... it's got to be a mistake. Cass Leary isn't stupid. There's no way in hell she'd agree to get involved with Ted Richards."

I let out a sigh. So this was no coincidence.

"You're out of your jurisdiction, Agent Cannon," I said. "Don't you belong back in Chicago? This is a state law matter."

"Tell me the truth," he said. "This is Thorne. He put you up to this."

I wasn't sure which Thorne he meant, Liam or Killian. Probably both. And there was no good answer I could give him.

"I can't discuss past or present clients with you, Cannon," I said. "That was true a year ago, it's still true now."

I needed to get the hell away from him, and fast. If Liam or even Killian *did* have eyes on me, being seen with an FBI agent would be problematic, to say the least. This was a mess. Through and through. But the flare in Cannon's green eyes let me know he wasn't going to leave me alone without saying what he came to say.

"Listen," he said. "Mark Channing was a friend of mine. He was one of the good guys. You don't want to touch this one, Cass."

"Mark Channing deserves justice," I said. "But you know how the system works. I'm one of the good guys too."

Cannon's face fell. "I never said you weren't. I'm counting on the fact you still are. But Ted Richards isn't. No matter what happens in this trial, Ghost Man's a monster, Cass. I'm surprised you don't already know that."

Ghost Man? The name sent a chill through me. It was familiar, but I didn't know why. Something must have registered on my face. Cannon grimaced.

"Jesus. Ghost Man, Cass. He's a contract killer. The Bureau has been trying to get him for over a decade. He's dangerous. Whatever Thorne is paying you ... whatever he's got over your head ... it's not worth it for you to be involved in this. You have no idea the risk I'm taking even meeting with you right now. If you won't listen to reason, you need to promise me you'll do your homework on this guy. Channing was … Shit. Just … be careful. But they want him … bad. Channing's just the tip of the iceberg. If that fucker walks … Cass, he *can't* walk. You need to hear what I'm telling you."

"Thanks for the warning," I said, but my heart was pounding practically out of my chest. Ghost Man. "But I can't talk to you about this."

The elevator doors opened to the lobby. A group of people stepped in, jostling me. I pushed past them and got out. Cannon played it smart. He didn't get out. When I turned to face him, his eyes bored through me, pleading another silent warning.

Ghost Man. Who the hell was he? And how was Cannon so sure Ted Richards was him? I turned my back on the elevator and headed out of the building.

Ghost man. Richards. Whoever he was, I was about to come face to face with my client.

Chapter 6

I STARED at the cold cement walls, folding my hands in front of me as I waited for the sheriffs to bring Theodore Richards in for our interview. Lee Cannon's words echoed through me. Ghost Man. He called the guy Ghost Man. I hadn't gotten a chance to do even a cursory google search to figure out what he meant. I knew one thing with absolute clarity though: if I had any hope of a successful defense, I had to keep the jury from hearing that name even once.

The metal door opened. A young deputy poked his head in. The kid barely looked old enough to be out of high school. He was fresh-faced, rosy-cheeked. He smiled too much to work in a place like this. But he had the compact build and posture of a wrestler. They always seemed to carry themselves with a constant awareness of their center of gravity.

"Your conversation is private, Ms. Leary," he said. "I'll be right outside."

"Thank you," I said. His nameplate read "Cox."

Deputy Cox gave me a nod and led Theodore Richards

into the interview room. I rose to my feet, ready to shake his hand.

Richards was big, but not tall. In my heels, he was maybe only three inches taller than me. But he had big, muscled forearms and a barrel chest. He was bald except for thin gray hair at the sides. He wore a goatee and filled out his gray prison-issue shirt and pants. The words "Wayne County Prisoner" were stamped in bold white letters along his pant-leg. He was in belly chains, wrapped around his waist and connected to shackles around each ankle. Even with all that, the man managed to walk with his back straight and a definite swagger. Most men could only shuffle when bound like that.

Cox ushered Richards to the seat across from me. Richards met my eyes. His were clear blue. He lifted both wrists, unable to directly shake my hand.

"Thank you," I said to Cox. "I'll let you know when we're through."

Richards settled into his chair. I waited until Cox left the room before sitting. I folded my hands in front of me again and managed a polite smile.

"My name is Cass," I said. "Cass Leary. I understand Mr. Thorne has already briefed you about my taking over your defense?"

Cox lifted his shackled wrists and scratched his chin. His nose twitched and I soon learned it was a tick he had. He leaned back, getting comfortable in his chair as he looked me over.

"Yeah," he said. "I signed some papers."

"Substitution of attorney forms, yes," I said. "I filed my appearance this morning and had a hearing with Judge Benitez about adjourning your trial date. I'm afraid it was denied."

"Good," Richards said, startling me a bit. "I want to get this over with."

"I understand that. But ..."

"You're supposed to be good," Richards said. "You worried you can't handle this case? Is that why you're in there begging for more time?"

"What? Of course not. It's just unusual for a judge not to grant a request like that in a circumstance like yours. You're up for first-degree murder, Mr. Richards. Your previous lawyer just up and died ..."

"Alan was a pussy," Richards said. I kept my face neutral. If he meant to shock me with the word, I wouldn't let him.

"I was going to fire him anyway," he continued.

"You want to let me in on what your conflict was?"

Richards leaned far forward. "I didn't like him. Let's see if you're any better. Liam thinks you are."

It was strange to take a compliment from Liam Thorne through the mouth of an accused murderer.

"There's one thing we need to make clear right here, right now. I don't work for Liam. I don't work for the Thornes. They may be fronting your legal bills, but they have no say in my defense strategy or how I do my job. If you have an issue, you bring it to me. If I find out you've been talking to them about any aspect of this case, I walk."

I kept my gaze locked with his. Richards's eyes went hard for a second, then his beefy face broke into a grin. "Well, I guess I already like you better than Alan."

I kept his stare and reached for a pad of paper from the side compartment of my messenger bag. "Now that that's out of the way, let's get down to it. I've just received your case file from Alan's office. It's going to take me the weekend to get familiar with it. Once I do, we need to meet again. In the meantime ..."

"In the meantime, when are you going to get me out of here?" he asked.

"I'm not," I said. "You'll get out if you're acquitted."

"I want bail!" He pounded his fists on the table hard. The echo of it bounced off the walls. I didn't flinch. It felt like another test on his part to see if I would.

"The judge already ruled against you on that."

"I told you Alan was a pussy."

"I didn't know Alan. I can't speak of his skills as a trial lawyer. But you're facing first-degree murder. You have a record. Let's see. Petty theft. Looks like you had a thing for bar fights. And most recently, you drove a truck for a living. If I were the judge, I wouldn't have let you out on bail either."

"All kid stuff. Twenty, thirty years past. That's a bunch of bullshit."

"Which part?"

Richards's nose twitched again. He cracked his neck. For the first time since he sat down, he broke my gaze. Everything about his demeanor seemed orchestrated to test me. Would I stand up to him? Was I strong enough? Never mind whether he was guilty of this. I'd known guys like Ted Richards all my life. Would the little lady buckle under? No. She would not.

"Did you know Mark Channing?"

He sucked his teeth. "I answered all this shit before."

It was my turn to test him. "I need you to answer it again. How did you know Channing?"

"I didn't," he said; his eyes flicked back to mine. "Never met him. Never even knew who the hell he was."

"I've read the police report. Your car was seen in Channing's neighborhood three times. Once the night before he went missing. Once the night before that. You do drive a silver Jaguar, F-Type Coupe? Hell of a car."

"Yeah. That's what I drive. But somebody's lying about the rest of it. I told you. I told the police. I told Alan Fitzgerald. I don't know where Mark Channing lives. This case is bullshit. All circumstantial."

"That doesn't matter," I said. "You can go to prison for life on circumstantial evidence. I'm going to comb through your statements to the police. Your interview with them was recorded."

He laughed. "It'll be a pretty boring show. I told them exactly two things. One, I never met Channing. Two, they got the wrong guy. Those are all the words I said."

I drummed my fingers on the table. "Well, you better hope they don't find someone who can refute your first claim."

"If they do, then he's a lying son of a bitch too."

"All right, so track your movements for me on October eighteenth and nineteenth."

"I was home. Alan probably has that in his notes. I was getting over some kind of stomach thing."

I let out a sigh. It was the shittiest alibi on the planet, unless someone had seen him. I'd seen enough of Fitzgerald's notes to know that he'd yet to find an alibi witness.

"And nobody can verify that. You didn't order pizza, didn't call anyone?"

"If I'd have ordered pizza, lady, I would have thrown it back up. And no. I don't remember calling anyone."

"What did your cell phone records show?" I'd only had a chance to peruse the basics of the police report. I hadn't done a deep dive into cell phone forensics yet.

"My phone was on the charger the whole time."

"Well, that's something. But that just proves your cell phone was home, not that you were. Give me a couple of days. We need to meet the first part of next week. I'll have to work fast, but we'll talk about your defense strategy then."

He shook his head. "The strategy is, I didn't do it."

He was like talking to a brick wall. If anything, Richards seemed irritated by all of this. I wasn't getting the kind of fear and anger I expected from a man who was truly innocent of the crime he'd been charged with. Whether I called him to the stand or not, he was going to have to work on that.

"Okay," I said. "Mainly, I wanted to make it clear with you today that I've agreed to take your case. For now. And to make sure we're on the same page. You're not to discuss this case with anyone. You keep your mouth shut in here."

"I'm in solitary," he said. "For my own safety, they say. I don't get it. Pretty sure most of the guys in here weren't big fans of some hotshot federal prosecutor."

"Do you want me to work on that for you?" I asked.

Richards shook his head. "No. It suits me. If I can't get out on bail, I just want to be left alone."

"All right. Is there anything else you need?"

He shot me a smirk that sent a chill through me.

"Fine then. I meant what I said. I don't care what your connection to Liam Thorne is. He's not your lawyer. If he reaches out to you again, you send him my way. Are we clear on that?"

"As a bell." Richards smiled.

"Okay. What about your family? I read you have a wife. I'll need to speak to her. I'm sure the police already have."

It was like a switch flipped inside Ted Richards. His entire head turned red and he let out a hissing sound.

"You don't go near her."

"You're kidding me, right? Where was she? If you were home sick, why wasn't your wife with you?"

"That's none of your fucking business."

I put my messenger bag back on the floor. "It's straight up the middle of my fucking business, Mr. Richards. If there's a problem between you and your wife, you need to tell me. You don't think the cops haven't already talked to her?"

"I said," he grimaced, "you don't go near her. This doesn't touch her."

I leaned forward. "Listen to me. Her statement matters. If you're still married to her, this absolutely touches her. Write down a phone number and an address where I can reach her. She's going to be my first phone call. And you better let me know right now ... did you give this same little speech to the cops?"

He grabbed my wrist and squeezed hard enough my eyes watered. His fetid breath blew in my face.

"Take your hands off me."

"You work for me," he said. His nose was less than an inch from mine. My heart raced.

"Ghost Man," I said. His eyes narrowed. "Is that what they call you?"

Richards let go of my wrist. His nose twitched as he sat back in his chair.

"Do your job," he said. "I didn't do this shit. How you prove it is up to you."

I held the pen in my hand, pointing it straight at Richards's chest. Somehow, I kept my hand steady. "Write your wife's number and address down. I take it she wasn't staying with you last October. We can table this discussion until I come back next week, but I'm going to need a good answer from you as to why. I'll have hers by this weekend."

He took the pen and scribbled on the pad of paper. Then he slid the whole thing across the table. I caught it just before it fell off the edge. I slipped the pad into my bag and rose.

"Get some rest this weekend," I said. "I need you sharp when we meet next week. And if you ever touch me like that again, I'll make sure you rot in here."

I didn't wait for a response. I kept my back straight even

though I could barely catch my breath. I knocked on the outer door. I felt Ted Richards's eyes boring into me, but I refused to turn around.

I didn't know how this case would end. I wasn't even sure how strong the case was against him yet. But as I waited for Deputy Cox to open that door, I knew with absolute certainty I had just looked in the eyes of a stone-cold killer.

Chapter 7

I HAD a text from Killian and three messages from my brother Joe by the time I left the county jail. I didn't feel like dealing with any of them until I took a shower. As a defense lawyer, I'd taken plenty of jailhouse meetings with clients. But I'd never felt as dirty as I did after ten minutes sitting across from Ted Richards.

Killian's message was simple. "Call me." My stomach dropped. The trouble was, after that meeting, Killian was *exactly* the person I wanted to talk to most. He still knew some of the secret parts of my heart. Over the decade I knew him, I'd confided things to him I'd never told anyone. And I'd cried on his shoulder during more than one dark time. He had been a hard habit to break.

As I stopped at a light on Woodward Avenue, I called him back.

"Cass," he said, answering before I even heard a ring. My breath caught. He was a hard habit indeed.

"I just met with Richards," I said, trying to keep things focused on the matter at hand. "And don't ask me how it went. I'll just say I made it clear that I'm running this defense. I'd appreciate it if you made that point to your brother."

"He's what I called to talk to you about," Killian said. "We've had a family meeting. Don't ask me how *that* went."

The light turned green. It took an angry horn behind me before I realized it. I stepped on the gas.

"You called to tell me the outcome," I said.

"Yes. You're safe, Cass. You and your family. It's handled."

There was a double meaning in Killian's words. There always was. He kept his promises. He expected me to keep mine. I'd brought these particular chickens home to roost. My mind drifted to my sister. I would have called in a million favors from Killian and the devil himself to keep her safe. She was now. She'd taken an extended vacation to Florida to help her daughter reconnect with family she barely knew. I missed her, but with everything swirling around how it was, I was grateful Vangie was gone for now. One less chicken to corral.

"Thank you," I said.

"Richards—" he started.

"No," I cut him off. "Don't ask. I mean it. The only way this works is if you and your brother stay out of it. On every level, Killian. No interference. No surprises. I don't care who this guy is. I'll build the best defense I can with what I've got. That's all. Are we clear on that?"

"I'd like to see you again," he said. I let out a sigh. Old habits. Fresh resolve.

"Killian, I need you to say it and mean it."

He chuckled. "Yes. No interference. No surprises."

"Good. Let me do my job. That's all I ask. We'll talk later. I need to get home."

"You want to tell me what's wrong?" he asked. How could he do that? How could he know just by the sound of my voice there was anything wrong at all? Joe's three messages nagged at me. There had to be something else going on with Emma. She stayed with me over the weekend and nearly threw a fit when I insisted she needed to go home. I couldn't be her refuge. Not now. Not until I had the Richards case under control.

"We'll talk later," I said, smiling.

"Good," Killian said. "I'll hold you to that." He clicked off before I could. I hit I-94, thankful I'd gotten out of the city before rush hour. Hopefully the worst part about the Richards trial would be the daily commute from Delphi. Though I doubted I'd get so lucky.

Joe called again. This time, I answered.

"What's up?" I asked, trying to sound cheery. Joe was just as good at Killian at reading my moods just from my voice or taking one look at me.

"I don't know," he said. "Emma took off again. I've got Josie calling me every two seconds. She's out of her mind, Cass. Emma's not answering her phone. I'm in Livonia today at a job site. I can't get away. Can you call Katy for me? Or swing by your place from wherever you're going? I'm thinking Emma probably went there. I *hope* she just went there. I called the boyfriend's house. His dad swears she's not there."

"Yeah," I said. "I'm just coming back from Detroit. I'll drive by your place on the way to mine. I'll stop by and grab Katy."

"Thanks," he said. "And I'm sorry for dragging you into this. I just ... I've got too many women up my ass right now."

"Joe," I said. "I'm worried about Josie. And more than that, I'm worried about Emma *with* Josie. She was pretty blitzed the other day when I went to pick up Emma. I'm just not sure it's a good idea for Emma to be staying there until she gets her crap together a little better."

"Yeah." Joe sighed. "That's what Katy's been saying. God. It's just such a cluster fuck with Josie."

"Emma's seventeen," I said. "Maybe I can try talking to Josie one on one. If Katy's willing, maybe Emma could just live with you guys her senior year. It shouldn't have to involve the court ... but if we need too ..."

"Shit," he muttered. "I know. Dammit. I know. I was just really hoping we'd get to the finish line with this stuff."

I laughed. "I don't have to be a parent to know there's never a finish line, Joe."

I hung up with Joe, the sense of dread building as I passed each mile. I knew this feeling. I grew up with it. The volatility. The emotional bombs ready to explode and you never knew when or over what. And I'd seen something so familiar in Josie's eyes the other day. She was headed down a dangerous path. Joe had tried to protect Emma from it. But you can't. It sticks.

I have a superstition. An old trick I learned when I was a little girl before my mother died. I would conjure up the worst-case scenario, thinking it would keep it from happening. Because I'm not psychic. If I imagine it, it can't come true. Reality will be much less harsh.

When I made the turn down Joe's street and rounded the corner to his well-kept brick house, I was once again confronted with how foolish it is to think anything I could do with my imagination would stop the bad things from happening.

Emma was in the front yard, red-faced, sobbing. Two Delphi P.D. patrol cars were parked in front of the house, one with its roof lights still spinning.

The neighbors were out. Gawking. Pointing. Talking behind their hands.

I parked across the street. As soon as Emma saw me, she let out a sob and ran straight to me.

"Cass!" she shrieked. She barreled into my arms, nearly knocking me over. My heart started beating again once I felt the solid weight of her. There was chaos all around, but Emma was whole. I would make her safe.

Then the floodgates opened. Emma was talking so fast I couldn't understand her. One of the deputies came out of the house. He was still writing things on his pad.

"Emma," I said, handing her the keys to my car. "Just get in the car and wait for me."

"I don't want to see her!" she screamed. "I'm done, Cass. I'm done!"

"Shh," I said. "Don't say any more. Just try to calm down and let me try to sort this out."

A second deputy came out of the house. He had Katy, my brother's wife, with him. She was crying too and her hands were cuffed in front of her.

"Jesus," I muttered. I turned back to Emma. "I mean it. You don't move out of this car."

I ran across the street. "Get back inside!" I yelled to a gaggle of Joe's old-lady neighbors. One of them gave me the haughty expression of judgment I'd experienced my whole life.

Katy fell apart when she saw me. "Cass," she said. "I didn't ..."

I held a hand up. "Not now," I said, glaring at the deputy. He was a young kid. God. Why does it always seem like they're so young?

"Mrs. Leary won't be making any statements until I have a chance to talk to her. She's represented ... by me."

The deputy glared at me, but nodded.

"Is that really necessary?" I asked, lowering my voice. I gestured toward the cuffs.

"She's going in for assault," the deputy said. His female

partner stepped around him. She had a look of sympathy in her eyes. Then all hell broke loose.

Josie came out of the house, ushered by another female deputy. She held her hand over her eye. When she saw me, she lowered it and a little of what must have happened became clear. Josie was sporting a cut under her right eye. God only knew what set her off, but Katy must have decked her.

"You keep that bitch away from me!" Josie yelled. She liked the show. More neighbors came out.

"Josie, stop," I said.

Her eyes, other than the shiner, looked clear. I couldn't decide whether I thought that was good or bad under the circumstances.

"You're out of your mind!" Emma yelled from the car. I turned around and glared at her.

"You're arresting her?" I asked the deputy.

She nodded. "Ma'am, you can sort all of this out with the judge. This one claims the other one punched her in the face. She's not denying it."

I shot a look at Katy; she knew to keep quiet.

I went to Josie. I pulled her aside. She was like a wild thing, snorting and stomping her foot.

"She hit me," Josie said. "She hauled off and hit me. She's going to jail for it. I'm pressing charges. I'm getting a restraining order. I will not have my kid around this nut a second longer."

"Josie, please. Tell me what happened?"

"I just did."

"She's a liar," Katy said, surprisingly calm.

"Katy, I swear to God," I said through gritted teeth.

This made no sense. Katy wasn't a volatile person at all. She was smart, even-keeled. At her worst, she was a control freak. Whatever happened, I felt certain Josie had pushed her into it. It didn't make it a damn bit better.

The female deputy gestured with her chin. I left Josie's side and went to her.

"Look," she said. "All we know is we got a call about a domestic disturbance. When we got here, your sister-in-law was sitting on the porch and Josie was sitting inside bleeding. The neighbor across the street saw the whole thing. Katy struck first. You know how this works."

"Cass, please," Katy said.

I went to her. "Katy, we'll figure this out. But you're going to have to go with the deputies right now. I'll meet you down there. I'll get a hold of Joe."

"Knew you'd take her side!" Josie yelled. "You're all a bunch of white-trash losers. This is over! Emma, get in the car. I'm taking you home!"

I looked back at the deputy. Her nameplate read Mullins.

"Deputy Mullins, I'm going to take my niece home with me."

She at least had the decency to look miserable, but she shook her head. "That part is a civil matter. If you can get a judge to …"

I held up a hand. "I know the drill."

Unfortunately, Emma knew it too. She rose from the back seat of my car. Josie ran across the street and threw her arms around her. I shot a look at Emma and mouthed "It's okay."

I had one fire to put out at a time. For now, Katy slid into the backseat of the patrol car. Fury filled her eyes as the deputy shut the door and drove her off to booking.

Chapter 8

JOE WAS outside my office the next morning, alone. His skin was pale, he had heavy bags under his eyes, and he wouldn't stop pacing.

"She spent the night in jail, Cass."

"I know," I said, putting a hand on his arm as I led him into the office. Jeanie was already inside. We had a big strategy session planned on the Richards case. She wasn't happy about my decision to take it, but I think she understood why. God love that woman. She might not always agree with me, but she'd fight at my side all the way down to hell if I asked her.

"Is Katy okay?" I asked. Joe's eyes went wild.

"Cass ... she's out of her mind. Josie's gone too far. I'll kill her ... if she came after ..."

"Stop it," I said. "That's the last time you say anything like that. Not to me. Not to anyone else."

"She's not going to drop this. Cass, you know Katy. She's not violent. She's a yeller, sure. But Josie provoked her. She was talking crazy. She tried filling Emma's head with all kinds of lies about me and you and ... just ... she's off the rails."

"Joe, I know. I've seen her. Josie needs help. This is a fixable problem for Katy. I'll get her through it."

"How?" Joe said. "She's a teacher's aide, Cass. She's been charged with assault. She could lose her job over all of this."

"One thing at a time. Right now, I need you to be a rock for Katy and Emma. Let me handle the legal stuff. I'll try talking to Josie in a day or two once things calm down. She's always liked me a hell of a lot better than you. It's going to be okay. Just promise me you won't do anything stupid. Stay away from Josie. Keep your cool with Emma. Don't go off ranting down at Mickey's Bar. Stay above it. Please. Can you promise me that?"

He reminded me of a bull ready to charge the way his nostrils flared. Joe was a good man. He knew how to fight for and stand up for his family. He was a far better father to Emma than he or I ever had with our own absent dad. He'd broken the cycle. I would *not* let this thing with his ex ruin his life. But I'd need his help in keeping it from getting worse.

"Yeah," he said, deflating. "Yeah."

"Good," I said. I went up on my tiptoes and kissed his cheek. "Go look after Katy. Tell her not to worry. I'll check in with her later today."

Joe looked like he'd aged ten years overnight, and it gutted me. But we'd get through it. We'd gotten through far worse. He said a quick hello to Miranda and turned down her offer of fresh coffee. I waited for him to head out the front door and get in his truck. Then I made my way upstairs.

Jeanie was busy organizing Alan Fitzgerald's case file. She had witness statements in one pile, crime scene photos in another. She had a red dry erase marker between her teeth and pulled the big white easel around to the end of the conference table.

"It's a hot mess, is what it is," she said, spitting out the marker. "The guy's got half his notes on little Post-its. There's no order to any of it. I tried talking to his secretary. She was cagey as hell. I think they were an item ... her and Fitz. She was pretty shaken up about his death, but happy as hell not to have to be dealing with this case. There's a story there. And maybe a warning."

I gave her a hard look. Jeanie had said her piece about my involvement in all this. I'd said mine. It was time to get to work.

"How'd your meeting with him go?" she asked. I filled her in on the highlights.

"You're sure you're going to be able to work this case without interference?" Jeanie asked.

I nodded. "Or I'm not going to work it at all."

She gave me a dubious expression.

"Don't start," I said. "I know the Thornes better than you do."

"Fine," she said. She turned back to the giant stacks of discovery. It pretty much looked like Alan Fitzgerald's secretary had thrown everything into a giant garbage bag and tossed it on us.

I went over to the easel and drew a straight line from left to right. "Channing was last seen alive at five o'clock on Friday, October nineteenth. Security footage from his office building parking structure shows him leaving at twenty-three minutes past. He never made it home. He vanishes off the face of the earth at that point."

Jeanie came over. She was still holding her marker. "You've got a C.I. telling the police a silver Jaguar was spotted trolling the streets in front of Channing's house on the nights of the fifteenth, sixteenth, and the eighteenth.

We've got a physical description of the driver roughly matching Ted Richards's description."

She marked those events on the rough timeline.

"Channing's body is found Monday morning in the basement pit where they're about to pour the foundation on his new house in Gross Pointe Farms."

"Nobody claims to have seen the silver Jag at that location?" Jeanie asked.

"I need to pore through more of these witness statements, but no. There's just the matching tire tracks leading away from the construction site."

"Damn, that's thin," she said. "Have you looked through the search warrant they executed for Richards's car?"

I sat at the table. I had a copy of the warrant in front of me. "The C.I. gave them a pretty good description. Benitez already ruled on Fitzgerald's motion to suppress. I can raise the issue again ... I will ... but the jury's going to hear about what they found in that car."

Jeanie took her marker and made a list in the white space on the right side of the easel. "You've got the black carpet fibers, blood evidence. How fucked are we on the forensics?"

"Still working on it," I said. "Same with the piano wire. I've got a call into a repairman I know. I don't know enough about the stuff and Fitzgerald's notes are like you said, a hot mess."

"I still can't believe Judge Beni wouldn't give you a continuance. No, I actually *can* believe it. I've always hated that guy."

"He's opening himself up to appealable error. I just don't *like* the idea that if we lose, it puts somebody in the position of having to argue I couldn't do my job."

"Someone," Jeanie asked. "Not you?"

"I agreed to handle the trial."

"What if you lose?" she asked.

"Jeanie, don't."

I hadn't yet told her about my conversation with Agent Lee Cannon.

"Jeanie," I said. "You ever heard the name Ghost Man?"

"What, like attached to an actual person?" she asked.

I tapped my chin with my pen. "I'm just ... trying to figure a few things out."

"What do you know about what Channing was working on? I've only just seen what the news outlets released. Some kind of big RICO case against a Saul Kinsell. Money laundering, fixing government contracts, all sorts of stuff. Look, I'm not asking you to break confidentiality on anything you might have done with the Thornes, but it does seem like the natural conclusion to draw. It's the only motive they've got for this. Channing was getting too close to something, so Kinsell hires Richards ... or whoever ... to take care of him."

"Yes," I said. "I need to call the U.S. Attorney's office. Fitzgerald wasn't aggressive enough with them, I don't think. He was given only the sparsest reporting. I'm not seeing any interview notes from Channing's former colleagues. I need to know who he was talking to."

Jeanie reached over me. She grabbed a cluster of Post-it Notes attached to business cards and laid them out for me. "Here's your notes."

My heart dropped. The three cards identified attorneys working for the Detroit office of DOJ: Ryan McGuinness, Laura Wyler, and Andrew Tate. Scribbled on each, he'd written "Call, don't call, no help."

"That's it," I said. "That's all you've found?"

"They've all given written statements that are in the police report," Jeanie said. "I don't even want to hazard a guess as to what Fitzgerald meant by the Post-its. Damn, Cass. I've been around a long time. Seen a lot of different trial prep strategies. I know guys who pretty much operate

straight from their heads. You're a little of both. I just have
the weirdest feeling that Alan Fitzgerald was trying to throw
this case. And I want to know more about how he died."

I nodded. "Look into it. I'm going to make an appointment to meet with these three. They won't like it. They
might even try to dodge the meeting. But I need to know a
lot more about what Channing was working on."

"What about his wife?" Jeanie asked. She pulled another
page from the police report. "Sally Richards. I did some
checking. She lives up in Traverse City. Near as I can tell,
they weren't living together. No formal separation or
anything. It was unlisted, but I got a phone number for her."

Nodding, I took the page from her. Jeanie had added her
own sticky note with Mrs. Richards's phone number. I pulled
out the pad of paper Ted Richards gave me when I asked
him to write it down. It was the first time I'd looked at it.
Instead of a phone number, he'd written, "Fuck you," on it.

"Real charmer," Jeanie said, reading over my shoulder.
"Christ, Cass."

"He was cool the whole time I met with him," I said.
"Until I brought up his wife."

"Call her," Jeanie said. "Call her right now. That's a cell
phone. She works as a cleaning lady for one of the major
hotel chains up there."

I raised a brow and slid the phone across the table. I
pressed the speaker button and dialed. The phone rang five
times. I was almost ready to hang up, but she answered. A
thin, frail voice said hello.

"Sally?" I said. "Is this Sally Richards?"

"Yes," she said. The woman had the ragged voice of a
long-time smoker. Jeanie put a piece of paper in front of me.
She'd written some basic bio facts for Ted Richards's wife.
Things she must have quickly pulled from the internet.

Sally was fifty-five, a high school drop-out, Baptist, no

political affiliation, no children, married to Theodore Richards since 1982.

"My name is Cass Leary, I'm calling because I've been hired to represent your husband in his murder trial."

She went dead silent. "Did Teddy tell you to call me?"

I decided to play it straight. "No." I couldn't really tell her how angry he became when I even suggested it.

"Is he still in jail?" she asked.

"He is."

"Good," she said. "I hope he rots in there."

Then the phone went dead.

"Shit," I said. I redialed. The call went immediately to a canned message saying the number was no longer in service.

"Son of a bitch," I said. "She just blocked my number."

Jeanie took out a fresh pad of paper. "I'll see if I can get someone up there to talk to her in person."

"Good," I said. "The sooner the better. I need to know if she's talking to the prosecution."

"Well, based on that reaction, hopefully she did the same thing to them. I'd say it sounds like Sally Richards is the last person we want on the stand."

I rested my chin on my arm as the Richards discovery file splayed out in front of me. Six weeks. I had a little more than six weeks to figure out how to untangle this entire mess.

Chapter 9

"ANOTHER?"

Scotty Teague stood behind the bar with a kind expression and a bottle of Jack Daniels in his hand.

"Why not?" I answered. He made me my second Jack and Coke. I was going to have a third after that. Maybe a fourth. The shouts from the crowd behind me reached a crescendo. There was a big fight on and the undercard just ended in an upset. The noise was good. So was the crowd. I very much wanted to get lost in either that or the whiskey tonight. It wasn't my usual style, but I needed it.

"Hit me up, Scotty. I'll just have one of those." A familiar deep voice behind me made me smile. I finished the last of my first glass and pushed it toward Scotty to grab the new one.

Detective Eric Wray sat on the stool beside me. There was a stiffness in his posture that wasn't there a few months ago. He was recovering from a serious gunshot wound that he'd taken for me.

"You look like shit, Wray," I said, though it was good to see him. A senior detective with the Delphi Police Department, Eric had gone on medical leave after the shooting. He left town to visit a sister in North Carolina. Though his muscles still seemed stiff, his eyes shone with a light I hadn't seen in him lately. The vacation did him good.

"Good to see you too," he said, nodding to Scotty as he took his drink. "I've heard rumors about you again."

"Uh oh, that's never good."

"The Mark Channing murder? You serious with that?"

I raised a brow. "Ah, so it's not rumors we're talking about." I turned on my stool so I faced him full on. The crowd behind us was getting even more raucous. I knew it made Eric uneasy. He had that constant vigilance cops have. Bar fights were pretty much a weekly feature here at Mickey's. Knowing Eric, he wouldn't be able to help himself from trying to get into the fray if one broke out. Which meant his even being here was a bad idea. With the way he was staring at me, I realized it wasn't just a coincidence. He came for me.

"It's what I do, remember?" I said. "Scumbag defense attorney. I'm working on getting the vanity plates." I took another sip of my drink.

He laughed. "Well, I can think of better phrasing, but …"

I lightly punched his arm. He faked pain.

"Seriously," he said. "I was kind of worried about you."

"I'm okay," I answered.

"That's not all I'm hearing, Cass. I'm talking about Joe and Katy too. I know she got brought in."

I let out a breath. Sometimes there is just not enough Jack Daniels in the world.

"Just your typical Leary family fun," I said, trying to lighten the mood. It was hopeless though. Eric was getting to know me too well.

"Is she okay?" he asked. "I mean, I don't want to get into

your business, but I know how Josie is. And I also know she's been struggling a lot lately. She was dating a guy in the department a few months back. It didn't end well. This might just be ... Is there anything I can do?"

"Thanks," I said, and meant it. "Right now, no. But I reserve the right to change my mind."

He nodded. "And I'm not just talking about Katy. I've heard some things, Cass. About this client of yours."

I finished my second drink. My head spun already. I should have stopped. I knew that. But when Scotty caught my eye, I asked for a third. No matter what else happened, I was going to need a ride home.

"It's a murder case, Eric. It's messy. And it's public. I've been here before."

"I don't know," he said. "This guy ... he's ..."

"Ghost Man," I said. Eric's eyes flickered. I knew I said what he'd been thinking. "That's the rumor, right? And you know I can't discuss that."

"Well," he said. "Then let's talk in generalities. I know some things about it. Guys talk. Guys in the department working on this task force or another. Ghost Man is one of the bad ones, Cass. Maybe the worst of them. The feds have been tracking him for over a decade. They think he's responsible for up to twenty murders. Some of the sickest shit they've ever seen. A contract killer, yeah, but more than that. It's like ... it's like they think he's pretty much the most dangerous serial killer out there, only he's figured out a way to monetize it."

"My client is Ted Richards," I said, hating myself a little for it. "And this case is about Mark Channing's murder."

"Are you safe?" he asked me. Eric was shrewd. He knew enough of my background and involvement with the Thorne family. It didn't surprise me how quickly it would take him to put things together. "Are they threatening you?"

I stared at the bottom of my empty rocks glass. Scotty had just slid me my third drink. I had to be careful what I said. I had to be careful of everything.

"I'm okay, Eric. You don't need to come to my rescue on this one." I smiled, but he wasn't buying anything I said.

"I do appreciate the concern though," I said. "I mean that. And I've been worried about you too. You're healing?"

He rolled his shoulder and winced. "Never better. I'm tough to kill."

"Lucky for me," I said.

"Listen," he said. "I don't like that you're on this case. It's given me all kinds of bad vibes. But I also know I'm probably wasting my time trying to talk you out of it. What I *would* like to do is maybe be a friend."

I touched his arm. "Thanks. But I really do mean it. I'm okay. And as far as Katy and Joe and all of it ... I don't know. I'm honestly more worried about Josie than I am Katy right now."

Eric took a drink. "Yeah. Me too. I'm not saying this for gossip's sake, but her break-up with the guy I know, it got ugly. I think he was worried she was going to do something, I don't know, nuts."

"It's tough on Emma," I said.

"God. I bet. How's she holding up?"

I shrugged. "She's tough. She's a Leary."

"Isn't she eighteen yet?"

"She's got about a year to go. I'm hoping we can just handle all of this within the family. Work something out. I figured I'd give Josie a few days to cool off then try and talk her out of pressing charges. Katy says she was saying all sorts of awful things to Emma when she just couldn't take it another second."

Eric laughed. "Katy's always been kind of a scrapper."

"She'd have to be to put up with my brother as long as she has," I said, smiling.

"I remember her tearing into Wendy once. This was, hell, a hundred years ago. Wendy and I were going through a rough patch, before we got married. We were on again and off again all through college. Anyway, it was girl drama over some other guy. Katy caught Wendy sniffing around her boyfriend and all hell broke loose."

"Sorry I missed that one," I said. "How is she? Wendy?"

Eric's face went blank for a second. I knew it was a hard subject for him. His wife, Wendy, had been cheating on him for years and he never knew it. She'd gotten into an accident close to two years ago now. She was in a coma and the doctors didn't expect her to ever recover. It had torn Eric apart. I watched as his eyes drifted to the wedding ring he still wore.

"She's ... just ..." He couldn't finish. He didn't have to. I put a hand on Eric's back.

"You're a good man," I said. Eric Wray was the kind of guy who, by virtue of his job, was forced to confront the worst in people on a daily basis. It hardened him. It didn't stop him from trying to do the right thing, even if it took him to the darkest parts of himself. On that, we understood each other.

"So are you," he said. "Good, I mean. But this case, if this Ted Richards is who they say he is, you can't walk back from that, Cass. This will change you. No matter what kind of verdict he gets. You shouldn't be near it. You shouldn't be near him."

"I can take care of myself, Eric. Most of the time, anyway. And thank you. I do appreciate the concern. I'll make a deal with you. You can pull me back from the dark side if you see it coming for me. And I'll keep doing the same for you. Hell, maybe we can come up with a code word and everything."

He laughed. "Sure."

It was easy between us then. I was glad of it. He ordered another drink. I finished my third and the hard edges of both the room and me seemed to blur. We talked for a while. We watched what we could of the fight. I had one more drink even though I knew I shouldn't.

After a while, Eric circled the conversation back to Richards. "How far into this are you?" he asked.

"Trial's a little over a month from now. I'm dealing with half-assed notes and a hot mess of a case file from a dead lawyer who was either a genius or just a ... well ... hot mess. Most of the world thinks my client might be evil incarnate and it's looking like the murder victim was on a short list for sainthood. So, I'd say things are shaping up about as well as they usually do."

This time, Eric's laugh was genuine. Deep enough he snorted whiskey through his nose. I slapped him on the back while he coughed. He twisted a bit; the pain from his healing wounds was ever present. But he recovered.

"Well, like I said. If I can help ..."

"Actually," I said. "I'm trying to get a good line on what Channing was working on. He was set for trial on a RICO case."

"You get a copy of the file?"

"Bits and pieces."

"They were looking into your guy though, I assume."

"That's my hunch, yes."

Eric narrowed his eyes. "This previous defense lawyer, he didn't subpoena what they had on him?"

"I'm still sorting through all of that. I'm probably going to make a trip back to Detroit in the morning. See if some of Channing's colleagues will talk to me."

"I wouldn't," he said. When I opened my mouth to argue, Eric cut me off. "I'm serious. You know they don't have to. If a partner of mine got offed like that, I'd be telling the scumbag defense lawyer to pound sand before I'd waste any more breath."

"Thanks for the tip."

"Just be prepared for them not to want to talk to you. That's all I'm saying."

"No, I get it. But I need to try."

The fight ended. The crowd in the bar started to thin out. I was well on my way to a bitch of a hangover and knew I'd probably said way too much to Eric about my case. We had an understanding and a dollar bill taped to my fridge at home that covered most of it. I was technically Eric's lawyer and he technically consulted with me on cases outside his jurisdiction. Still, it wasn't the greatest idea talking about any of this here at Mickey's Bar.

"I better get going," I said. "I've got a lot of sand to pound this weekend if I'm going to get ready for this trial."

I slid off the stool and the ground started to spin on me. Eric caught my elbow.

"Whoa there, cowgirl," he said. "Let me drive you home."

I looked back at the bar. Though I'd had a head start, Eric had quickly caught up with me on the Jack and Cokes. He saw where I looked and shrugged.

"Okay," he said. "Maybe we split a cab."

I slid the strap of my purse over my shoulder. "I'm just going to give Joe a call. Something tells me he'll welcome the excuse to get out of the house. Can I trust you to find your way home?"

"Cass," he said. Something changed in Eric's face. His focus went over my shoulder.

I turned around. My gaze settled on a dark tailored suit

and blood-red tie. My eyes went up. Killian stood there, still as stone except for a muscle twitching in his jaw. He stared straight at Eric, his eyes lighting with fire as he saw Eric's hand on my elbow.

I put a hand to my forehead. "Eric Wray," I said, putting a hand on Killian's chest. "This is Killian Thorne." I turned to Eric. My brain wasn't quite caught up with my mouth. "Sorry," I said. "I mean vice versa."

Eric slid off his stool and actually puffed out his chest. Shit. There was more testosterone flying between these two than what I'd seen on the main event.

"What are you doing here?" I said to Killian.

"I tried calling you," he said. "Stopped by your place. Your neighbor told me I might find you here. I thought perhaps you'd need a ride home."

"It's taken care of," Eric said. There was no use pretending. Eric already knew exactly who Killian was.

"Eric," I said, turning to him. "I'll catch up with you later."

He was fuming. I could see it in his eyes. But I didn't want a scene. Killian wouldn't have just shown up again in Delphi if it wasn't important. Whatever it was, instinct told me to keep Eric Wray as far away from it as possible.

"Come on," Killian said. "I've got a car right outside."

"Cass," Eric started. But he saw something in my eyes and figured out I wasn't kidding. He stood down but for the fiery gaze he kept on Killian. I could feel it boring into my back as I took Killian's arm and left the bar with him.

Chapter 10

FIRE BURNED THROUGH MY THROAT. I woke up cotton-headed. I rolled to the side and instantly regretted it.

"Whiskey," I whispered as I pressed my fingers to my throbbing temples. "Why did it have to be whiskey?"

I barely remembered leaving the bar. Was Eric with me? Shit. What had I said to him?

As I sat up and found the floor, I heard a deep, steady voice coming from downstairs.

I was wearing a tank top and underwear. My heart flared with alarm as I looked at the empty space in the bed next to mine. The pillow was dented. I clapped my hand to my forehead. No. I didn't. I couldn't have.

The smell of eggs and bacon cooking downstairs made my stomach roll. I made it to the bathroom and brushed my teeth. It made everything instantly better. I splashed cold water on my face and grabbed a pair of sweatpants from the closet.

I walked gingerly down the stairs, anxious about what I might find. The kitchen table was set. Two steaming plates held my waiting breakfast. That steady, chanting voice came to me again and my heart caught.

Killian was sitting on the porch, facing the lake. He prayed the rosary in deep, murmured tones. His morning ritual.

The haze from last night's events cleared a bit. He'd shown up at Mickey's while I was talking to Eric. I was at least three drinks in by then. He drove me home. I remembered sitting in the living room talking to him. I remembered giving him the ten cent tour of my house. Then everything else was a blank.

I stood watching him, feeling a little like a thief. He wore a plain white tee shirt and a pair of jeans. Last night he'd been in a suit. He was barefoot, casual, unguarded. I knew I was one of the only people he ever risked letting see him like this.

Killian had a lean build, tall, muscular, with a tapered waist. He breathed through a Hail Mary, working the beads on his rosary in a fluid, delicate grace the way I knew his mother taught him. This was his solace. His meditation. I waited.

The smell of coffee hit me and I padded into the kitchen to grab a cup. The lake was quiet and calm this morning with a gentle, smoky mist wafting over it. It lent it an almost haunted air.

Killian finished. I watched him pocket his rosary. He turned and his face brightened as he saw me. I poured a second cup of coffee and brought it to him. He slid open the patio door and came in to join me.

"You didn't have to do all of this," I said, sitting at my place at the table. His warm smile still melted me a little. But I had questions that needed answering.

Killian blew over the steam on his coffee cup. He gave me his laser focus through those ice-blue eyes of his.

"So, I don't remember a whole lot after we left the bar last night. Do you think you can put me out of my awkward misery and tell me what happened?"

Killian's eyes sparkled. I knew the answer in them immediately. Killian could be a dangerous man, but I had always known him to be a gentleman.

"I put you to bed," he said. "And I slept on the couch."

I turned to said couch. Had I just looked there in the first place, I might have saved myself the worry. The pillows were rearranged and one of my grandmother's Afghans was draped over the end of the big couch against the wall.

"I have a guest room," I said. "You were welcome to it."

"I tried that," he said. "You still snore pretty loudly. It was more peaceful down here." He winked and I felt my cheeks flame red.

"Well, thank you. I don't usually let myself get that far. It's just ... it's been kind of a long week."

"Richards," Killian said, his expression hardening.

I set my coffee cup down. "Richards and a lot of other things."

"Your family?" he asked.

I stabbed at my eggs. Killian was a master in the kitchen. If he hadn't joined the family business, he could have made it as a professional chef. The eggs were light, fluffy, and seasoned to perfection. I didn't know how he did it. I didn't even know what to do with half the spices in my cupboard, but Killian turned them into something divine.

"Yes," I said. "But nothing I can't handle. What about you? Why are you here?"

He took another sip of coffee. "Do I need a reason?"

I considered his question for a moment. It was complicated with Killian. For so many years, he was the only person I had been willing to let close to me. I didn't regret that, but it would be so easy to fall into old patterns.

"Yes," I said. "I think we both do."

He set his cup down. "I was worried about you. I know I've asked a lot of you. I wanted to make sure you were okay. It seems my instincts were right. You were in bad shape last night."

"I had one too many drinks," I said. "I wouldn't call that bad shape."

"That man you were talking to ..."

So there it was. A little knife twisted in my heart and I didn't like myself for it. Part of me liked the jealous flare in Killian's eyes. I hated that it mattered to me whether he still cared, but it did.

"He's a friend," I said.

"He's a cop," Killian said.

"How do you know?" Now I felt protective of Eric. Had Killian already checked into him?

He gave me a boyish, crooked smile. "I can spot 'em a mile away, Cass. So can you."

I let out a sigh. Killian might be playing me, but he was right.

"So," he said. "How close a friend?"

"Stop," I said. "This doesn't work for me. I have a life here now. You don't get to just swoop in and start questioning how I live it."

"Well, I'm not sure your friend is in it just for that. I can spot that a mile away too."

"He's married," I said. I wasn't even sure why. I didn't owe Killian that. It seemed all my old patterns emerged just from sitting in a room with him for five minutes.

In any event, my answer barely satisfied him. But I thought the tight-lipped expression he gave me meant he would move on from it, for now. I was wrong.

"And we're still engaged, technically."

I couldn't help it, I barked out a laugh. "Killian ..."

He put a hand up. A twinkle came back into his eyes. He was teasing me and I walked right into it.

"You're right," he said. "It's no longer my right to tell you how to live your life. I'm sorry. I can't help that I still worry."

"And yet, that doesn't stop you from requiring payment of your debt," I said.

"I would have asked for your help with Richards whether you owed me something for it or not. And you're being paid handsomely for your time."

The edge of anger in Killian's voice made his skin flush.

"Killian, if I'm going to mount a proper defense for this guy, I need to know everything. Mark Channing was building a solid case against the Kinsell organization. You're connected to them. I need to know how."

"There's nothing for you to worry about," Killian said, giving me his standard, evasive answer.

"I think there's probably plenty for me to worry about. If Kinsell goes down, are you next? Is that what's driving all of this? You and Liam are worried about some domino effect. Christ, Killian, after ten years and all the promises, things are as bad with your family business as they ever were, aren't they? Were you lying to me the entire time we were together? How hard are you really trying to turn the business legitimate?"

Killian gripped the handle of his coffee mug so tightly, I thought he would crush it. "I've never lied to you. I swore to you I wouldn't, and I haven't. That doesn't mean I can always tell you everything. You need to believe me when I say I have things in place for the future of my business. I'm *so* close to being able to walk away from the shit my father and grandfather mired us in."

"Except Liam doesn't want that. He's never wanted it. And now I'm in the middle of it. Again. Let me guess, your allies still think I'm a liability. That's why you really want me on this case. So you can prove to them I'm still one of you. Is that it?"

"No," he said. I wasn't convinced.

"If you're playing me on this, it's going to come out," I said. "It's a conflict of interest for me."

"It isn't," he said. "I wouldn't put you at risk like that. And I wouldn't have come to you if I didn't think you were up for this."

"Put me at risk," I said, my own anger rising. "How can you sit there and say that to me? Killian, I still have nightmares about the last time my involvement with you put me at risk."

The color drained from his face.

"Cass ..."

Once I started, I couldn't stop. "I've never told you how bad it got," I said. "Killian, your brother put me on that yacht with the intention I sink to the bottom of Lake Michigan."

He flinched.

"Sometimes I can still feel the zip ties cutting into my skin. I knew I was going to die that night. And for what? I had one meeting with someone your brother doesn't trust."

"Liam believes you were going to turn evidence against the firm over to the FBI." It was a statement and an accusation.

"I had a conversation," I said. "And that's the truth. Your brother still wants me dead."

"And you know I can handle him."

"I don't want to be in your debt for handling him. I want to be done with this. Forever. After the Richards case is over ... no matter what happens ... I need your word. And I'm never going to call you again. Ever."

I could see the pain flash behind his eyes. I wondered if he could see it in mine.

We stared at each other like that for a few moments. I took Killian's silence for acceptance.

"Richards," I finally said. "I need to know what you know about him. And I need it to be the truth."

Killian sat back a little straighter in his chair.

"Ghost Man," I said. "That's who the feds think he is."

"You've been talking to them?"

"Enough," I said. "This is about me doing the job I was hired to do. Nothing else. Is Ted Richards this Ghost Man? Has he murdered before? How many times?"

Killian raised a brow. "I don't know. Anyway, you're the lawyer, Cass. Prior bad acts and all? What difference does any suspicion around him for other bad deeds have to do with the burden of proof in this case?"

"I need to know for me," I said.

Killian smiled. "Bullshit. I know you better than that. You forget, I've seen you in action. I know how much you love the arena. And I know how much you believe in the system, flawed as it is."

He was right. He knew so many things about me I wish he didn't. But I knew just as many about him.

"Cass," Killian said. He leaned forward and took my hands in his. "I know you can handle whatever they throw at you in the courtroom. And I can't give you the answers you seek about Richards. I don't know them. But I do know he's dangerous. Never forget that. Never let him too far in."

I smiled. I slid my hands out of Killian's. "Do you know how many people told me the same thing about you?"

He dipped his head, conceding my point. It was enough for now.

"You'd better go," I said.

He nodded. "I know."

Killian rose from the table. He walked over to the living room and grabbed his shoes and set of keys.

"I'll go," he said. "But I won't go far. Not until after the case is over."

Though I didn't expect it, I found myself relieved that he said it.

"Okay," I said. "But you need to promise me you won't interfere. If this thing starts to go south, whatever your interests are in the outcome ... this case has to be above board or I'm out."

Killian smiled. "Wouldn't have it any other way."

He twirled his keyring on his index finger and smiled. Then he turned and walked out the door.

Chapter 11

"As BAD IDEAS GO, this one's next level, Cass." Jeanie spoke between crunchy chews on the raw carrot she was eating.

"Yeah, I know," I said into the phone. I took my own lunch in my car, a stale bagel with strawberry cream cheese. I'd found a spot on Fort Street two blocks from the Department of Justice building in downtown Detroit. I'd left three messages for Mark Channing's colleagues in the Criminal Division – Violent and Organized Crime Unit. They weren't answering and they weren't calling back.

Every instinct in me screamed that Alan Fitzgerald had dropped the ball here, big time. The statements Channing's co-workers gave seemed cooperative, but vague. Channing was set to go to trial in the RICO case against the Kinsell organization in just a few months. I was hoping at least one of the lawyers in his office would agree to give me even five minutes of their time. Fitzgerald should have deposed them. I still might. But I'd probably need to file another motion with Judge Benitez asking for more time.

Through one of Jeanie's contacts, I'd learned Channing's office liked to take lunch in Greek Town on Wednesdays. It was within walking distance of their office and today was the first day we'd hit over sixty degrees since last November.

"Well," she said. "Don't say I didn't warn you."

"You always warn me," I muttered.

"And you never listen." She said a few other things, but my attention went to the crosswalk at the nearest intersection.

Two men and two women had just emerged from the building. I looked down at the printout I'd made of Ryan McGuinness and Andy Tate's social media profiles. That was them all right. McGuinness was tall and lanky with unkempt blond hair. Tate was nearly a foot shorter than his colleague and twice as wide. According to their statements Tate was working the RICO case with Channing.

"Gotta go," I said, hanging up on Jeanie and tossing the remains of my bagel on the passenger seat. I needed to head them off. If luck was with me, they'd let me buy them all lunch. More than likely, I was about to run into four middle fingers. Their friend was dead. Murdered. To them, I would seem like the enemy.

"Mr. McGuiness!" I yelled, raising a hand to hail the group. I caught them just as they left the crosswalk and headed straight for me.

McGuiness looked at Tate. Of the two women with them, one looked close to forty, tall and toned. Pretty, but with a hard edge to it. She wore her brown hair pulled tightly back in a bun probably lacquered with a pound of product. She was a lawyer, for sure. Probably Laura Wyler. The second woman was much younger. She barely looked old enough to be out of high school. If she weighed a hundred pounds I'd be surprised.

"Mr. McGuiness," I said, finding a quick smile. I was breathless from the jog from my car. The wind kicked up.

The younger woman wore a pleated skirt that flared up. She was awkward, practically doubling over to catch it.

"I'll cut right to it," I said, knowing they'd appreciate it. "I'm Cass Leary. I was hoping to borrow you, Mr. Tate, and Ms. Wyler for a couple of minutes. If you'll let me walk with you even …"

"Cass Leary?" Tate asked. He was as unkempt as McGuiness and Wyler were neat. His tan suit jacket was rumpled as if he kept it in his car most of the time. There were coffee stains on his tie. From everything I gathered, he was a formidable trial lawyer. But Mark Channing was supposed to be the star.

"Yes," I said. "I know this is pretty unorthodox of me. But, lawyer to lawyer, I'm hoping you'll give me …"

"Lawyer to lawyer?" Tate said, not bothering to mask his instant contempt. "You're a bottom feeder."

"Andy," Wyler said. "Something you want to share with the class?"

"You've been calling my office," Tate said. "She's Ted Richards's new lawyer."

The charming grin on Ryan McGuinness's face melted. The young girl between him and Tate bit her bottom lip. She didn't look shocked though. In fact, her eyes seemed to register recognition when I said my name.

"Yes," I said. "I have. I was just hoping to ask you a few simple questions."

"We've already given our statements," McGuinness said. "Unless you've got a subpoena on you, you're just in my way."

"Don't be a dick, Ryan," Laura Wyler said. "Listen, we're not trying to be rude."

"And I understand why you don't want to talk to me. You're absolutely right that you don't have to …"

"I'm Laura Wyler," she said. "I'm guessing you already

know that." Laura extended her hand to shake mine. I took it.

"And this is Victoria ... Stockton. My paralegal." Victoria looked scared to death. She forced a smile and shook my hand.

"Were there other threats?" I asked, jumping right into it. In another second, McGuiness and Tate would probably tell me to fuck off. "Were any of you threatened?"

"We get threatened all the time," McGuinness answered. "Comes with the job."

"Was Channing worried about any of it?" I asked.

"Just stop," Tate said. "You wanna call any of us to the stand, that's your prerogative. We're not doing your job for you. This asshole you work for? You need to understand just how big a monster he is."

"Ghost Man," I said. "You think that's who he is?"

A look passed between them. Laura Wyler put a hand on McGuinness's arm. His face had gone snow white.

"He's a fucking monster," Tate said. "That's what he is. And he's going down for this. Channing was just about to ..."

"Enough," McGuinness said. "Jesus. You have your answer. You can serve your subpoenas on the office just like everybody else."

"The rumor is," I said. "Channing was being groomed for higher office. Were you aware of that?"

Andrew Tate lost his shit then. He stuck a finger in my face. At least it was only his index finger. "Mark Channing was the best man I know. He was better than all of us. He was going to take down Kinsell. That was just the beginning. Your boy's lucky he's only behind bars. He's probably safer there. And for you to come here, expecting ... what ... for us to help you? Jesus. Lady, you're out of your damn mind."

"Andy, enough," Laura said. She tugged on Tate's jacket.

"No," Tate said. "I want to make sure I'm crystal clear. You stay away from my office. You stay away from me. And if I find out you've tried reaching out to Mark's wife ... God ... that woman's been through enough. Did you know she's pregnant?"

"No," I said. "I didn't."

"Found out two weeks after we buried Mark," he said. "She's due in June. The jury's going to love her."

There were tears in Andy Tate's eyes. Ryan McGuinness looked downright homicidal. Laura tried to placate both of them. But it was their young paralegal, Ms. Stockton, who caught my eye. She was blinking rapidly. She'd gone a little pale. I couldn't figure out why. At first, I wondered if maybe she was just one of those people who shied away from conflict. If so, what the hell was she doing working in the U.S. Attorney's office?

"Listen, I pretty much hate this as much as you do," I said. "Do you think it's my idea of fun getting chewed out and called the worst kind of scum in the middle of the street? I get it. I do. Mark Channing is the victim here. Believe me, I want to see that justice is done as much as you do."

"Bullshit!" Tate yelled. "We know who hired you. We know the Thornes probably better than you do. Did your boss bother briefing you on what your client is capable of?"

"How do you know what my client is capable of?" I asked. It was almost a throwaway question, but Andy Tate flinched.

"Don't you read your own damn discovery?" Tate asked. "It's in the fucking report."

Alan Fitzgerald's file had little more than summary reports of the investigation into the Kinsell organization. Basically, I knew Channing was lead counsel on the RICO case. I knew the crux of the case centered on the operation of a strip club in Detroit allegedly used for money laundering. There were alleged kickbacks on a construction contract for a new parking structure downtown. But my gut told me that was probably the tip of the iceberg.

As I stood there, I got the sinking feeling there might be something missing from the materials Fitzgerald's office sent over. I didn't want to ask Tate exactly what report he meant. Like it or not, he was my adversary in this. I had another tree to bark up and fast.

"He was the best man I know," Andy Tate said again, but the anger had left his voice. He spoke from a place of deep grief and my heart broke a little for him.

"Catherine's like a sister to me," he said. My mind spun. Catherine was Mark Channing's wife. I fully expected Abbato to call her to the stand. Probably first.

"I'm sorry," I said. "I truly am."

"We're done here," Ryan McGuinness said. He gestured with his chin to his colleagues. Laura Wyler gave me a sympathetic eye. I was grateful for it. Andy Tate stormed off and McGuinness followed him.

Only the young paralegal seemed to hesitate. Then McGuinness called for her and she picked up her step, almost running to catch up to the others.

Chapter 12

JEANIE CALLED me thirty seconds before I got to Tony Abbato's office. Thank God for her. Her timing saved me from tanking my credibility with Abbato and maybe Judge Benitez after that. But her news didn't solve the larger problem.

"It's here," she said, breathless. "Dammit all to hell. It's here."

"You have this Ghost Man report? I mean ... how the hell did we not see it?" I had briefed Jeanie on Tate's reference to a report.

"No," Jeanie said. "I have a receipt for it. Well, not even a receipt. It's buried here in an enclosure list on one of Abbato's discovery responses. It was supposed to be on a flash drive."

The wind picked up. The warm front we'd enjoyed would be blasted off by the lake effect in another few hours. I pulled my jacket tighter around me.

"I'm not even going to ask you if you triple checked. I know you did. You think Fitzgerald's office never forwarded it."

"Yeah," Jeanie said. "At least I think that's the angle. I

mean, I suppose it's possible Tony just *said* he sent it, but
didn't. It's just ... these discovery responses were served
almost four months ago. Alan Fitzgerald would have received
them back before Christmas. I know his secretary, Cass. She
was always on top of things with him. If Abbato forgot to
send these, she'd have noticed."

"All right," I said. "I need to meet with her. I need to
figure out what happened to the rest of Fitzgerald's files. If
worst comes to worst, I can explain it all to Abbato and ask
for a second copy. I just don't like the way that looks."

"Me either. And I've got a bad feeling about this anyway.
I've had it during every conversation I've had with Fitzgerald's office. You need to get to the bottom of this. I've already
called over there. They know you're coming. Fitzgerald was a
solo practitioner, but he shared office space and some
support staff with two other lawyers. I used to date one of
them. It was a million years ago ... we're talking the Carter
Administration. But ... he's a good guy. Paul Lovelace.
Theresa Shuler is the office administrator you want to talk to.
She kept both Alan and Paul organized. If anyone knows
what the hell happened to that flash drive, it'll be Theresa."

"Thank you, Jeanie," I said. I knew how much she hated
all of this. Nothing would have made her happier if I'd just
thrown up my hands and walked away from this case altogether. But regardless of her personal feelings, Jeanie would
always have my back.

Alan Fitzgerald's office was all the way out in Allen Park.
A jack-knifed semi on I-75 turned it into a two-hour drive.
With each passing minute, I felt my chances to win this case
slipping away. And I wasn't sure if that was good or bad,
considering who my client might be.

It was an old office building buried behind a strip mall.
The law offices of Alan Fitzgerald had a tiny little listing on
the lobby sign. He'd been sandwiched between a dentist

office, a chiropractor, an insurance agency, and a real estate brokerage. I took the stairs instead of the elevator, not trusting the smell of the place.

There was no other marking on the dented brown door other than "Law Offices." I barely got my hand around the knob before someone inside buzzed me in. Sure enough, I spotted a security camera mounted high in the corner of the ceiling.

An older man stood at the receptionist's hub. He had a thick head of carefully styled white hair and deeply tanned skin. He stood with the rod-straight posture of a military man and I guessed right away this was Paul Lovelace. He was handsome with a ruddy complexion and a loud, gravelly voice when he greeted me. Oh yes. He was Jeanie's type all right.

"Hi," I said, shaking Lovelace's hand. "I'm Cass Leary. Thanks for seeing me on such short notice. And I'm very sorry for the loss of Alan Fitzgerald."

Lovelace eyed me up and down. It wasn't lewd in the way he did it. It felt more like a measure of my worth.

"It's no problem," he said. "I'd do just about anything to stay on Jeanie Mills's good side."

"Wouldn't we all." I laughed. The receptionist answered a call and turned away from us.

"Jeanie said you wanted to talk to Theresa. Theresa's been taking some time. Alan's death threw her for a loop. She'd worked for him for almost twenty years. They were close. You understand."

"Thanks," I said. Although this was beginning to sound like a classic runaround. "Is there somewhere we can talk in private for a few minutes?"

Lovelace nodded and ushered me down the hall. He took me to a small conference room. The place was a mess with boxes stacked nearly to the ceiling.

"Sorry," he said. "Let's just say this place only runs smoothly when Theresa's here."

"It's fine," I said. I waved him off when he offered me something to drink. Then Lovelace sat in a chair opposite me and folded his hands beneath his chin.

"I'll cut right to it," I said. "I assume Jeanie's already filled you in on the highlights anyway. There were some items missing from the case file my office received on the Ted Richards' murder case. In particular, I'm looking for a flash drive that would have contained detailed reports from an FBI investigation the victim had access to."

Paul Lovelace let out a sigh that felt more theatrical than honest. I had lost my patience hours ago.

"Look," I said. "I have a murder trial that starts in just over four weeks. I have no doubt Alan Fitzgerald was a great man and a good lawyer. I don't know what was going on with him in the last few weeks of his life. But he left a giant, heaping turd on my lap with this case. Discovery materials were missing from the file I received. I've got an asshole of a judge who refuses to grant a continuance. The *good* news is that this all might be reversible error if I lose. The bad news is, my client's going to have to file his appeal claiming he didn't have adequate counsel. I really don't want that hanging around my neck. I'm sorry Ms. Shuler is distraught. But she made assurances to my office ..."

"Stop," Lovelace said. All polite pretense drained from his face. His eyes went hard.

"Do you know where my missing flash drive went?"

Lovelace wiped a hand across his face. I couldn't tell whether he was getting angry or just irritated. I decided not to care.

"You need to understand how this all went down."

Great. With that sentence, I understood Paul Lovelace

knew *exactly* what happened to my missing flash drive and it wasn't just some oversight.

"I really don't care how it went down."

"Theresa is ... this is killing her. Alan kept promising to marry her. And *she* kept telling him this case was going to be the death of him. She was right."

I felt like I had cotton in my mouth. I regretted not taking Lovelace up on his offer of refreshments. "Do you think something sinister happened to Alan?"

Lovelace's eyes went wide. "No. God, no. Ms. Leary, I was with him when he died. It was right here in this room."

My skin started to crawl a little. I lifted my hands from the arms of the chair.

"Alan was overweight. He had high blood pressure and he wouldn't take his meds for it because he didn't like how sleepy they made him. His cholesterol was out of control. He drank too much. We'd had a big lunch just before ... We were sitting here talking. Alan went gray. It was like he turned to stone right in front of me. Clutched his chest and keeled over. That was it. Out like a light. Poor bastard never had a chance. Doctors said it wouldn't have helped if his heart seized up like that right on the operating room table. His aorta ruptured. It was lights out. There was nothing sinister about it."

I relaxed a little. "I'm sorry. I wasn't trying to make you relive anything."

"I'm trying to apologize to you. And I'm doing a shit job of it." Lovelace reached into his breast pocket and pulled out a small black flash drive. He put it on the table between us.

"I don't get it," I said. I didn't wait for an explanation. I reached over and picked up the flash drive.

"I'm getting her some help," he said.

I twirled the flash drive between my fingers. "Wait a

minute. You're saying Theresa did this on purpose? She kept this?"

"Jeanie explained it all. She sent me a screenshot of Abbato's letter listing the attachments to his discovery response. I showed it to Theresa. She started to cry. When I pressed her, she spilled everything. She's been a wreck for six weeks. We're all worried. Like I said, after this ... It's obvious. I'll make sure she talks to some professionals. She's convinced Alan was murdered. I'm telling you, he wasn't. She's just looking for a way to make sense of all of this. She's looking for someone to blame. Your client ... Alan's client is like a ready-made boogeyman for her. I swear to you, I had no idea she was hanging on to that thing. I don't even know what's on it."

I shook my head. This was insane. If Theresa Shuler held on to this, what else might she have done?

"Mr. Lovelace, I need to be frank. As I just explained, I'm out of time. Now you're sitting here telling me Alan Fitzgerald's secretary withheld part of the case file from me out of some misplaced sense of grief or outrage or ..."

"Yeah," he said, growing irritated. "I told you. That woman is a wreck. I'm worried she's suicidal."

"How can I be sure this is the only thing she tampered with?"

"She didn't tamper with it," Lovelace said. "She just ... hung on to it. I think she was trying to make sure Richards would go down for this murder, no matter what."

"Well, this is unacceptable. And it changes things. You're telling me I've got a member of my client's former defense team actively trying to sabotage his defense. I have to report this. At a minimum, I need to report this to the judge and try to get a continuance ... again. I need to cross-check everything with the prosecutor to make sure your secretary hasn't altered what's on here."

"I'm telling you she didn't," Lovelace said.

"A minute ago you told me you couldn't believe she would do something like swiping this in the first place. I'm sorry if your assurances aren't good enough. I've got a job to do."

"Why is that?" Lovelace said.

"Excuse me?"

"Why are you defending this guy?"

"I think we're done here. I expect an affidavit from Theresa Shuler on my desk by morning."

"This isn't your neck of the woods," Lovelace said. I rose from my seat. He didn't. "Nobody comes to Wayne County unless they make a practice out of it. You don't. So, it's got to be the money. That's why Alan did it. He regretted it though. I can tell you that. You asked me if I suspected foul play. I don't. But the stress of this case helped bring on that heart attack. *That* I'm sure of."

"Theresa Shuler is a good woman," he continued. "I don't want to see her dragged through the mud. Not for this guy. Make no mistake, Ms. Leary, you're defending a monster."

I palmed the flash drive. "Have a good afternoon, Mr. Lovelace. I'll give Jeanie your regards."

Chapter 13

THE NEXT MORNING, Paul Lovelace faxed Theresa Shuler's affidavit. In it, she spelled out just about everything Paul had told me the day before. That was the good news. The bad news, Judge Benitez didn't care. Abbato agreed to resend everything on the flash drive so I could cross-check it. But the trial date would stand.

Jeanie stared into space as I sat across from her at the conference room table. Miranda, bless her heart, stayed at the office with me until almost midnight, helping me print out the entire contents of the flash drive. We had it spread out in more or less neat piles across the table.

I hadn't slept. If Miranda hadn't forced the issue, I wouldn't have even eaten. I rested my chin on my arm amid the mounds of paperwork.

Most of it was heavily redacted with thick, black lines. But what we *did* have was daunting. There were phone transcripts. Report summaries. Photographs. Timelines. Travel reports. Listings of key witnesses in the Kinsell case detailing when and where Mark Channing spoke with them. And there was one very special file devoted to a suspect identified as "GM." Ghost Man.

"We sure Alan Fitzgerald just up and croaked?" Jeanie asked.

"Lovelace was pretty convinced Fitzgerald died of natural causes. I mean, it happened right in front of him," I said. I didn't want to discount the possibility. But it didn't make sense.

"How far did you get with this?" Jeanie said. She pushed her copy of the Ghost Man file toward me. "They've listed over twenty homicides he's suspected of carrying out. Look at page five, Walter Dunham."

I already had. I flipped open to the page. A grainy black-and-white photo of Dunham stared back at me. It was his Facebook profile. He smiled at the camera, leaning casually against the guard rail on a yacht with blue waters churning behind him. He wore a light-blue polo shirt with a sweater knotted over his shoulders. Deeply tanned with aviator sunglasses, the man had a craggly face and capped teeth. I knew the man. Years ago, with the Thorne Group, I'd briefly represented him in a fraud case.

I flipped the page. Dunham went missing three years ago. No body had ever been found, but I was looking at a transcript between one of the agents and a confidential informant. The man identified himself as "Loomis." Loomis claimed to have been paid by Ghost Man to make a cyanide spray. He told the FBI Walter Dunham had been the test case to see if it worked.

"It's ingenious," Jeanie said. "Coroner doesn't know to look for it. The victim will appear to have just had a heart attack."

"But they can't prove it," I said. "They never found Dunham. They just have his statement with no other corroboration."

"You think he was lying?" she asked.

"I think it doesn't matter. This isn't something Abbato could even use. It doesn't match the manner of death in Channing's case even remotely."

"But it matches Alan Fitzgerald's death," she said.

I closed the file. "Except Ted Richards has the perfect alibi for that. He was already in jail, Jeanie."

She rubbed her eyes. "God. I don't know. I'm losing my mind looking at this stuff. I think we could both use a break."

I ran a hand through my hair. "It just doesn't make sense," I said. Granted, my brain wasn't exactly fresh, but I'd pored over the reports of all twenty-two suspected hits Ghost Man had allegedly carried out.

"There's a theme here," I said. "A pattern."

"He's creative," she said. "That cyanide thing is impressive. Quick. Mostly untraceable. Mostly clean."

"But he doesn't always operate that way." I flipped through the packet to another victim.

"Here," I said. "Jerome Haggerty. Went missing from St. Petersburg, Florida six years ago. He was a bookie connected to Kinsell. His body turned up a few months after he was last seen. Garroted. Just like Channing."

Jeanie opened her copy of the file to the same page. "Piano wire," she said. "God. And that other one, the doctor in Queens. He was chopped up. It's like there's no clear M.O. to these. I mean, as a whole. Sometimes it's messy. Sometimes it's so clean it's almost clinical. And they've only ever found three bodies. Well, four if you count Channing."

"That's the thing though," I said. I picked up a pen and started drawing circles in the corner of one of the report pages.

"What. I recognize that tone in your voice. And you only resort to doodling when your brain is on fire."

I sat up and smiled at Jeanie. "These killings. They're

over almost a twenty-year period. Twenty-two named victims. And this C.I. is talking about at least a dozen more that he doesn't know by name. Thirty-four victims. And with the exception of Channing, there's no physical evidence to connect them to Richards or anyone else."

I got up from my chair and started to pace. I twirled the pen in my hand.

"He's a specialist," I said. "Murder made to order. Sometimes it's clean and clinical like Dunham, if that's what really happened. Sometimes it's gorier than a horror film. And he leaves no trace."

"Ghost Man," Jeanie said. "That's why law enforcement started calling him that."

"And it's why it took so long for them to zero in on Richards." I moved over to the case file materials I'd already been working with. I had a listing of all the most damning evidence against him in the Channing murder behind me on the whiteboard. I dropped the pen and picked up a marker.

"Piano wire still wrapped around Channing's neck. That's not how they found Haggerty. And to just leave him to be found on his own property?"

Jeanie nodded, tracking my line of thought. "The three victims they did find it was pretty much by accident. Haggerty was found at the bottom of a ravine after a hiker took a spill. If he hadn't, the poor bastard might still be down there."

"And there was never anything else. No hairs, no blood evidence, no DNA. Nothing to draw a straight line to Richards. Until this time."

"You think it was a copycat?" she asked.

I put my hands on top of my head. "I don't know. I really don't. I just know I'm going to have to fight like hell to keep all of this from coming out at trial. But if I fail, this is how

I'll have to use it to my advantage. Ghost Man isn't this sloppy."

Jeanie nodded. "That could backfire, Cass. If I were Abbato, I'd tell the jury I never said Richards was Ghost Man. I just said Richards killed Channing and there's plenty of physical evidence to support it. And if any of them still think Richards is Ghost Man, they'll convict based on that alone. It's a win-win strategy."

"Maybe. I still say I've got enough for reasonable doubt."

"Probably," Jeanie said, her shoulders sagging as if the effort of conceding the point weighed on her. It probably did. "I just know if I had my pick, I like Abbato's case better than yours right now. So, what are you going to do?"

"I'm going to keep digging. I still feel like I'm missing something."

"That's my girl," she said. "But if you don't take a break, Miranda's going to come in here with a bullwhip. Don't laugh. I've seen her do worse."

I smiled. "So have I."

Jeanie shut the file she was looking at. "So let's talk about something more refreshing. How's Katy?"

I sat back in my chair with a thud. "Holding up. I've at least managed to get her, Joe, and Josie to their neutral corners. Emma's been a help with that. She's gotten good at handling Josie. I hate that she has to."

"Is she staying there now?"

I nodded. "During the week. She's been at Joe and Katy's on the weekends."

"You get anywhere convincing Josie to drop those stupid assault charges against Katy?"

"Not yet," I said. "I've still got some time. Even if she doesn't, I don't think Katy's facing much. She's got nothing in her background but a Minor in Possession charge when she was seventeen. She got caught with a beer at some party when she was a junior in high school. Pretty sure LaForge will work with me to plead her down. And maybe I can talk him into dismissing altogether."

Jeanie shook her head. "Still. You sure that won't cause her grief at work? She's a reading specialist at the elementary school, right?"

"That's the kicker," I said. "But ... the principal over there is well aware of Josie's ... er ... issues. I'm hoping they'll overlook all of this. They love Katy. I just hope their hands aren't tied. There are a few hardasses on the school board who are still looking for any reason at all to screw over somebody named Leary."

"Right," Jeanie said. "So you try to work your magic with Josie. I'll think positive."

"Emma blames it all on some new boyfriend of Josie's. She can't prove it, but she thinks he's the one who got Josie using again. I haven't mentioned any of that to Joe yet. He'll go bananas."

"Well, shit," Jeanie said. "Josie's always been her own worst enemy."

I opened my mouth to agree with her. My phone buzzed on the table in front of me. Before I could pick it up, Jeanie saw the caller ID too. It was Killian.

I shot Jeanie a look. She'd crossed her arms again, disapproval darkening her eyes.

I let the phone go to voicemail. Ten seconds later, Killian's text lit up the screen.

"We need to meet. Call me as soon as you can."

"Don't," I said to Jeanie before she could start.

"I didn't say a word," she said.

"You were thinking plenty."

She sighed. "Yeah. I was. I'm just worried this guy has clouded your judgment on this whole thing. And don't tell me I'm overreacting. I already know you went home with him from Mickey's the other night."

Of course she did. This was Delphi, after all.

"Don't judge me, Jeanie. I can stand just about everything but that. It's ... complicated with Killian. It always has been. I'm not ..."

"Save it," she said. "You don't owe me an explanation and I'm not asking for one. Just promise me you'll be careful."

Jeanie stood. She came around the table and put her hands on my shoulders. She kissed the top of my head.

"I worry about you, kid. That's all. I always have."

I covered her hand with mine and smiled up at her. "I know."

"You know what you're doing?" she asked.

I paused. I couldn't pretend with her. She'd see right through it. I valued her counsel and her opinion of me far too much.

"Not always," I answered honestly.

She patted my arm and headed for the hallway. As soon as I heard her going down the stairs, I picked up the phone and called Killian back.

Chapter 14

KILLIAN PICKED me up and at my suggestion, took me to a little restaurant I liked. An upscale place, ten miles from town, tucked away on a man-made lake. It was called The Wayside and it seemed perfect. The place was practically empty on a Wednesday night. Killian marveled at the price of the lobster.

"You're not in Chicago anymore." I smiled and sipped my Pinot Grigio. It was just the one glass for me tonight. I didn't want a repeat of the Jack and Coke situation.

He was quiet, pensive. Killian ordered nothing more than ice water. He was so careful that way. He would never have so much as a drop of alcohol if he were driving himself. That was rare too. He usually preferred traveling with his driver/bodyguard. It told me that whatever he wanted to talk to me about, it was absolutely private.

"I won't ask you how the Richards case is going because I know you won't tell me."

"I have concerns," I said. In the day since I'd read through the FBI's Ghost Man file, much of it was seared on my brain. The victims weren't always strangers. Other than my former client, I saw names I recognized. Ones I'd heard before in conversations I'd had with Liam over the years.

"You think he's guilty?" he said.

"I don't think in those terms," I answered. "Not in the way non-lawyers do. I think there are real problems with the prosecution's case on this one. But I need you to promise me again that you've dealt with your brother."

I expected him to smile in the way he always did. I expected his answer to be immediate, unequivocal. Killian was the alpha dog between Liam and himself. Any time Liam tried to step outside the bounds, Killian smacked him down. This time, there was no mistaking the troubled lines around his eyes.

"You don't have to worry about Liam," he finally said. "But I need to know whether you're truly committed to this case."

"Is that what you wanted to talk to me about?" I asked. "Is that why we're here? That's a phone conversation, Killian."

He smiled. "I asked you here because I wanted to see you. I like spending time with you. I understand all your reasons for leaving Chicago. I just don't see why that should stop me from having dinner with you. I still miss you."

I could pretend, but I couldn't lie. Sometimes, in spite of everything, I missed him too. There was a question in his words. One I wasn't ready to answer just now. I found myself grateful we were here at The Wayside and not somewhere closer to Delphi. The whole town knew Killian took me home from Mickey's the other night. So far, my brothers hadn't grilled me about it. I didn't yet have a good explanation for them.

"It's complicated," I said. "And for the next few weeks, I need to focus on this case only. Plus, my involvement with you tends to land me in trouble I don't need. My life is simpler now. It makes more sense to me. I belong here."

He blanched. I don't know if he thought he would talk me into coming back. It shocked me a little that he still thought I wanted to.

"I worry about you," he said.

"Don't."

"Force of habit. And from what I've seen, your life is only about work. When's the last time you went out like this?"

His question had a double meaning and he didn't even try to hide it. A little bit of anger rose in me.

"My personal life isn't your business anymore, Killian."

"I don't think you have a personal life anymore. That's the point I'm trying to make."

The waiter brought our food. We both went with the shrimp. We ate in companionable silence for a few minutes. Killian savored every bite.

"See," I said. "Southern Michigan cuisine is just as good as Chicago for about a tenth of the price."

"Is that an invitation?" He was teasing me.

"I couldn't see you fitting in down here," I said. "You like your fancy hotels and room service too much."

"I'm more adaptable than you give me credit for. And you're changing the subject. Be honest with me. More importantly, be honest with yourself. When's the last time you went out for a nice dinner with someone who wasn't your family?"

"I hang out with Jeanie. And Miranda. And ..."

He put his fork down. "Jeanie Mills is your mother's age. So is your secretary. And you work with them. They aren't your friends."

"And how is it you know so much about how I spend my time? I swear to God, Killian. If you've had me followed ..."

"I haven't," he said. "Only what you know about. And that was enough to make me concerned."

Last year, during the Aubrey Ames trial, I received a few death threats. Killian took it upon himself to assign me a bodyguard.

"Well, don't be," I said. I had more to say. I was angry. I also felt more defensive than I should. Maybe some of what he said hit home. But I was happy. Content. I meant everything I told him about feeling like I was finally someplace I belonged.

My phone rang, cutting off the argument I was gearing up to make. My heart jumped when the caller ID came up. I held up my index finger to Killian and turned in my seat so I wasn't facing him.

"Emma?" I asked.

Her words came out in a rushed, sobbing torrent. There was screaming in the background. A man's voice.

"Emma? Slow down. What's going on?"

"I don't know what to do!" Emma cried. "She's lost her mind ..."

Her words were cut off by an angry, staccato shout. I could make out Josie's voice, yelling, but there was someone else with them.

"Emma," I said. "Where are you?"

"It's my mom," she said, sniffling. "Aunt Cass ... I can't call my dad ... I need ..."

I heard glass breaking. This time, Emma screamed. A door slammed and I heard heavy footsteps. When Emma came back on the phone, she whispered so softly, I could barely hear her.

"Can you come get me?" she asked. "I don't care about the custody order. I don't care. I can't stay here. He's nuts."

"Emma," I said. "Listen to me. Are you safe?"

"Just, please come," she said. Then she hung up.

Squeezing my eyes shut, I slipped my phone in my purse.

"Cass?" Killian asked. For a moment, I forgot he was

even there. Memories flooded back. It wasn't Emma hiding in some closet while hell broke loose in the kitchen. It was me.

"I have to go," I said. "It's ... family trouble."

"Come on," he said. Killian took two hundred-dollar bills out of his wallet and placed them on the table. Our waiter was about to walk home with a hundred-dollar tip.

I rose to my feet. I didn't want him near this. Old instincts flared. This was a Leary problem. We didn't let in any outsiders. Only I didn't have my car.

"Cass," he said. "I heard enough of that from the other end of the phone. Was that your niece? Was that Emma?"

"Yes," I said. "Her mother's been ... and there's a boyfriend ..."

I could barely get the words out. A new fear flared in me. God. If this new boyfriend of Josie's had laid a hand on Emma ... I'd kill him.

Killian knew me well enough to read the expression on my face. A muscle jumped in his jaw and his expression went hard as stone.

"Come on," he said. "You can tell me the directions on the way."

Killian drove with the precision of a NASCAR driver. I kept checking my phone. Emma hadn't called back. I debated calling Joe. Guilt tickled the back of my mind. But I knew he'd rush right over and his temper would do more harm than good for whatever was going on. Katy was under a no-contact bond with Josie. It was just better for all of them if I could get Emma out of there without their help.

"There," I said. Killian turned down the side street to Josie's house. I let out a breath I hadn't realized I'd been holding. I expected to see a patrol car, an ambulance, or at least a gaggle of neighbors gathering outside. There were none of those things and I wondered if that made it more ominous or not.

Killian parked at an angle, blocking the drive. I recognized Emma's little blue Honda and Josie's red Taurus, but there was a third car in the driveway I didn't know.

"Can you just wait here a second?" I asked. No sooner had I got the words out before we heard more glass breaking from inside.

"The hell I will," Killian said.

He didn't wait for me. He slid out of the driver's seat and stormed up the front walk. I had to run to keep up with him.

I pounded on the front door. Killian stood beside me, fists curled and nostrils flaring. He was a sophisticated man now. A multi-millionaire with houses all over the world. But at his core, Killian Thorne was still a brawler who grew up on the streets of Belfast. If there was a fight behind that door, he'd be ready.

No one answered. We were treated to more yelling.

"Come on," I said. "I've got a key to the back door. Emma's probably in her room."

Killian followed me, towering at my side.

I didn't need the key. The back door stood wide open. From there, I saw the source of all the yelling.

Josie stood in the kitchen, red-faced and crying. A man loomed over her. He was bare-chested, wearing tattered jeans. He kept his fists curled at his side.

"You believe that little slut over me?" he shouted.

"Fuck you, Deke!" Josie yelled.

Josie picked up a plate out of the sink and frisbeed it at the man's head. Deke ducked it neatly and charged her. He got his hands on Josie's wrists and shoved her hard into the counter. She yelped. He cocked his fist back.

"Oh shit!" I yelled.

Killian moved, coming down on Josie's companion with

the force of an avalanche. He caught the asshole's fist mid-air and threw him back against the wall.

Josie took a staggering step backward, her eyes wide with shock.

"You in the habit of raising your hand to your woman?" Killian said through gritted teeth. When his emotions were high, his Irish brogue grew thick. He pushed the guy back into the opposite counter just like he'd done to Josie a moment before.

"Where's Emma?" I yelled.

Josie blinked hard, still trying to register what just happened.

"Take her," Deke yelled. "Get that little bitch out of my house!"

"Your house?" Josie more or less came to her senses and started screaming again. "This is my house. Don't you dare stand there and lie to me, Deke. This is Delphi. Everything comes back to me!"

Josie lost it then. She charged Deke and spit her words at him over Killian's shoulder. For his part, he stayed remarkably calm. Only his flaring nostrils belied the bubbling rage inside of him.

"Josie," I said. "Back off. Emma!"

I called out once more. Finally, Emma emerged. She too had been crying.

"He's a lunatic!" she said. "Don't you see that now? Jesus. He's been cheating on you since day one."

Emma threw something on the kitchen table and my heart shattered. She held a crack pipe and a rock. Josie's eyes went dead as she saw it too.

"You think I didn't know?" she said. "Aunt Cass, Deke's her dealer."

Deke tried to shove Killian back. For his efforts, Killian smashed his forearm beneath Deke's chin.

"Cass," he said, his voice remarkably calm and controlled for the thunderous fury I knew he held within him. "Take your niece out of here."

With his free hand, he reached into his pocket and tossed me his keys.

It was in me to protest. Emma was my family. This was the kind of mess it was my job to contain. Then I saw the look in Killian's eyes. Emma saw it too. She pulled at my sleeve.

"Please," she said. "I just want to get out of here."

"Killian," I started.

His lip twitched as he looked at me. He jerked his chin in a gesture that told me he had things under control.

Emma started crying again and all thoughts of doing anything other than protecting her melted away. I put my arm around her and led her outside.

She ran toward Killian's car. I slid behind the wheel and drove her back to my place.

She fell apart when we got there. On the way, I called my brother. Emma didn't want me to, but I gave her no choice. I left out the worst of the details. There would be time for that later. Right now, I just wanted to make sure Emma was safe.

She was still crying when we went inside. I pulled her against me on the couch and let her sob into my shoulder. "I've been telling her for weeks he's bad news, Aunt Cass. He's been running around with her friend Christine from the salon. It finally got back to her and he went nuts. Started blaming everything on me. He thinks I'm the one who told her. He said so many awful things. And she's using. You saw. He brought that into her life."

"Shh," I said. "It's going to be okay. You don't have to go back there."

I was already writing the emergency motion in my head.

There was no way in hell I was letting Emma spend another night under Josie's roof.

"She's not bad," she said. "Mom's just ... why does she always pick such losers?"

Emma cried a little more. Then she started to calm down. I knew Joe was on the way and so did she. My next trick would be to make sure he kept his own shit together. We both needed to stay calm for Emma.

She sniffled and wiped her face. "Who was that guy anyway?" she asked.

"That was ... a friend," I said.

"He was ... I mean ... Deke's such a bastard and a bully. I didn't think he could ever be scared of anyone. But your man had him terrified. I can't help that I loved that."

"He's not my man," I said, smoothing the hair away from her face. "He's just ... well ... he's Killian."

There was movement at the door. Joe moved so quietly, I hadn't heard him come in. His eyes flashed with anger. I held a hand up, trying to gesture to him that it was all right now. I hoped it was.

I knew he wanted to ask me a million questions. I'd tell him my plans to deal with the legal side of all of it. For now, he just needed to get Emma home and let her go to sleep.

"Thank you," Joe said. "Emma, you should have called me."

"It's taken care of," I said. "I'll handle it."

Joe nodded. When Emma put her head against his chest, all of Joe's fury melted. For as tough as she was, Emma would always be his little girl. She'd been terrified tonight. And brave. She needed her father and he would be there for her. He would give her the things neither of us ever had growing up.

He mouthed a "thank you," and started toward the door. Just as he was about to walk out, Killian appeared. The two of them silently sized each other up. But Emma pulled my brother along. His questions could wait. His daughter couldn't.

Killian closed the door behind Joe and locked it.

I'd kept my emotions tightly controlled from the moment Emma called. Now I felt them all unraveling. It was too much. All of it.

Killian came to me. His eyes held an answer to the question I hadn't asked. This may be my family mess, but he'd stepped in and taken care of it in a heartbeat.

He took me by the hands and pulled me against him. When Killian tilted his head toward mine, our lips met. I had a million reasons to pull away. But that night, I didn't.

Chapter 15

I woke in a haze. For a moment, I felt suspended in time. Killian's rhythmic breathing beside me, his scent, the past fourteen months seemed to dissolve. Only the sound of a distant pontoon boat motor snapped me back to the present.

He slept on his stomach, his face in profile. Peaceful, content. I was anything but. I padded to the bathroom then slipped on a pair of running shorts and a tank top. I needed to clear my head.

There were a dozen unanswered texts on my phone. Jeanie, Joe, and even my sister Vangie tried to check in. Vangie wasn't due back from Florida for another couple of weeks. Though I missed her, I was grateful to have one less person to worry about while I sorted through this trial.

I heard the tell-tale zing of fishing line at the end of the dock. I twisted my hair into a topknot and grabbed my running shoes. When I got downstairs, the coffee was already brewing. I knew Killian's schedule as well as my own. He probably woke at least an hour ago to say his morning rosary. Then he went back to sleep.

I went out the front door, shutting it quietly behind me. I

wasn't ready for a conversation with Killian or anyone else. I wouldn't be that lucky though. My brother Matty had put the dock in last weekend. Now he stood at the end of it, casting his line.

"Shit," I murmured. This wasn't some coincidence. No doubt he'd already talked to Joe. He'd of course be most worried about Emma. So it was just like him to send my younger brother here to check up on me.

Matty didn't turn as I made my way down the dock. The air was crisp, but had a warm weight to it that meant winter was finally giving up.

I put a hand on Matty's back. His shoulders bunched as he reeled in his line with quick skill. Both of my brothers had a pole in their hands before they even learned to walk. He slipped it into the holster attached to the side of the dock.

"You okay?" he asked, finally turning to me. My brother looked tired. The last year had been as stressful on him as anyone. He'd been on and off the wagon. His wife Tina had been threatening divorce since before Christmas. To be honest, I wasn't sure where he was sleeping lately. For a while, it had been right here. I reached up and smoothed the hair away from his eyes. Matty wasn't quite thirty yet. To me, I would always see that six-year-old boy who looked to me to fix his world when we lost our mother in a car wreck.

"I'm fine, Matty. I suppose you've heard Josie's drama."

"Yeah," he said, looking up toward the house. Killian's car was still parked in the street where I'd left it. I never even bothered to ask him last night how he made it back to my place. Killian Thorne was ever resourceful.

"That's not why you're here though," I said. "Joe sent you to check up on me. Don't pretend."

"I'm not pretending," he said. "Is that him?"

"If by him you mean Killian Thorne, yes. He's here."

I waited for a beat, my back going up. No matter what

else happened, I couldn't take Matty's judgment right now. I had no regrets about last night, but I wasn't in the mood for a post-mortem about it with my baby brother.

Whatever passed through Matty's eyes though, it wasn't judgment. He just pursed his lips and gave me a nod.

"I just woke up," I said looking down at my texts. "My phone blew up. Please tell me everything's okay over at Joe's."

Matty raised a brow. "Uh ... yeah ... they're more than okay. That's what he's been trying to call you about. I don't know what you did, but he got a call from Josie's lawyer about an hour ago. She's dropping the charges against Katy. And Joe said she's willing to sign an order letting Emma stay with him now. She's not planning to fight him on visitation or anything."

My heart dropped. I wanted to act surprised but something stopped me. In all the chaos last night, I'd never even mentioned a word to Josie about the legal ramifications of what I saw. It was on my list of things to deal with today. I planned to call Jeanie and have her start drawing up a motion. I looked back up at the house. This was Killian. It had to be. What the hell had he done after I left?

"Does he know where Josie is now?" I asked.

Matty shook his head. "Nope. I don't think he much cares. Katy's got her hands full trying to keep him calm. He's in the mood to bust some heads. Er ... one head anyway. That Deke Martin is a piece of shit, Cass. I had no idea that's who Josie was hooking up with lately."

"She needs help," I said. "Serious help. I'd like to get her into rehab."

"Is that really your mess to clean up?" he asked. "I mean ... it seems like you've got enough of your own."

So there it was. Matty at least had the decency to blanch after he realized how that might have sounded.

"Matty ..."

He put a hand on my arm to stop me. "I'm not trying to give you shit. I mean ... not more than normal. But I'm not going to pretend I'm not worried ... that we're all not worried. Joe's afraid this murder trial of yours is going to stir things up like when you defended Aubrey Ames last year. The shit they're saying about that Richards guy in the paper. And what about him?" He gestured with his chin toward the house.

"What about *him*?" I asked, my anger starting to rise.

The him in question opened the back door and started to walk toward us. You'd never know Killian had just tumbled out of bed. He was back in his dress shirt and tie but with the sleeves rolled up. He shot my brother a wry smile as he came down the dock.

"Matty," I said, taking a breath. "This is Killian. Killian, this is my younger brother Matty."

Killian smiled. He extended a hand. Matty shook it roughly as they sized each other up. I had a quick fantasy about shoving both of them sideways, straight into the water.

"It's good to finally meet you," Killian said.

Matty tilted his jaw to the side. He gave me a quick smile. "Same," he said.

"Catch anything?" Killian asked. He too had grown up on the water.

"Uh ... no keepers. We've got mostly walleye, catfish at night, some crappie."

Then the two of them started speaking the universal male language of fishing. Killian expressed genuine interest in the shiny lures my brother fashioned using a pair of my old earrings. They practically touched heads, discussing the finer points of their techniques.

I took the opportunity to slip away. I went back up the house, summoned by the strong, rich smell of freshly brewed coffee. I tapped Jeanie's number, hoping she wasn't calling to bust my ass about Killian next.

She answered the way she always did, in mid-sentence. "Good news," she said. "Miraculous really. Well, sort of. I just got off the phone with Tony Abbato's office. He's changed his mind about stipulating on a request for a continuance. He's going to go bat for you with Benitez. We just bought more time."

My shoulders dropped. I'd almost forgot about my Hail Mary request for a little more prep time on the Richards trial.

"You're kidding."

"Nope. But don't get too excited. He bought you an extra week. Judge Beni had another trial settle after yours."

"A week." I ran a hand through my hair. Matty and Killian were still deeply entrenched in their fishing lure discussion. I wouldn't be surprised if it ended with Killian offering to take Matty out on Lake Michigan. Lord. I wasn't sure whether that would be a positive step or a disaster. No matter what else happened, I wasn't willing to move backward in my life.

"Tell me what you want me to do?" she asked. "You can file a motion anyway. It'll be a harder sell because Tony will waltz in there spouting off how reasonable he tried to be. But a week ..."

"Is a week," I finished for her. "Can you call Tony back and tell him we'll take it?"

"You sure?"

"No," I said. "Not about anything. Richards has the thinnest of defenses. I'm sitting on a mountain of discovery that I'm only partially sure is complete. Fitzgerald's secretary pretty much tried to sabotage this case on the way out as a final eff you to Ted Richards. And I have nothing more than a funny feeling about how I left things with U.S. Attorney's office."

Jeanie chuckled in my ear. "I'd say a week sounds just about perfect then."

I shook my head. "Yeah. Thanks."

"Everything okay over at Joe's?" she asked. Boy, things sure got around in this town fast.

"Yeah," I answered. "More or less. I've got some loose ends to tie up for him. But Emma's safe. Josie is ..."

"Say no more," she said. "Josie is Josie. You coming into the office?"

"Yeah," I said. "Give me an hour."

"Good enough," Jeanie said. She clicked off without saying goodbye. Also one of her trademarks. I set the phone on the counter. Matty and Killian were walking up the dock. Killian said something that made Matty laugh. They shook hands again. This seemed more good-natured, less Alpha male. Matty saw me watching and waved. Then he climbed into his truck and drove away.

I took a sip of my coffee. Killian came back inside. I poured him a cup. I felt awkward. I wasn't ready for a deeper conversation about last night. I needed to get back to work.

"Can I ask you something?" I said. Killian was still attuned to my moods. He drank his coffee, but grabbed his suit jacket. He would make his getaway.

"You can ask me anything," he said. "You know that."

"After I left with my niece last night, I need to know what you did."

He raised a brow. "Did?"

I pointed to my phone. "I got a text from my brother. It seems his ex has had a change of heart on a few things since last I saw her. She's dropping the assault charges against my sister-in-law. And she decided not to fight Joe on custody of my niece anymore. I expect a call from her lawyer any minute. I need the truth, Killian. Did you threaten her?"

His smile dropped. "Cass, I think you know me better than that. I don't go around threatening women. I'm not my brother."

"You did something though. What was it? Did you pay her off?"

His silence partially answered the question. I wasn't sure if I really wanted the full story. I rubbed my temples, feeling a monster of a headache coming on. He rolled his sleeves down and buttoned his cuffs.

"I helped you solve a problem," he said. "Is your sister-in-law guilty of assault?"

"What? No. I mean … it's complicated," I said. He finished my sentence with me.

"Is your niece better off living with her father for now?"

"Yes," I answered. "It's just … I didn't ask you to do any of that. Whatever you did. And I can't … Killian … I can't owe you any more than I already do."

His face fell, then hardened again just as quickly. He finished the last of his coffee and swung his suit coat around his shoulders, snapping his arms through the sleeves. My words came out harsher than I meant. God. I don't even know what I meant.

Killian's face became a mask for me again. He gave me a polite smile. "You needn't worry, love," he said. "Your debt is almost paid."

He grabbed his keys off the counter, shot me a devastating wink, then turned and walked out the door.

Chapter 16

I WAS NOW on a first-name basis with several of the officers at the Wayne County Jail. Judge Beni's gift of a one-week extension evaporated, as I knew it would. It was now the first Friday of May. Monday morning, we would begin jury selection. This was my last chance to talk to Ted before he sat beside me at the defense table.

I sat in the interview room, waiting for Ted Richards to come. The smell of this place lingered on my clothes hours after I left. I began to feel like the case itself might stick to me in the same way.

The heavy metal door opened and Ted Richards walked in. He had a casual gait. This time, he wore no belly chain. Just simple wrist cuffs. He had a smile for me as the deputy closed the door and took a position outside.

I pulled a blank notepad out of my messenger bag and gestured for Ted to take a seat. He cocked his head to the side and his neck cracked. It echoed. The sound of it sent my pulse racing. I was starting to get antsy around this guy and needed to get a handle on it.

"I don't like this delay," he said. "You're supposed to ask me about things like asking for a postponement."

"It was my request," I said. "I needed more time to review new discovery."

Ted sat back. "New discovery? What new discovery?"

"Well, not so much new. New to me. There were ... complications with the file transfer from your former lawyer's office. It's sorted out now."

Ted's nose twitched. It gave him an almost canine appearance. He took a deep, snorting breath. "You trying to tell me Fitz tried to screw me over from the grave?"

"Not exactly," I said. I caught myself before going any further. I felt strangely protective of Theresa Shuler, despite what she'd done. I had to sort out whether keeping that information from Ted Richards was at odds with his own best interests. For now, I didn't think it had any bearing on his defense.

"The FBI was investigating you," I said.

"Was?"

"Ted, you know the crux of the prosecution's case as far as motive. They think you killed Mark Channing to silence him on behalf of the Kinsell organization."

"And that's got nothing to do with anything. Motive's not an element of the crime."

It seemed an odd thing to say. He was right.

"It'll come out," I said. "I can't keep the jury from hearing it. It's relevant, Ted."

"Well, the FBI's got the wrong man."

"Twenty-four murders," I said. "That's the number they have. Dates. Times. Details. It's damning. Fatal, maybe."

"Only if the jury hears it," Ted said. Again, he hadn't claimed innocence.

I found my focus drifting to his hands. They were rough and calloused. Strong hands. I couldn't help but imagine those same hands tightening the garrote around Jerome Haggerty's neck. In my mind's eye, I could see his crime scene photos from the portion of the FBI file I had. The M.E.'s report postulated Channing was strangled from behind. Haggerty had died facing his attacker. But if I ended up having to rest my defense on that grisly detail, I might as well give up now.

"Your demeanor in front of the jury is just as important as any piece of evidence they hear. You need to be aware of that," I said.

"My demeanor?" he asked. "Would you like me to smile pretty for them?"

"No," I said. "No matter what else happens, a man is dead, Ted. By all accounts, Mark Channing was a decent man. He had a wife. The jury is going to hear from her. Probably first. It's what I'd do. And she's heavily pregnant now."

Richards smiled. "She sure it's his?"

"You can't lose your temper in that courtroom. Not even once. You can't look bored or irritated like you are now."

He cracked his neck again. That sound. It was loud and distracting. This seemed like a habit of his he'd need to break.

I was about to tell him just that when his entire posture changed. He relaxed his face, letting his mouth turn down. His eyelids became hooded. He shifted low in his seat, almost in a slouch. In one breath, he was cocky, arrogant. In the next, he looked beaten down, weary. He sat that way for a beat. Then the chameleon changed his stripes and his mouth lifted in a smirk. He sat up straight and zoned those cold eyes in on me.

"I have no witnesses to call, Ted. There's no one who can put you at home at the time of the murders the way you claim."

"Claim?" he said. "I'm not claiming anything, Cass. It's just the truth."

"The bulk of my defense work will come in cross-examination. They may call your wife. You have to prepare yourself for that."

The facade fell. Ted's eye twitched. I felt the rage bubbling up in him.

"And I told you Sally's off limits."

"I can't stop the prosecution from calling her. And if you react the way you just did, she won't even have to open her mouth for the jury to believe the worst of you. I couldn't even get her to talk to me."

"And I told you not to try. It doesn't matter. The jury will believe me."

I took a steadying breath. "They're not going to hear from you."

Ted's eyes flashed. "Well, that isn't really your decision to make now, is it?"

"I believe it is," I said. "There's nothing whatsoever to be gained by putting you on the stand. We're better off leaving the state to its proofs and chipping away at the weaknesses."

"I disagree," he said. "I'm not going down for this. I told you, I wasn't anywhere near Mark Channing when he died."

It wasn't a direct denial. It left me with more questions than answers.

"And statements like that are exactly what could get you into trouble on the witness stand," I said.

"I was at home," he said.

"But you can't prove it."

He slammed his fist to the table. "I don't have to prove anything. They do. Isn't that what you just said?"

"There's evidence, and then there's perception. This case will be won and lost on the jury's perception. You have things in your favor. Big things. The prosecution has plenty of circumstantial evidence. I'll succeed in keeping some of it out. For the rest, I can raise questions in the jury's mind."

"I'm damn well gonna get up there and tell those assholes what really happened."

I crossed my arms. "What is that, Ted? What really happened?"

He went deadly silent. Ted Richards had an almost reptilian quality about him when he was brooding over something. It looked like he stopped breathing. Only the slightest movement of his eyes gave a window into his thoughts. The problem was, it would be easy for someone to see him like this and cast him into the role of a killer.

The crime scene and autopsy photos I'd been studying came to the surface of my thoughts. If the FBI was right, the man sitting just two feet away from me was one of the most calculating serial killers in history. He did it for sport. He did it for art. He did it for money.

"The car," I said. "Your Jag."

"What about it?" he said.

"You get on the stand, they're going to ask you about it."

He smiled. "It's a work of art, isn't it?"

It was such a strange and damaging thing for him to say and he seemed totally unaware of it. Abbato was going to tell the jury how Mark Channing's body was transported in that car.

"You'll have to answer questions about it on the stand if I put you there. Guys who do what you do for a living can't afford cars like that, Ted."

"Don't have kids," he said. "I've got the Jag."

"On paper, you earn forty thousand dollars a year in a good year. You pay a giant chunk of that to Sally in spousal support until she dies or remarries."

I wanted to swallow my words. I forged on. "There's no

way you can afford the payments on that car. But you don't have any. There's no loan on it."

His eyes widened. "Yes," I said. "That was pretty easy for me to find out. You can be sure Tony Abbato knows it too. So that's going to beg the question where you got the money to pay for it."

"None of his fucking business. It's not relevant to any part of his case. Seems to me that's the kind of thing you should be able to keep out if you're doing your job. You telling me you're not capable of doing your job?"

I was getting to him. Good. "Sure," I said. "I can raise hell about relevancy. Then the jury wonders why I'm so bent out of shape about keeping them from hearing how you can afford the car. Or, I lose the objection and Judge Benitez makes you answer. Do you have a good answer for that, Ted? Got a rich aunt we don't know about? Did you declare that gift with the IRS?"

His nose twitched. "What's your fucking point?"

"My fucking point is that's just one of probably a thousand rabbit holes Tony Abbato might lead you down if you take the stand. And I'll be damned if I do and damned if I don't as far as objections. You'll do more damage to your case on the stand than off it. You have to trust me on that."

"It's my life we're talking about!" he shouted. "And I didn't fucking kill that asshole."

"What about the rest of them?"

I shouldn't have asked.

Ted narrowed his eyes. He leaned forward, clinking his cuffs against the table. "I'm good at what I do, Cassiopeia. Aren't you?"

"Yes," I said without hesitation. "So good that this is a deal breaker for me. You're right about something. This is your defense. Your life. You really want to testify, I can't stop you. But then you're on your own. I'm tapping out."

His cold smile sent a shiver down my spine. "Bullshit."

"Try me," I said.

"You think I don't know why you're sitting there? You think I don't know who pulls your strings?"

"We're done here," I said. "I'll file a motion to withdraw before the end of the day."

Ted blinked. But he recovered just as quickly.

"I think this shit's not up to you anymore. I think if you have to file a motion, that means you can't get out unless your favorite judge lets you. And I think he's not going to let you. You're stuck with me, cupcake. Trial starts Monday. It's too late for you to back out of this."

"You'd be surprised what I can pull off, Mr. Richards."

"I know exactly what you can pull off," he said. Something shifted in him. The hostility was gone. If anything, he seemed amused now. The air in the room seemed to thicken. There was a strange familiarity about his eyes.

"Thorne," he said. "You think he's the one who recommended you?"

I bit my lip. I wasn't sure which Thorne we were talking about.

Then Richards answered that question and I let out a breath I hadn't realized I'd been holding.

"Liam's a smart man. But he's not anywhere close to as smart as he thinks he is." Ted's grin widened. "I asked for you special, Cassiopeia. You're sitting here because I want you to be."

I didn't dare breathe or blink. I didn't want to give him the satisfaction of a reaction. He could be lying. But somehow, I knew in my gut he wasn't. I wasn't Liam or Killian's idea at all. Ted Richards had been pulling the strings all along.

"We're done for the day, I think. Are we clear on what's

going to happen Monday morning? I'll have your suits sent over early."

He waited a moment, then lifted his hands. He pulled off an awkward shrug in his handcuffs.

"Whatever you say, boss," he said. "You just better hope you're right about calling me to the stand."

"Is that a threat?" I said. "Because if it is …"

"Nah," he said. "I don't make threats. If I'm coming for you, you'll never even know."

The deputy opened the door. Our time was up. I rose from my seat and slipped the strap of my bag over my shoulder. Ted sat looking straight ahead. As I stepped around the table, he shrugged his shoulders again. The crack of his neck echoed through the room.

Chapter 17

MONDAY MORNING, and a dreary haze settled over downtown Detroit. I hoped it wasn't an omen. As the deputies led Ted Richards into the courtroom, I realized he took my words about his demeanor to heart. He gave me his measurements. Miranda went out and got him three suits to wear. Maybe he'd lost weight in jail. But the sleeves hung a little long and the jacket had too much room in the chest. It made him look smaller, and he walked with a shuffling gait that reminded me of a young boy trying to figure out how to work dress shoes for the first time. As he made his way to the defense table beside me, his eyes caught mine and he gave me a devilish grin. Yes. Ted Richards knew exactly what he was doing.

The moment Judge Benitez took the bench, Ted's grin faded to a scowl. Two minutes later, Judge Beni called for the jury.

I'd gotten some of what I wanted after voir dire. We'd impanelled eight men and four women. Most of them were in their forties. As the last juror filed in, I let out a breath. He was tall, balding, and chivalrous as he held the chair steady for the woman he would sit beside. Juror number seven. A retired cop. I'd fought like hell to keep him out, but lost.

Tony Abbato was smiling at number seven as he took his seat. I knew his opening statement would be delivered straight to him. I also knew chances were the rest of them would vote him in as foreman. Lucky seven as far as the prosecution was concerned.

"You ready to go, Mr. Abbato?" Judge Benitez asked as he straightened the papers in front of him.

"Yes, Your Honor. Ready when you are."

Benitez just gave him a quick nod. Tony straightened his tie and stepped up to the lectern.

"Ladies and gentlemen of the jury," he said. "You've already been through a lot. Thank you for your patience and your service."

He paused, letting his expression darken. "Today, I want to tell you about someone else who understood the importance of civil service. I want you to get to know a man who dedicated his life to it. That man was Mark Channing. He dedicated his life to his country and serving justice and the freedoms we all enjoy. Because of it, he was cut down in the prime of his life. Make no mistake, Mark Channing was a casualty in a much larger war. A war that threatens to touch every single one of us in this room."

Ted bristled beside me. As discreetly as I could, I gave him a cold stare. Any negative reaction from him at all could sink this case before it really got started.

Abbato clicked his pointer and the projector behind him flared to life. It was a giant picture of Mark Channing in his marine uniform. He was handsome, with bright eyes. Young. Vibrant. Patriotic. Then Tony flipped the image to Mark's government ID photo. He wore a crisp black suit for this one, the American flag draped behind him.

"This man was a hero," Abbato continued. "The best of

us. He served nobly during Operation Iraqi Freedom. He took a shrapnel hit after an IED exploded near him. He lost three of his buddies during the same attack. When he came home, he could have lived a quiet life, gone into private practice near his small hometown in Indiana. He didn't do that though. Mark Channing chose a different way to fight for all of us. He took a job in the U.S. Attorney's office. For the last few years, he won over two dozen convictions against some of the most dangerous criminals in the country. He stayed a soldier in the fight against organized crime."

Ted murmured beside me. "He was a marine, not a soldier, dumbass."

I put a hand on his sleeve. The jury was still focused on Tony Abbato.

"Then," Abbato said, letting the jury absorb his words, "Mark Channing was murdered in cold blood. He was too good at what he did. He was getting too close to bringing down one of the worst gangsters the FBI has ever seen."

It was working. The jury was riveted. Juror number seven had a stony expression and he clenched his jaw.

"Mark Channing might have been president one day," Abbato said. "Two weeks before he died he told his wife he was going to accept a nomination to fill a U.S. Congressional appointment. I would have liked to have had Mark Channing fighting for me and winning in this new war. He was already a champion. But he never got the chance. Mark Channing wasn't just murdered, he was assassinated. This hero. This soldier of justice lost his life because he tried to do the right thing. Because he wasn't afraid to stand up for you and against the worst criminals in the country."

"This man." He pointed to Ted. Ted's shoulders dropped. He was still trying to make himself appear smaller. "The evidence will show that this man was paid to murder Mark Channing. Because he was getting too close. Mark

Channing was winning the new war he volunteered to fight and that couldn't stand.

"Mark Channing was a soldier. He was a family man too. You'll hear what kind of man he was from his wife, his colleagues, his friends, and neighbors. And I'm sorry for it. So sorry. Because I know in my heart each and every one of us is less safe today because Mark's no longer here to fight for us."

"Mark Channing's murder was brutal, heinous ... it ... there aren't enough words to describe what happened to him."

Abbato paused. I truly believe he hadn't intended it, but he stumbled on the last few words. His voice broke.

"He didn't deserve it," he said. "And this man ... Ted Richards is the one who murdered Mark Channing. You'll be asked to weigh whether there is reasonable doubt he committed this crime. I struggle to even call it a crime. It was an abomination. An affront to everything good and just in the world. Ladies and gentlemen, there is evil in the world. And you will be forced to look straight at it and call it out. It's what Mark Channing did his entire life. Now it's up to you."

With that, Abbato gave the judge a grim nod and returned to his chair.

Ted Richards seemed to turn to granite beside me. He needed a softer face. Right now, even before the first bit of evidence was presented, the jury was trying to decide if he was a killer. Did he look like one? His hands. They were large and calloused. His ill-fitting suit couldn't truly conceal how big a man he was. For now, I just needed him to keep his composure. And I needed to keep mine.

"Counselor?" Judge Benitez looked at me.

"Thank you, Your Honor," I said, rising. "And thank you, members of the jury. My name is Cassiopeia Leary. I represent Mr. Richards."

I took my own pause, walking deliberately to the lectern. The jury would size the lawyers up as much as they did the defendant. If they liked me, that alone could turn a few of them. If they liked the prosecutor better, they might side with him no matter what the legal evidence showed. It happened that way sometimes. Every word, every gesture counted. I folded my hands and rested them on the lectern.

"Mr. Abbato is right. Mark Channing was a true hero. And he didn't deserve what happened to him. He was a champion for justice. That's also true. He believed in the system designed to protect innocent people from being sent to prison for crimes they didn't commit. No matter how heroic the victim, justice demands you weigh the evidence presented to you not on emotion, but by the rule of law. That's what Mark Channing fought for. It's what I fight for too.

"Theodore Richards deserves justice too. He deserves the benefit of the doubt. The law demands that he receive it. The presumption of innocence. That means that each and every one of us is innocent until proven guilty. It's not just a slogan or a movie title. It's real. It matters. It's what Mark Channing fought for, just like Mr. Abbato told you.

"You will want someone to pay for what happened to Mark Channing. I know I do. Mr. Abbato is right about that too. This was a brutal, heinous killing. A man was snuffed out in the prime of his life. You may hear about all of it. It may disturb you. I know I'll take the things I learned in preparation for this trial to my grave. No matter the outcome, Mark Channing will never be far from my mind. I'll think of him every time I step up to this lectern and I hope I can honor his sacrifice in some small way by doing my job. By serving justice. By fighting for the system we have. It may not be perfect, but it's the best in the world. Mark Channing believed that too.

"Mr. Richards is innocent, ladies and gentlemen. No matter what the prosecution will want you to believe of him, he did not commit this crime.

"Mark Channing was every bit the warrior Mr. Abbato described him as. I wish I'd had a chance to get to know him. I think I would have liked him. And if what Mr. Abbato says is true about his political ambitions, then we've all suffered in some way from the loss of him.

"Marine, hero, champion, victim. Mr. Channing did not deserve what happened to him. It's up to us to make sure he didn't die in vain. It's up to you to make sure that the system he devoted his life to protecting works. Even when he became the victim. Ted Richards did not commit this crime. If you honor what Mark Channing fought and perhaps died for, then Mr. Abbato is right. But justice demands no innocent man should go to jail for a crime he didn't commit. That is what Mark Channing fought for. And so do I. Thank you."

I went back to my seat. Jeanie sat behind me. She'd been watching the faces of each jury member. I would rely on her read. But not now. Judge Benitez cleared his throat.

"Mr. Abbato," he said. "You may call your first witness."

Chapter 18

"THE STATE CALLS Catherine Channing to the stand," Tony said in a clear, thunderous voice.

I felt each staccato click of her footsteps like a tiny knife to the heart of my case. Catherine Channing didn't need to say a single word to get the jury to like her.

She was small. Pretty, but plain. She wore her light brown hair in a low ponytail, with strands coming loose at the sides. She had on a red cardigan sweater over a simple black maternity dress. No makeup. She was already trembling as she raised her hand to be sworn in. As she turned to climb into the jury box, they saw her in profile; her great, swelling stomach looked almost too heavy for her to carry with her small frame. The bailiff extended a hand to help her up. She thanked him and took her seat.

"Mrs. Channing," Tony started. "Thank you for being here. If you need a break, will you please let me know?"

He looked at Judge Benitez who gave him an affirming nod.

"I'm okay," she said. "I just want to get this over with."

So did I. Lordy, so did I.

"For the record, can you identify yourself?" he asked.

"Catherine Royce Channing. Mark Channing was my husband."

"How long were you and the victim married?"

She tried to smooth back one of her errant locks of hair. "We got married on January first of last year. So we were married a little over eight months when Mark ... when he was killed. I didn't find out about the baby for about a week after."

"So he never knew," Abbato said.

"No," she said. "We were trying though. Mark wanted to have kids right away. He was older than me. He'd just turned forty. I'm twenty-nine. And he just ... with his job and what he did before that in Iraq, he needed it. It was time."

"I understand. Mrs. Channing, I wish there was another way for me to do this. I wish it had been anyone else ... but ... I want to cut right to the night in question. And I will, but first, if you'll indulge me just a little."

Ted was scribbling notes on a pad beside me. I shot him a look. He narrowed his eyes and put down his pen. As he did, I saw what he drew. It was a shockingly good likeness of Catherine Channing on the stand.

"Mrs. Channing, do you know what your husband did for the Department of Justice?" he asked.

"He was a prosecutor," she answered. "Like you. He worked in the Organized Crime Division. There's a long name for it. I can't remember it. But Mark didn't talk a lot about what kind of cases he was working on. Most of the time, I found out after the fact while reading the news online."

"Of course. And what about the last case he was working on? Did you know what it was?"

She nodded.

"I'm sorry. This young lady seated in front of you has to

transcribe everything we say. Can you answer verbally for me? Do you have any knowledge about what your husband was working on before he died?"

"Oh, sorry. Yes." Catherine leaned forward so her mouth was closer to the thin microphone in front of her. "I know it was a big RICO case. He told me that much. And I knew that he was about to go to trial on it about two weeks after he died. We were planning a vacation around it. And I know the defendant was a Saul Kinsell. I asked Mark a few times about it. I mean, I looked Kinsell up online. I always did that when he was about to go to trial. I mean, Mark was gone a lot, preparing. I wanted to try and figure out what had him so stressed, you know? But I promise he never told me any details about that case. I would just hear him talking on the phone every now and again. To the other lawyers."

"Sure," Tony said. "If I may, I'd like to take you forward in time a bit. Can you tell the jury how you came to know about what happened to Mark?"

Abbato's face was genuinely pained from the question. It wasn't perfect. I could have objected to form. But Catherine Channing was Mark's grieving, pregnant widow. I would score no points coming hard at her with objections or on cross. I hadn't even completely decided whether I would subject her to cross. The best strategy might just be to get her off the stand and out of the jury's view as soon as possible. Still, my heart bled for her and part of me wanted her to know it.

"Um ... well ... he was ... On Friday, October nineteenth, we had plans to go to dinner. It was kind of our anniversary. It was one year to the day of our very first date. He called me at four o'clock in the afternoon. He said he'd be a little bit late. He was trying to get out of the office by five. We had reservations for seven thirty at this restaurant in Greektown. He told me to just meet him there because he was going to work until seven instead. I was angry. He knew I was angry. I hate driving into downtown Detroit. We ... we sort of had a fight about it."

Catherine Channing lost her composure. Tears rolled down her face.

"When did you end the call?" Abbato asked, trying to keep her focused.

"Um ... I'm not sure. They pulled my phone records. The police. You can look. I think it was maybe a ten-minute phone call. Mark told me to call an Uber and he'd drive us home after. I hated doing that too. It scared me. I don't even like riding in cabs."

"So you think you hung up with Mark by four fifteen?" Abbato asked.

"Objection," I said. "Counsel's starting to lead the witness."

I hated doing it. But if I didn't set some boundaries for Abbato early, he'd try to walk all over me later.

"Apologies," he said before Judge Beni could even rule. "Let me start over."

"Ms. Channing. What happened next after you hung up with Mark?"

"I got ready to go. I did end up calling for a car. I texted Mark a few times but he didn't respond. I thought he was still mad at me."

Ted started scribbling again. Before I could gesture for him to be still, he slid his notepad toward me. He'd written two words above the doodle of Catherine Channing.

"Trophy wife."

I put my hand over the writing. But Ted wasn't done. He wrote a second note. "Ask her how they met."

"Mrs. Channing," Abbato said. "Can you tell me what happened next?"

Catherine cleared her throat. She really was pretty in a

wholesome sort of way. Ted was wrong. She didn't look like a trophy at all to me. What she looked like was perfect for a man being groomed for political office.

"I got to the restaurant late. It was almost eight. There was a backup on the Lodge. I was feeling kind of sick to my stomach. I didn't know it then but it was probably morning sickness."

"Sure," Abbato said. "Then what happened?"

Catherine wiped her eye. "I kept waiting. Mark wasn't answering his phone. I started getting worried. But I mean ... not terribly worried. Not yet. I was still so angry."

"Why were you angry?" Abbato asked. It stunned me a little that he did. It was a risk. In fact, it was one of the questions I had for her on cross.

"He left me there," she said. There was a hard edge to her voice that surprised me. "I was just waiting. People were looking at me and I knew they felt sorry for me. Mark didn't answer his phone or his texts and I was just so mad. I mean, how could he do that?"

There was a tiny break in Abbato's rhythm. Catherine's answer wasn't what he expected. And that right there was the problem with the way he asked it.

Ted Richards was a lot of things. Dumb wasn't one of them. I saw the corner of his mouth twitch. He knew exactly what was happening too.

"Mrs. Channing, can you tell the jury what happened next?"

"I left," she said. "I was so embarrassed and angry with Mark for doing that to me. I had to call another driver. It was hard to find somebody on short notice. Mark was supposed to drive me home. He never showed. I got home around ten o'clock and I went to bed."

It was my turn to scribble like mad.

"Then what happened, Mrs. Channing?"

"I woke up around eight, I guess it was. Still no Mark. No calls. No texts. His car wasn't in the garage. We were supposed to meet with a contractor out at the new house Mark was building. In Gross Pointe Farms. I wanted to move somewhere really nice. He promised me when he proposed. So I went out there."

Tony paused. He walked back behind the lectern. The worst things that Catherine Channing could say were coming up.

"Mrs. Channing, please tell the jury what happened when you got to the construction site?"

She started to fidget with her sleeve. Once again, Catherine Channing looked so small and girlish. Her skin paled.

"I found Mark," she said, her voice breaking.

"I'm so sorry to have to make you relive this," Tony said. "But I need you to tell the jury what you mean by that."

"I saw tire tracks. It had rained a little the night before. The ground was kind of wet. I parked next to them. Got out. The contractor hadn't shown up yet. He was late too. Why are men always so late? They say women are but I'm always on time."

Richards wrote again. "Except for at the fucking restaurant."

I bit my bottom lip.

"I found Mark in the middle of the house. Or ... what would be the house. He was lying face down in the mud. I almost didn't see him. He was so dirty."

"What did you do then?" Tony asked.

"I screamed," she said. "I mean ... because I knew. He wouldn't just be lying there like that if he wasn't. But ... I had to check. You know? Like maybe it was a heart attack or something. He could still have been breathing. So I climbed down into the pit. I tugged at him. Tried to roll him over. But he was so heavy. Anyway, I knew then it was too late. I knew he was dead."

"Why?" Tony asked.

Catherine was sobbing now. "Because he had this awful wound. His neck. I thought he'd been stabbed. But it was a wire. It was all sticky with mud and blood but his skin was open. His whole head kind of rolled back. His eyes were open and staring and he was gone. Just gone ..."

Catherine's sobs became uncontrollable. "I have nothing further," Tony said. "Thank you Mrs. Channing. And I'm so sorry for your loss."

The courtroom went deadly silent except for Catherine's crying. Judge Benitez waited a moment. Then he leaned over.

"Dear," he said. "Would you like a few minutes to compose yourself? This lady here needs to ask you a few questions."

Catherine blew her nose into a tissue. She smoothed her dress and looked up, staring straight at me.

"No," she said. "No. I don't want to break. I want to be done. Ask your questions."

"Thank you," I said. "They are brief. Mrs. Channing, I too am so sorry for your loss. You're brave to be here. I cannot imagine how hard this is."

"Thank you," she said. Not once had she looked over at Ted Richards. When I turned to gather my notes, he was staring straight at her with a smirk on his face.

I turned back to Catherine Channing.

"Mrs. Channing," I said. "You indicated you didn't arrive at the restaurant until almost eight and you waited about an hour for your husband. You said you tried to call and text him a few times during. Was there anyone else you tried to call?"

I knew the answer already. I'd reviewed the phone forensics report.

"I called my sister," she said.

"Do you remember what you talked about?"

"Not really. I kind of unloaded on her about how Mark wasn't there yet."

"What was her reaction?"

Catherine shrugged. "She didn't have much of one. I mean, she told me to keep calling him."

"Did you?"

"I left a voicemail for him right before my driver got there."

"Do you remember what you said on that voicemail?"

She sniffled. "I was pissed, okay. I didn't know ... I didn't imagine ... I ... I told him don't bother coming home."

"Had he ever done that before? Not come home?"

She shook her head. "Sometimes. He slept at the office sometimes. When he was working late."

"Was it his custom to call and tell you if he'd be spending the night at the office?"

"Yes."

"But he never said that this time?"

"No."

"Did you try calling him at his office?"

"No."

"How often would Mark choose to spend the night at the office during your marriage?"

Catherine looked down. "I didn't keep count."

"Once a week? Once a month?"

"Probably a couple of times a month."

"Thank you. And those times when he slept at the office, he always called you to tell you of his plan?"

"Objection," Abbato said. "She's already answered that."

"Sustained," Benitez said.

"So, is it fair to say the fact Mark didn't call or text you of his plan to sleep at the office was out of character for him?"

"Um ... it was. He always called."

"Thank you," I said. "Did you call the police at any point that night? I mean, after he didn't call or didn't come back home?"

"No, ma'am," she said.

"And the next morning, you said you hadn't heard from him either. You didn't call the police then?"

"No. I just assumed he'd meet me at the construction site for our meeting with the contractor."

"So you weren't worried at any point up until you got to the site?"

She looked at Abbato. Catherine's color went a little pale. "Um ... no."

"Because it was Mark's habit to occasionally not come home."

"Um ... I mean ... I suppose so. Yes."

"But it was not his habit to not call you if he wasn't going to come home."

She looked down again. "He usually called, yes."

"Thank you," I said. "I have nothing further. Thank you again, Mrs. Channing. I wish you the best."

She gave me a weak smile. I turned back to the table. Ted's expression was unreadable. Jeanie was hiding a smile.

"You're up, Mr. Abbato," the judge said.

Chapter 19

THE STATE CALLED Detective Carla Ellis Whitney to the stand next. She looked as strong as Catherine Channing had looked frail. Impeccably dressed in a cream-colored suit, her dark skin stood out in luminous contrast. She wore her braids gathered into an intricate bun. Detective Whitney's voice was calm and almost melodic as she took her oath and answered Tony Abbato's establishing questions.

Whitney had joined the Detroit Police Department after serving with the Wayne County Sheriffs for twenty years. In her over thirty-year law enforcement career she'd served on multiple drug task forces and earned both state and national commendations. She was flawless, likable, formidable. She had worked as a homicide detective for more than a decade and cleared hundreds of cases including one of the oldest cold cases in Michigan two years ago. The jury sat with rapt attention and admiration, hanging on every word this woman said. Then Abbato got to the scene of the crime.

"Detective," he said. "Can you tell the jury what you found on the night of October nineteenth?"

"Well, it was actually in the morning of the twentieth,

Counselor. I was called to the scene at approximately eleven a.m. We had reports of a white male victim, late thirties, early forties. When I got there, the area had been cordoned off by our crew. The Crime Scene Response Team arrived when I did. I coordinated with their efforts and took statements from the uniformed officers. Mrs. Channing was still on scene. She was visibly upset. She had been placed in the back of a patrol car to get her out of view of any onlookers."

"Were there onlookers?" he asked.

"Well, we had quite a presence at that point. I think it was six or seven patrol cars. The CSRT van. The tape was visible from the street as we didn't want anyone else coming in or out. The property is located in a wooded area. The construction site where the house was being built was at the end of a winding, quarter-mile drive. The main road leading into it is rather well trafficked. So yes, cars were beginning to slow as they drove by. We wanted to make sure we controlled who was coming in and out."

"What did you find when you arrived?"

"Well, the victim, as I said, was a white male, approximately forty years old. He was lying at the bottom of a pit dug for the foundation of the house. He was wearing a business suit. He was wearing only one shoe. He appeared to have been strangled. Garroted, actually. We found wire around his neck which was later determined to be piano wire. It was embedded into his flesh approximately one inch."

There was an audible gasp from one of the jurors. Juror number seven remained stoic, respectful as Detective Whitney delivered her testimony with cool reserve. I knew what was coming next.

"May I direct your attention to what's been marked as exhibit four for identification?"

Whitney cleared her throat and lifted a photograph.

"Do you recognize this photo?" he said.

"I do," she answered.

"Can you describe it?"

"This is a photo of the victim as I first saw him, lying supine on the ground."

"So it is a fair and accurate representation of the scene as you came upon it on the morning of October twentieth?"

"It is," she said.

"Your Honor, the state moves to admit exhibit four into evidence."

Benitez looked at me as Tony leaned back from the lectern and handed me a copy of his exhibit.

"No objections," I said.

"So admitted," Benitez said.

A moment later, Tony put the crime scene photo up on the overhead projector.

Catherine Channing was no longer in the room. Two members of the jury went completely pale.

In death, Mark Channing looked ghoulish. His eyes bugged out, his lips were purple and swollen. The wound around his neck shocking. There wasn't much blood, but the skin was torn straight through.

"How did you come to make an arrest in this case?" Abbato asked.

Detective Whitney sat straighter in her seat. Her eyes came into sharp focus and she zoned in on Ted Richards. For once, he stopped doodling.

"The critical pieces of evidence found at the scene were the murder weapon itself, it was left in the victim's neck. As I indicated, it was 0.035 inch piano wire. Steel. Approximately two feet in length. The medical examiner concluded there were no other wounds."

"Objection," I said. "Foundation."

Abbato gave me a nod. "Let's just stick to the evidence

you collected, Detective. Tell me the basis for your arrest warrant."

"Of course," she said. "We were able to analyze the tire treads going in and out of the property. As I indicated, it had rained the night before. There was only one set of tracks coming into the property. Mrs. Channing's vehicle was parked near the street. She came to the construction site on foot. We identified the make and model of the tires from the tracks. They were of a high-performance type. Carpet fibers on the victim's clothing and in his hair came up as a match as coming from a 2014 F-Type Jaguar. The tires were consistent with that make and model as well."

"Can you explain what that means?" Abbato said.

"Well, Mr. Channing wasn't killed at the construction site. He was placed there. We believe he was transported in the defendant's trunk sometime after his death and dumped there."

"But you're not claiming those carpet fibers and tire tread alone would be enough to prove Mr. Richards is the killer?"

"No, sir," Whitney continued. "The morning after the murder, my office was contacted by an Agent Leslie from the Federal Bureau of Investigation. I had just completed an interview with Mr. Channing's colleagues at the U.S. Attorney's office. They began to advise me of a RICO case the victim was getting ready to prosecute. Agent Leslie called me with information he thought might be relevant to the case."

"And what information was that?"

"Special Agent Leslie had a file on the defendant. Other suspected killings ..."

"Objection!" I couldn't get to my feet fast enough. "To the extent this witness is about to testify about any other suspected criminal activity of Mr. Richards, we have a 504 issue."

Benitez frowned. I wanted to wring Tony Abbato's neck. This was a cheap trick. Even letting Whitney get into this territory in front of the jury was dangerous and he knew it. Now they'd heard me object and even if I won, he got their attention.

"Judge," Abbato said. "We can move on to another topic."

"By all means," Benitez said.

"Detective Whitney," he continued. "Just tell us what else made you request the arrest warrant?"

Whitney uncrossed then recrossed her legs. "I was put in touch with a confidential informant working with Special Agent Leslie. He believed this witness had information relevant to the Channing murder."

"Did he?"

"Objection," I said. "To the extent this witness is about to testify about anything she was told by this alleged informant, we're in hearsay territory."

"Sustained," Judge Benitez said. "Stick with what you did, not what you were told."

"Of course, Your Honor," Whitney said. "I felt we had probable cause to arrest Mr. Richards based on the carpet fiber and tire treads matching a vehicle registered to him. Additionally, I had information that Mr. Richards was seen parked outside the victim's home two consecutive nights before he went missing. When we executed that arrest warrant and searched Mr. Richards's vehicle, we found blood evidence inside the trunk matching the victim's blood type."

Abbato introduced photographs of Ted's car and inside the trunk. He admitted the lab report on the blood. He moved to the table and held up a coil of wire, marking it for identification.

After establishing chain of custody, he asked the question that riveted the jury most.

"Detective Whitney, can you tell the jury what this is?"

"Yes," she said. "This is a loop of piano wire we found in the defendant's garage the night he was arrested."

"And can you tell me if there is anything else significant about it?"

"Well," she said. "It matches the type used to choke Mark Channing."

"Anything else?"

Detective Whitney hesitated. She tilted her head slightly. "Well, yes," she said. "We searched Mr. Richards's residence, of course. There was no piano on the premises. He doesn't own one."

"Thank you, Detective. Your witness, Ms. Leary."

I straightened my jacket.

"Thank you," I said. "Good afternoon, Detective. I just have a few questions. Regarding the Jaguar, you can't be one hundred percent certain the carpet fibers came from that exact vehicle, can you?"

She leaned forward. "Correct, though it is the only vehicle of that exact type registered to an owner in this county."

Shit. I walked right into that.

"And this blood evidence, I need you to be more specific. What was the victim's blood type?"

"O positive," she said.

"Do you know Mr. Richards's blood type? Did you have occasion to test it in your investigation?"

"Yes, ma'am," she said. "He is also O positive."

"Did you recover any DNA evidence at the crime scene other than the victim's?" I asked.

"No, ma'am, we did not."

"No DNA evidence from the victim in the Jag?"

"No."

"No DNA evidence from the victim present at Mr. Richards's home?"

"No, ma'am."

"And this informant you speak of, to your knowledge, was he or she offered anything in return for cooperating?"

"Well, I don't have the specifics on that. But I believe so, yes."

"So I'm clear, the principal evidence you relied on to make this arrest include carpet fibers and tire treads matching a Jaguar Mr. Richards owns. The presence of piano wire at his home. And blood found in the trunk of this car matching both the victim's blood type as well as the defendant's and more than a third of the entire human population. Correct?"

I heard Tony Abbato grumble beside me, but he didn't object.

"That and the testimony of the informant. I can't speak to what the informant said. I understand they will be available to testify. I'll leave that up to you."

"Thank you, Detective. I have nothing further."

Shockingly, Tony Abbato did not ask the detective anything on redirect. The judge advised Detective Whitney to remain available under her subpoena, then excused her for the day.

I stole a quick glance at the jury as I made my way back to the defense table. The only thing I knew for sure was that their attention had held. Other than that, this thing could go either way.

Chapter 20

DETECTIVE CARLA WHITNEY left the witness stand just before four o'clock. Judge Benitez adjourned us for the day. In a moment, the deputies would come to escort Ted back to his cell. They would wait until the jury was out of the room.

"It's bullshit," he said. "All of it."

During my cross, Ted had been busy with his doodle pad. He'd made a detailed sketch of me with my back to him at the lectern. Over my left shoulder, he'd drawn Detective Whitney, exaggerating her features to the point she looked ghoulish.

"We start up first thing in the morning," I said. "It would help if you had some family or friends in the gallery, Ted. The jury notices this stuff. The more they can view you as something cold and detached, the easier it will be for them to bring back a guilty verdict."

"That's why you need to put me on the stand," he said.

"We've been over this. And right now, we're focusing on one witness at a time. I can score points with the science they trot out tomorrow. I laid the groundwork today. But they're putting the coroner up. Things are about to get a lot rougher."

Ted finally put his pencil down and gave me a gruff laugh. Two deputies came to his side. Ted put his wrists up as he stood so he could be cuffed. He started whistling as they led him away.

I gathered my things. Jeanie was at my side.

"I still don't know what to make of that fucker," she said. "It's like he's barely interested in his own trial. They noticed, Cass."

I slid my bag over my shoulder as we turned to walk out of the courtroom.

"How'd it go?" I asked her. Jeanie was my eyes and ears in the courtroom. Her instincts and read of other people were accurate enough to seem otherworldly sometimes.

"You scored some points with the wife. I don't know how you did it, but they were paying attention to that stuff about her not even bothering to call the cops on Channing when he didn't show up for dinner. It was weird."

"Yeah," I said. We pushed our way through the gauntlet of spectators and made our way downstairs. "I took a risk with that. I honestly had no idea."

"Right," Jeanie said. We took the stairs over the elevator. "Whitney was tough though. And you screwed yourself a little on the car."

I let out a sigh. She was right. I left Carla Whitney an opening and she blasted right through it mentioning how Richards owned the only Jag of that type in the county. I had to be better. "Don't worry," Jeanie said. "There's a hell of a lot of trial left and you may have done some damage with the blood evidence. Depends on how skillful Abbato is when he presents the particulars tomorrow. Most of these people think they're DNA experts from watching the friggin' O.J.

trial. They're liable to think the lack of it means more than it means."

We'd reached the ground floor. "Yeah. Still, it's a pretty thin thread to try and hang a whole defense on."

"You heading back to the office?" she asked.

I took a breath. It was warm again, thank God, over seventy degrees. Pure Michigan weather. We'd had a thirty-degree swing since early morning.

"No," I said. "I need to clear my head for tomorrow. I'm heading home. I think a glass of Riesling and a pontoon ride will do me some good."

Jeanie nodded. "I'll check in with Miranda. As long as she doesn't have some emergency for us, I'll see you bright and early."

Jeanie gave me a sloppy salute, and headed toward her car. I slipped on my sunglasses and found my own vehicle.

I got lucky, hitting the freeway about ten minutes ahead of the thickest part of rush hour. I made it home in less than an hour. Another reminder why I preferred practicing in Woodbridge County over anywhere else. As I made the final turn toward Finn Lake, I felt the day's tensions sloughing off. I only wished the water was warm enough for a swim. It would take another few weeks for that.

As I pulled into my drive, a little of the tension came back. Two trucks were parked along the street. Both of my brothers were waiting for me.

I stashed my sunglasses in the visor. I slipped off my heels. They dangled from my fingers as I made my way bare-foot out to the dock.

Matty sat on the end of the pontoon, his pole in the water. Joe came out of the shed carrying a gas can. He stopped short when he saw me.

"You done for the day?" he asked.

I shot a look out to Matty. I caught him quickly turning back to the water, trying to play it casual.

"Something tells me I'm not. Am I allowed to at least go change into a pair of shorts and grab a glass of wine?"

Joe smiled. "Bring two beers down with you."

I made a courtly bow and headed into the house. What I really needed was a shower. I didn't suppose my brothers would wait that long though.

As I made a quick change out of my suit, my phone buzzed. It was Killian. His ringtone sent my heart fluttering for a moment. I was just glad I was out of Joe and Matty's earshot.

"Hey," I said, answering.

I could hear traffic sounds in the background. "Hey, yourself. I heard it went reasonably well today."

"Of course you did," I said, setting my teeth on edge. It didn't surprise me one bit if Killian had spies in the gallery. I knew him well enough to know he would closely monitor anything that might impact his business in any way. A shudder went through me at the prospect of just how much he knew about Ted Richards.

"It went," I said. "It's just day one. And you know I'm not going to talk any more about it with you."

"Fair enough. I want to make plans though. To see you."

"Killian, it's a bad idea on about four different levels. I need to focus on this trial. It will take at least a week. And it's ... it's just not a good idea for me to be seen with you right now."

He paused a beat. "You sure that's all it is?"

I closed my eyes. It was a hard thing to admit to myself, but it felt good when he was around. Too good, maybe.

"I'll call you later," I said. "Promise. I've got a lot of work ahead of me tonight to prepare for tomorrow. You know how this goes."

He laughed. "I know exactly how this goes. That's why I want to see you. I know how you get during trials, Cass. You forget. I've been the one taking care of you during them. I know what you need."

I sat down on the edge of the bed. The man did tend to have a sixth sense into my moods. For years, I wouldn't let anyone else near me during trial week but him. He knew not to ask too many questions. He would make every other aspect of my life effortless so I could focus. I missed that. And I knew how dangerous it was to think that way.

"I'll call you later," I persisted. "Promise."

"Make sure you eat," he said. "I arranged to have Edwardo's delivered to you in about an hour. I won't invite myself over to share it with you this time. I've got a few things of my own I need to take care of."

At the mention of Edwardo's my stomach growled. God, this man knew me well. Edwardo's was my favorite deep dish pizza in Chicago. I knew better than to question how he managed to get it to me. That was Killian. He just did things like that.

"Thank you," I said.

He clicked off before I could say goodbye. My brothers were still waiting on the boat. Matty had just snagged a large-mouth bass and worked on getting the hook out of its mouth. I went downstairs to pour the wine and grabbed a bottle of Bud and a Coke for Matty.

Joe pulled the boat a little closer to the dock so I could step on. He sat in the captain's chair. Nineties alt-rock played softly through the speakers. I put Matty's pop in the cup holder closest to him as he cast his line again.

We sat in companionable silence for a while as Matty snagged a few more fish and Joe tinkered with the bimini cover. I put my feet up on the bench seat, letting the sun warm my face. The rhythmic sway of the boat nearly put me to sleep.

I finished my wine and put the glass down, turning to Joe.

"How's Emma?" I asked.

He swiveled his chair so he faced me.

"Better," he said. "She's relieved not to have to go back to Josie's right now. Or really ... ever."

"Any luck getting Josie into a program?"

Matty holstered his fishing pole and took a seat on the back of the pontoon above the motor. He cracked open his Coke. I knew how much he wished it were a beer.

"I'm out," Joe said. "It kills me to see her in the state she's in, but she's made it too damn hard. Katy's not handling it very well."

"I can imagine," I said, wishing I'd just brought the whole damn bottle of wine down.

"The case against her got dismissed formally today," Joe said. "No charges. That helps."

I nodded.

Joe was staring hard at me. I didn't know what he expected me to say. If he was gearing up for a lecture, I wasn't in the mood to hear it.

"Thank you," he said. "And thank ... thank Killian. I know he was behind this. Josie won't say as much, but I know."

"He didn't threaten her," I said. "You know that, right?"

Joe shrugged. "No, that wouldn't have worked anyway. He just figured out the thing to give her that I never could. He paid Josie off, Cass."

I pressed my fingers to the bridge of my nose. I wasn't sure if Joe meant that as a question, an accusation, or just a statement. I decided to assume it was a mere statement.

"You're seeing him again," Matty chimed in. Joe shot

him a look. Apparently, whatever plan they'd cooked up, Matty had just veered off script.

"Look ..." I started.

"No," Joe said. "Just don't. I don't want to hear about how he's different or how I shouldn't believe everything I read. I've seen enough, Cass. I'm not an idiot. I may not have lived in a fancy apartment or had the money you did. But don't blow me off on this."

"I'm not," I said, meaning it. "Joe, I'm not. I didn't ... I didn't ask Killian to do anything where Josie was concerned. But he was there. Emma called me. What was I supposed to do? Not come?"

He threw a beer cap into the garbage can by his feet. "No. Shit. I don't know. I'm grateful. I won't pretend this isn't a fuck ton of a load off my mind. It's just ... I don't want to owe that guy anything."

"You don't."

"And I don't want you owing him anything either. Not for me. If you ... if he ..."

Heat flared through me. I sat up straight. "Jesus, Joe. Do you think I whored myself out to him for you and Emma?"

His eyes snapped wide. "Fuck. No ... I didn't ..."

I let the anger roll through me and dissipate a little before saying anything.

"Cass," Matty said. "We just worry about you, okay? This whole thing. This guy you're defending. This Thorne fucker showing up again. I know you're not doing it for the money. The case ... I mean. So it makes me wonder what *are* you doing it for? Did he threaten you?"

I didn't answer instantly. I didn't mean anything by it, but my hesitation was enough to clue Joe in.

"Shit," he said. "He threatened us."

"No! Killian would never hurt me or anyone I love. You need to believe me on that. He's not the enemy."

"It was something though," Matty said. "Jesus, Cass."

"Enough," I said. "I don't want to talk about my job with either of you. You both ought to know me well enough by now to trust my judgment. I'm just doing my job. That's all. And just this one job. I'm not leaving Delphi. I'm not going back to work for Thorne. As far as how I choose to spend my personal life ... well ... I'm sorry, but it's none of your damn business."

Joe and Matty went deadly silent. They looked at me. They looked at each other. Then they both burst out laughing. Matty doubled over from it. Joe wiped a tear from his eye before he recovered enough to talk again.

"You're a Leary, Cass. Did you miss a day or something?"

I rolled my eyes and threw a flip-flop at him, hitting him square in the chest.

Things were easier between us and I was glad of it. Three mallards paddled by us at the end of the dock. I sat back and watched their slow progression. It was one female and two males. The males hustled after her, flapping their wings. The female turned and bit back, letting out a sharp quack. The males spread their wings, puffed their chests, then settled back to follow a few inches behind her.

When the sun dipped below the horizon, a driver pulled up with my pizza. I ignored my brothers' questioning looks and invited them in for dinner.

Chapter 21

ABBATO PLAYED things exactly as I would have the next morning. He put his science on before the big punch of the day. And he took the bait I'd left the day before.

"Detective Fanning," he said. "Can you tell me why there was no DNA evidence in the suspect's trunk?"

Detective Burt Fanning was a year from retirement. Fanning was built like a Mack truck. Solid, wide, and he had a low, gravelly voice that vibrated across the floor when he spoke. He was smart. No nonsense, but his dry delivery was beginning to put the jury to sleep.

"You don't sometimes," he said. "And the trunk appeared to have been recently shampooed. We found trace chemicals that were consistent with a common carpet cleaner, as well as bleach."

"In your expert opinion, can you estimate how recently this cleaning took place?"

"It was recent," he said. "Probably within the last twenty-four hours from when the vehicle was seized."

"How do you know that?"

"Well, for one thing, the interior carpet was still damp to the touch. Also, when I opened the trunk, the smell of bleach and cleaner was pungent. It hit me in the face, so to speak."

"Thank you," Abbato said. "I have no further questions at this time."

Judge Benitez turned to me and gestured. I went to the lectern.

"Detective Fanning, did you find any of the victim's DNA in the trunk of the Jaguar?"

"No, we did not."

"Did you find any of the victim's DNA in or on any other part of the vehicle?"

"We did not."

"Did you find any hairs matching the victim's in or on the Jaguar?"

"No, we did not."

"And you didn't find any fibers from the clothing the victim was found wearing, did you?"

"No, ma'am."

"You found no mud or dirt inside the trunk."

"No, it was cleaned pretty thoroughly."

"You're aware the victim was missing a shoe, correct?"

"I was told that, yes," he said. "I didn't personally observe the condition the victim was found in."

"Nevertheless, did you find the other shoe in the car?"

"No, ma'am," he answered.

"And you can't say for sure whether the victim's body was ever in that trunk, can you?"

He let out an irritated breath. "I testified we found matching carpet fibers from the trunk on the victim's body."

"That's not what I asked you. You can't say for certain that Mark Channing, alive or dead, was ever in that trunk. You can only say that carpet fibers from an F-Type Jaguar were found on his clothing. That's your testimony, correct?"

"Yes."

"And the blood evidence. You found three drops of O positive blood inside the trunk. Correct?"

"Yes."

"Where was this blood located?"

"It was found just inside the trunk, near the latch."

"You're aware the defendant's blood type is also O positive, correct?"

"I was made aware of that, yes."

"So, you can't say for certain whether that blood belonged to the victim or the defendant."

"No, but there were no open wounds on the defendant when he was taken into custody."

"No open wounds. Can you tell me exactly how long that blood was in the trunk?"

"No, I can't."

"Days, weeks, months? Is it possible that blood was there weeks before the car was seized?"

"It's possible, yes."

"Thank you. I have nothing further."

The jury started to wake up. Judge Benitez checked the clock.

Tony waived redirect.

"We've got about forty-five minutes before I want to break for lunch. Call your next witness, Mr. Abbato."

The jury perked up as Tony called Dillon Paley, the medical examiner, to the stand.

Dillon looked younger than Matty to me. He had a fresh face and rosy cheeks that reddened even further as he was sworn in. He wore a crisp blue suit and combed his thick blond hair back. He was handsome with wide brown eyes. God, he barely looked old enough to shave. But he came with some of the most jarring evidence Tony Abbato would present.

Tony went through his establishing questions quickly. I knew he would have preferred if Paley were called after lunch when the jury was fresher. So would I. Even if he got through his direct in forty-five minutes, Judge Benitez would break for lunch before I could cross. That would give his testimony an hour to gel in the jury's minds before I could crack into it.

Dr. Dillon Paley had been with the Wayne County M.E.'s office for almost two years. He received his medical training at the University of Michigan Hospital. He had performed the autopsy on Mark Channing the Sunday morning after he died.

Tony laid his foundation and moved for admission of four photographs from Mark Channing's autopsy. The first showed him prone on the examination table, his bulging eyes staring up at the ceiling. The next photograph showed a close-up of his neck wound where it had been sliced through with the wire. This is the picture that drew the biggest reaction from the jury. All except for juror number seven. He remained stoic, only once letting his gaze wander over to Ted Richards. Ted Richards, mercifully, put away his doodle pad.

"Dr. Paley," Tony said. "Were you able to determine a cause of death for Mark Channing?"

"Absolutely," Paley said. "The victim was strangled. The exact cause was cardiac arrest. In the simplest terms, the main artery in his neck became compressed when the pressure was applied. It cut off the blood supply to his brain."

"He didn't suffocate," Abbato asked.

"Not technically, no. His windpipe wasn't crushed. That's actually somewhat of a myth regarding strangulation injuries. It's the arterial damage that often proves fatal, which was the case for Mr. Channing."

"Dr. Paley, how long did it take Mr. Channing to die?"

"Objection, lack of foundation," I said.

"Try again, Mr. Abbato," Judge Benitez said.

"Dr. Paley, in your medical opinion, could you estimate how long an injury like you've described would take to cause death?"

Paley nodded. "More or less, yes. Once adequate pressure is applied to close off that main artery, death would have likely occurred within a minute or two."

"Can you be more precise? Are we talking up to sixty seconds, ten seconds?"

"Sure," Paley said. "Understand there is no way to determine conclusively exactly how long, and also understand that the victim may well have lost consciousness prior to the point of medical death, but death would have occurred in a few minutes. He would have lost consciousness much sooner though."

"Thank you," Abbato said. "Your witness, Ms. Leary."

I picked up my notes and passed Tony as he made his way back to his seat.

"Thank you, Dr. Paley," I said. "Can you tell me how tall the victim was?"

Paley had his report in front of him. He briefly looked down. "He was six foot four and a quarter," he said. "One hundred and eighty pounds."

"Thank you," I said. "You anticipated my next question. In your examination, isn't it true that you found no evidence of defense wounds on the victim?"

"That is true," he said.

"You did not find the presence of any DNA not belonging to the victim, correct? No skin under his nails. No scratch marks, no bruising."

"No, ma'am," he said. "The victim's nails were clean."

"Dr. Paley, were you able to determine whether Mr. Channing was standing or seated while he received this injury?"

"Objection," Abbato said. "Calls for speculation."

"Your Honor," I said. "I believe I just asked the witness whether he was able to determine that upon examination. I'm not asking him to guess at anything. He's the state's expert."

"Overruled."

Paley cleared his throat. "Well, not conclusively, no. But the character of the wound would indicate that the perpetrator was in an elevated position to the victim."

"Can you explain how you know that?" I asked.

Paley sat straighter in his seat. He had a pointer in his lap and asked to refer to the slide showing the close-up of Channing's neck wound.

"See here," he said. "The wound ... the wire caused an injury in a more or less U shape. The angle of it would indicate that the perpetrator applied pressure in an upward motion."

Paley did a fairly credible impression using his fists and jerking them upward as if he were pulling the wire up and back.

"Thank you," I said. "Your Honor, the state has previously stipulated that the defendant is five foot ten inches tall."

Benitez said, "Understood."

"You said the victim was six foot four, correct?" I asked Paley.

"Correct."

"Within a reasonable degree of medical certainty, would you be able to opine whether the victim was facing the perpetrator?"

"What? Oh. No. I wouldn't think so. The perpetrator was most likely standing behind the victim when he or she wrapped the wire around Mr. Channing's neck. The deepest ligature marks were in the front of the victim's neck, not the back."

He gave me a small gift with that. So tiny I was hoping Abbato didn't catch it. It would be a definite straw grasp, but I would take what I could get.

"Dr. Paley, if I could direct your attention to the toxicology report on Mr. Channing," I said. It stunned me a bit that Abbato hadn't brought it up himself.

"Can you tell the jury what Mr. Channing's blood alcohol level was?"

"Well, understand the victim had been deceased for over twenty-four hours by the time my examination took place. But his blood alcohol content was 0.12."

"And you're aware the legal BAC limit for driving purposes in this state is .08?"

"Of course, yes."

"So we can say that Mark Channing was legally drunk at the time of death?"

"It would appear so, yes."

"Thank you. I have nothing further for this witness at this time."

"Redirect, Mr. Abbato?" Judge Benitez said.

"Just a few," Tony said, rising.

"Dr. Paley, you indicated that the perpetrator was in an elevated position to the victim while he was strangled?"

"Uh. Yes. That's correct."

"What Ms. Leary actually asked you was whether you could determine whether Mark Channing was standing when he was attacked. Is that something you were able to determine?"

Paley looked at his notes. "Um … not specifically no. Just that the character of the wound is consistent with the perpetrator using an upward motion. There are any number of scenarios where that would play out. If the victim were significantly shorter than the perpetrator, sure. But he also could have been seated. Or the perpetrator could have been standing above the victim on a step."

"Thank you," Tony said. "I think that clears things up. I have nothing further."

With that, Dr. Dillon Paley and the jury were excused.

Chapter 22

PATRICK JOHNSON WORE a light-green polo shirt and tan cargo pants that needed pressing. He was skinny, no more than a hundred and ten pounds, I guessed. He rubbed his hands on the front of his pants before he raised his hand to be sworn in.

He wouldn't look my way or anywhere near Ted Richards. Ted was smirking as Johnson took the stand. He held his pencil over his doodle pad, poised to render the kid on paper as God knew what. I resisted the urge to take the pencil away from him. To the jury, it looked like he was just taking notes. That wasn't the worst thing, I supposed.

Tony Abbato took longer than usual to gather his notes and step up to the lectern. When he did, he had a deep scowl as if up until the very last minute, he still hadn't decided how to play this. The jury might have been fooled, but I wasn't.

"Mr. Johnson," Tony started. "Can you tell me where you lived October of last year?"

Johnson's Adam's apple quivered as he leaned forward and spoke into the slim microphone.

"I was living at 1304 Ember Street, Southfield,

Michigan." The feedback from the microphone pierced the ears of everyone in the courtroom.

Benitez calmly told Patrick Johnson he didn't need to swallow the thing to be heard.

"Sorry," Johnson said and repeated his former address.

"Where is that in relation to where Mark Channing lived, if you know?"

Johnson nodded. "I lived two streets to the east of Turner street. The Channings lived in Hickory Circle. That's the newer subdivision. Ember Street is older, but they're connected by a through street, Bradley Drive."

Abbato had a satellite map of Hickory Circle and its adjacent neighborhoods that we had stipulated admission of. Johnson pointed out where his house was and then the Channings.

"Thank you. I'd like to direct your attention to the first and second week of October of last year. Were you aware of what happened to Mark Channing?"

"Yeah," Johnson said. For the first time, his eyes darted in Richards's direction. He swallowed hard and tried to focus on Tony.

"How so?"

"Um, I saw a bunch of police cars around the Channing house. I didn't know who lived there before that. Though I seen Mrs. Channing, the blonde lady, she used to run in the neighborhood in the morning. Sometimes I'd see her out my front window or if I was getting the mail. But I take walks too. I've got a Pitt mix, Titus. I would take Titus for walks three or four times a day. Sometimes I'd see Mrs. Channing on her runs."

"Did you know her to say hello?" Abbato asked.

"Um ... no. Not really. I mean, she'd smile at me. She seemed a little nervous about Titus though. I get that a lot because of his breed and how big he is. But Titus is more likely going to lick somebody to death as much as anything else."

"Did you know Mr. Channing?"

Patrick shook his head then leaned forward. "Sorry, no. I mean, I knew he drove a silver Lexus. I used to see it parked in front of the house. And ... I'm sorry ... this is probably not nice now ... but I used to get pissed because he wouldn't always park it all the way up. It would sometimes block the sidewalk and then I'd have to go around. And their sprinkler system was on a lot. I don't get why they don't turn those things on at night. I mean, there are a lot of people using those sidewalks."

"Mr. Johnson, let's talk about the days leading up to October nineteenth. Did you notice anything different in the neighborhood?"

Johnson cleared his throat. "Yeah. I mean, I told all of this to the cops."

"What did you tell the cops?"

Johnson looked down at his lap. His voice got quieter.

"There was this car. A silver Jaguar. I seen it parked across the street a few houses down from the Channings."

"Can you describe the car?"

"Yeah. It was sweet. Like I said, silver. Black interior. V-8. Looked like it had all the bells and whistles. The kind of thing you notice ... you know ... if you're into cars. I am."

"When was this, if you recall?"

"Um ... the first time was Monday evening, October fifteenth. It was parked at the end of the street."

Johnson pointed out a location roughly four houses away from the Channing residence.

"Was anyone in the vehicle?"

"Um ... I didn't notice, not that first time."

"There were other times?"

"Yeah. I saw it again, I think two nights later, so on

Wednesday. But parked a little further up. There was a guy sitting in the front seat. He was on his phone. I thought about stopping and asking about the car, but I don't know. Something about the guy just didn't strike me as friendly."

"Mr. Johnson, can you identify the man you saw in the Jaguar on the night of October seventeenth?"

Johnson's shoulders slumped. "Um ... I can. Yeah. It was him." He lifted a shaking finger and pointed at Ted. Ted stared hard back.

"Let the record reflect that the witness has pointed toward the defendant, Theodore Richards."

"Mr. Johnson, was that the only time you saw this car or the defendant?"

Johnson sighed. "Um ... no. It wasn't. The next night too. So that'd be Thursday the eighteenth. Only then he was parked right in front of Channing's house. And he was home."

"How do you know?"

"Well, I mean, his Lexus was parked in the driveway."

"Was it blocking the sidewalk?" Abbato's tone was sarcastic. His smile immediately dropped though as he must have realized how badly that might play.

"Actually, yeah," Johnson said.

"And to be clear, did you see anyone in the Jaguar at that time?"

"Yeah. Um, yes. It was that guy again, Mr. Richards. And he was looking straight at the Channing house. It was creepy."

"Objection," I said.

"Sustained," Judge Benitez said before I could even go further.

"Did you ever speak to the defendant?"

"No, I didn't."

"Did you tell anyone else about what you saw?"

"No. I mean ... not until after. I mean, first it came on the news that Mr. Channing had been found murdered. They showed his picture and I recognized him. That freaked me out. Then there was a hotline, you know? Like Crime Stoppers. It said if anyone had any information they should call. So I did. I called the hotline and I told them that I saw that car and that guy watching Mr. Channing's house that week."

"Thank you, Mr. Johnson, I have no more questions for now."

Judge Benitez cracked his knuckles. "If you're ready to proceed, Ms. Leary, let's get this in before our morning break."

"Thank you, Your Honor," I said, as I stepped up to the lectern.

"Mr. Johnson, if I may ... you indicated the Jaguar you saw outside of Mr. Channing's residence caught your eye because you're interested in cars?"

"Um ... well ... yes. I'm sort of a buff," he said.

"I see. And according to your statement to the police you noticed a man in the driver's seat the second and third time you saw this car?"

"That's right. I'm not saying he wasn't in the car the first time, it was just that I noticed the car more than the person inside of it. At first, I mean."

"What was it that you noticed about the car?" I asked.

"What?"

"What caught your eye?"

"Oh, it was just that it was a Jaguar F-Type. It's kind of my dream car."

"Got it. What color was the interior again, from your recollection?"

"It was black. Leather seats in charcoal."

"That's very specific," I said. "Have you ever owned a Jaguar yourself?"

"No. I can't afford that."

"Have you ever shopped for one?"

"No."

"Do you subscribe to any publications for car buffs like you?"

"No, ma'am."

"So how can you be so specific about the exact color of the interior?"

"Objection," Tony said. "This question has been asked and answered. The witness identified the car."

"Sustained," Judge Benitez said.

"I'll move on. Mr. Johnson, did you notice the license plate on the Jaguar parked on the street the first time you saw it?"

"What? Oh. No."

"Did you notice the license plate the second or third time you saw that car?"

"No. No, I didn't."

"So you can't say for absolute certainty that it was the same car on all three nights," I said.

"Well, you don't see too many Jags like that. And it was in roughly the same parking spot. I mean within a few houses. And I definitely noticed Mr. Richards behind the wheel the second and third time I saw the car."

"Okay," I said. "But you didn't bother to mention your sighting of this car in front of Mr. Channing's to anyone else, isn't that right? I mean, before you reported it to the police after the fact."

"Um ... no."

"Did you encounter other neighbors on your dog walks on any of those nights that you saw the car?"

"I don't remember that. I might have. The weather was nice. Indian summer. There are usually people out."

"And you never mentioned to Mr. or Mrs. Channing that you saw this vehicle in front of their home?"

"No, I didn't. I regret that now. But I mean it just parked there."

"After you realized what happened to Mr. Channing, did you discuss your sighting of the car to anyone else in the neighborhood?"

"Um ... no."

"To your knowledge, has anyone else from the neighborhood or anywhere else come forward to report the sighting of this Jaguar on Mr. Channing's street or in Hickory Circle within that time frame?"

"Uh ... I don't know. I was never told that. I don't think so."

"Got it," I said. "Mr. Johnson, when did you move into the house on Ember Street?"

"Um ... I moved in at the end of July of last year."

"Do you still live there?"

He cast a furtive glance over at Tony Abbato.

"Objection," Tony said. "Relevance."

"I'll allow it. Son, you don't have to give your address. Just answer her basic question," Benitez said.

"No, I don't live on Ember anymore. I was just renting. I moved out at the end of October of last year."

"I see. Mr. Johnson, there was a cash reward associated with information leading to an arrest in the Mark Channing murder, isn't that right? How much was it?"

He looked down. "I think it was ... I'm not really sure."

"Did you or did you not receive a five-thousand-dollar reward for the information you provided to the police?"

"I'm not lying," he said. "I told them what I saw. I saw a silver Jag with dark leather seats and black carpeting on three different days the week before Mark Channing died. That's the truth."

I tapped my fingers on the lectern. "Did you approach the Jaguar on any of the occasions you saw it?"

"I don't know what you mean ... I didn't go up and talk to the guy, no."

"Were you walking on the same side of the street as the car?"

"I was ... I was I think twice on the other side of the street, and the last time, the evening of the eighteenth, I was on the same side. I walked right by it and got a good look at the defendant."

"You indicated in your statement that it was almost nine o'clock at night. If the reports say sunset occurred at seven forty-two that night, does that sound right?"

He scratched his head. "Um ... yeah. That sounds right. The street lights were on that last night."

"So it was dark?"

"It was dark," he said. "But I told you, I got a good look at the guy."

"But not the carpet," I said. "You wouldn't have been able to see the carpet on the floor of the car at night."

"What? Oh ... no. I wasn't looking that far into it."

It was almost a throwaway question, but adrenaline coursed through me. I could hear Richards doodling behind me. I could hear Jeanie breathing.

Something was off about this guy. Very off. But it didn't mean he was lying.

"Thank you," I said. "I have nothing further."

"Just a couple of quick questions," Tony said, rising.

I took my seat. Ted had written in bold letters, "Lying sack of shit," on his doodle pad. I put a hand over his then flipped the pad over.

"Mr. Johnson," Tony said. "Just to reiterate, you testified that the first two times you saw the defendant in the Jaguar, it was broad daylight?"

"Yes," he said. "The middle of the day the first time, late afternoon the second. The third time was the only time it was at night."

"Thank you," he said. Tony gave a nod to the judge and went back to his seat. Judge Benitez adjourned for lunch.

The deputies were ready to take Ted back to his holding cell. We had no time to talk. It was for the best because it was Jeanie's ear I needed.

We waited until we had the courtroom mostly to ourselves and I turned to her.

"You think he's lying?" she asked.

"I don't know. There's just always been something nagging at me about that guy's statement."

I held Fitzgerald's discovery notes on Patrick Johnson in front of me. I looked again at his background information. There was something there, I just didn't know what.

"Jeanie," I said. "Can you call your investigator? We're running out of time, but there's something I want him to try and track down."

Her face split into a grin. "On it," she said.

I packed up my things and we made plans to grab lunch at the diner down the street. As we walked to the back of the courtroom, a young woman sat against the wall, her face drawn. She caught my eye and for a moment, I thought she meant to say something. Then she turned and started putting her own notes away. She looked familiar, but I couldn't place her. She was young, very thin, with straight brown hair and a pale complexion. Before I had a chance to put a name to her face, Jeanie got through to her investigator. She turned to me.

"Okay ... time to clue me into where your brain is," she said, smiling.

Chapter 23

ABBATO FINISHED the week calling Mark Channing's co-counsel, Andy Tate, to the stand. His testimony was short and terse. A seasoned trial attorney himself, Tate knew not to take his story too far into the realm of speculation or hearsay. He presented only the public charges filed against the Kinsell organization.

"You believe the defendant was on the Kinsell payroll?" Abbato asked.

Tate nodded. "We have evidence from the FBI. They tracked wire transfers from an account belonging to KLC Limited to the defendant, Ted Richards, yes. Those payments totaled almost one hundred thousand dollars over a three-year period."

"What were those payments for?" Abbato asked.

Tate looked down. "Mark was preparing to meet with a witness over the weekend with information about the nature of those payments. We were optimistic that that witness would be able to confirm the FBI's working theory."

"And what was that working theory?"

"Objection," I said. "This calls for speculation."

"I'll allow it," Benitez said. He'd been shooting me down all afternoon. Tate's answer here was the lynchpin of Abbato's entire theory of the case on motive.

"Their theory was these payments were compensation for a mob hit on one of Kinsell's competitors. We believe Mr. Richards was a hired killer on behalf of Kinsell and his associates."

"Mr. Tate, if that theory were confirmed, what would it have meant to your case?"

"Objection!" I nearly threw my pen across the room. Benitez scowled at me.

"You're overruled."

Jeanie sat on the other side of me. Richards kept right on doodling. She whispered in my ear. "He's out of his mind. This gets thrown out on appeal."

But it didn't matter. Since the second I walked into his courtroom, I knew in my heart Francisco Benitez meant to hand Tony Abbato a conviction.

"There's no way to tell," Tate answered. "It would have been explosive testimony, to be sure, if we got that far. But you never know what a jury will do with information like that. We were just hoping we could bring it to light."

"Thank you," Tony said. "I have nothing further."

"It's four o'clock," Judge Beni said, shocking me even further. "We'll adjourn for the day. You can take your crack at the witness first thing in the morning, Ms. Leary."

I couldn't believe what I was hearing. "Your Honor," I said. "I would prefer to begin cross-examination right now."

"We're adjourned," Benitez said, banging the gavel. If I needed any further proof of his intentions, the echo of wood on wood provided it. For the first time, I began to wonder if Judge Benitez was on the take.

The jury filed out. Ted Richards remained remarkably

calm at my side. He was even smiling when the deputies came in to haul him away.

"Have a good weekend, darlin'," he said, sneering at me. The cold expression in his eyes hollowed me out inside.

"I'm losing my mind," I said as soon as he was out of earshot.

"It's not over yet," Jeanie said. I gathered my things, looking forward to getting the hell out of Detroit for a couple of days. I had to figure out a way to undo some of the damage Abbato just did while the jury had two days to let Andy Tate's testimony harden in their minds. It was a complete disaster.

Andy Tate hurried out of the courtroom, but not before throwing me a glance, thick with contempt. Ryan McGuinness and Laura Wyler waited for him out in the hallway. Tate stopped and said something I couldn't hear to the young girl with the brown hair sitting against the wall. It dawned on me then who she was. It was the paralegal I'd seen walking with them outside the DOJ building downtown.

As Tate waited for her, she looked even paler than the day before. Tate stopped, holding the door for her. He gave her an exasperated look as she gathered her purse.

She rose and scurried after Andy, looking like she was about to be sick.

"What's with that one?" Jeanie asked.

"No idea," I answered. "Stockton! Victoria. Damn, I thought I was losing my mind. That's her name. Hopefully, she's smart enough to recognize bullshit when she sees it. Richards could be guilty as sin, but what happened up there was insane."

"Come on," Jeanie said. "Let's get gone before the traffic gets murderous."

She was right. Wyler, McGuinness, and Tate stood against the wall as I left the courthouse. Victoria Stockton stood among them; she wouldn't meet my eyes. Maybe there was hope for her yet. It took almost the entire drive home for my nerves to calm. When this was over, I didn't want to set foot in Wayne County for a good long while. My only silver lining was having the weekend to decompress. Still, there was something nagging at me about the whole picture Tony Abbato painted.

As I waited at a stop light, I pulled up my contacts. I taped my finger on the screen. This was ludicrous, but I felt like I had no other choice.

He answered on the first ring, my name no doubt flashing on his caller ID.

"Agent Cannon," I said anyway. "It's Cass Leary. Do you have a minute?"

Chapter 24

HE MET me at a hole-in-the-wall burger joint off I-75. I had enough time to order a beer before he arrived. When he did, Special Agent Lee Cannon came through the back, working his way past the growing Friday night crowd. He slid into the booth opposite me and ordered a beer of his own and the slider combo platter.

"Thanks for meeting me," I said.

"I need to have my head examined," he said. "Anybody figures out I'm here, it's bad for both of us."

"I know that better than anyone." His eyes flashed, but I wouldn't elaborate. Lee Cannon would never know how dangerous my last association with him had been for me. Because of it, Liam Thorne still wanted me dead.

"How's the trial going?" he asked.

I raised a brow. "You think I would have risked meeting with you if it was going swell?"

"I warned you," he said, raising his voice. He lowered it as the waitress came bearing his drink.

"You did," I said. "And you knew a hell of a lot more about this Ghost Man than I did. And I know you still do."

"Not my circus, not my monkeys."

I let out a sigh and leaned back against the leather seat. "Right. Which is why you took it upon yourself to come all the way out to Wayne County when I filed my appearance a few weeks ago. You could have just called or sent a message. But you showed up in person. And you showed up tonight. What, you just happened to be no more than an hour away when I called? You're orbiting, Cannon. These may not be your monkeys, but you're here for the circus."

"Mark Channing was my friend, okay?" he spat. "He was one of the good ones. He wasn't perfect, but he was a hell of a lot better than most."

"And you've read the file," I said. "Don't pretend you haven't. You know what the Bureau was trying to build against Richards, Kinsell, the whole lot of them."

He tore into his fries as soon as the waitress set them in front of him. "There's nothing I can give you, Cass. We've already been down this road. But you keep picking the wrong side. You're trusting the wrong people. You've been seeing Killian Thorne again."

My blood flared hot. He'd been checking up on me

"Killian's not his brother," I said. "And my personal life isn't any of your business. I'm here to talk about Richards."

"And you know I can't. So what did he do this time? What did he pay you to get involved?"

I didn't answer.

"No," he said. "It's not the money. It was never the money, right? Jesus. Cass, I can't help you if you don't let me."

"I thought you said you can't help me, Lee."

He threw down his napkin. "God, you're impossible."

"What I am is good at what I do. Forget all the rest of it if you can. For a minute anyway. You said you know Mark

Channing was one of the good guys. I believe that. So are you. And I also know you think I am."

He paused, his stare growing more intense. "Are you? Are you still, Cass?"

I exhaled. "Yes. I try to be."

"Ted Richards is a monster. You need to know that."

I nodded. "He may be. But ... Lee ... this case. I'll say it again. I know you've seen the file on him. His other alleged victims. His M.O. Tell me the truth. None of this tracks with what happened to Mark."

Cannon ran a hand over his chin. "Are we really doing this? Yeah. I've seen the file. Talk to me about Jerome Haggerty. Piano wire is one of Richards's weapons of choice, Cass. You have any idea what kind of death that is?"

"Tell me again why the Bureau calls him Ghost Man."

He pushed his plate away. "Isn't this a violation of your ethical duty? Attorney-client privilege and all?"

"You call him Ghost Man because he disappears. Generally, no bodies. No evidence. Nothing but thin air. But this ... Mark ... you think he transports him in his own car? And dumps him where he's for sure going to be found less than twenty-four hours later? Not to mention supposedly parking right in front of Channing's driveway the night before? And in the neighborhood two other times before that. Does that sound like a ghost to you? To me that sounds like someone wanted to make sure he'd be seen."

He clenched his jaw, then his fists. Lee Cannon dropped his head and let out a sigh. "Cass ..."

"And why kill Channing? It's not like his murder was going to make the case against Kinsell go away. I mean, that's the working motive, right? The rest of the victims in that file ... some of them you say were going to testify against other bad guys. Two of them your people think crossed made men. Retribution. Witness tampering. But offing Channing does none of that. Andy Tate, Ryan McGuinness, and Laura Wyler are ready to step in and prosecute Kinsell. It doesn't make any sense to kill Channing. You know it doesn't."

He didn't need to say another word. I had my answer.

"It's bullshit, Lee. Somebody set Ted Richards up. So why the hell aren't you guys tracking down that lead?"

He sat there like a statue.

"Seems to me if Kinsell ordered a hit, it would have been on one of the informants. Channing met with somebody he identified in the files as Witness X. The guy gave him all sorts of shit on Kinsell's operations. He'd be a better target if Kinsell really wanted to try and throw a wrench into the RICO case. There are others. Channing was cutting immunity deals left and right. All of those witnesses are alive and breathing. It doesn't make sense. Never mind the murder doesn't fit his M.O."

"I don't know about any Witness X. There were multiple investigations going on. We have our own turf wars within the Bureau. People are protective of their C.I.s. It wasn't my case. Richards got sloppy, or cocky ... that's all. It happens. It's how we catch these guys in the end, Cass."

"Shit," I said. It was my turn to throw down my napkin. "Richards is being railroaded on this one. You want a win so badly, you're all willing to let the real truth about what might have happened to Mark Channing die with him."

He turned into a stone wall. I didn't really know Special Agent Cannon well. We'd had a half a dozen phone conversations. This was only the third time I'd met him in person. But I could read the signs. He was shutting down on me.

He put a fifty-dollar bill on the table.

"Lee ..."

"No," he said. "It's on me. I've tried. I can sleep at night now knowing that. I thought I could help you. But you just can't be saved from yourself, Cass."

He rose and turned his back on me. I stared at the fifty-dollar bill. Ulysses S. Grant stared up at me, grinning as Cannon disappeared into the night.

Chapter 25

I SHOULD HAVE TURNED BACK AROUND. I should have slept at the office. When I pulled into my driveway at nearly ten o'clock that night, the figure at the end of the dock filled me with dread.

My tires crunched over the gravel as I parked. I gripped the steering wheel. He hadn't turned yet. The solar-powered dock lights lit up like an airplane landing strip, their reflection sparkling off the water. He took a slow drag from his cigarette then pitched the butt into the water. Asshole.

I shut the car door and walked over to him.

"What the hell are you doing here?" I said, keeping my voice to barely more than a whisper. Sound carried across the lake. You could hear conversations all the way down the shore if you listened.

"I'm paying your legal fees, remember?" Liam said. He didn't bother to give me his usual sly smile, so there was that. He was in shirt sleeves, his tie pulled loose. Sand covered his leather dress shoes. Good. I hope he fell in. I had the brief fantasy of pushing him over.

"You're checking up on me. I thought we agreed you'd stay the hell out of Delphi."

"I've heard reports," he said. "It doesn't sound like things are going very well for Mr. Richards with you at the helm."

"I think Mr. Richards has been the captain of his own ship a hell of a lot longer than I've known him. And I'm not talking about this with you."

"You need a win, Cass," Liam said.

"The trial's not over. The state hasn't even finished its case in chief." I wanted to kick myself for getting defensive with him. But I wanted to kick him even harder.

"I've honored my part of this bargain," he said.

"This is a jury trial, Liam. And your boy's been very bad. You left a few things out when you came to see me."

He put his hands in his pockets and walked toward me. I stayed on the shore. He came to the end of the dock.

"Are you going to put him on the stand?" he asked. His tone changed. He fell into old patterns. All of a sudden, this wasn't Liam Thorne, the aggressor and aggrieved. This was Liam Thorne, my colleague again. It might be easy for him to forget the last year and a half, but I couldn't. Not ever.

"You'll hear the verdict the same time I do," I said. "At least ... I assume. You've got a spy in the courtroom, I take it."

My mind spun. It was a throwaway comment, but the moment the words came out, I knew it was true. I started remembering the regular court spectators. None of them looked like Liam's people. I knew the reporters by name. The U.S. Attorney's office had their own mole in their young paralegal, Victoria Stockton. My heart raced. I'd seen pure fear in her eyes whenever I glanced at her. I wondered ... It would make a certain amount of sense.

"We're doing this your way," Liam said. "That was our

agreement. You wanted no interference from me. But if you're losing …"

"Stop. Go home, Liam. I'd hardly call this an agreement. Those require mutual assent. You threatened my family. You called in the last favor I owe your family. I'm representing my client to the best of my abilities. But this may be an unwinnable case."

The truth was, I didn't really believe that anymore. But I'd be damned if I was going to let Liam Thorne feel smug. And I sure as hell wasn't going to give him any ground. I'd spent too many years looking the other way at some of his methods. And I couldn't go down this path with him. How many past trials had he rigged in our favor? Thinking of the myriad number of ways he might have used me to his own ends turned my stomach.

One more week, I told myself. Two, tops. Then, for better or worse, the Richards trial and Liam Thorne would be in my rearview mirror for good.

"There's no such thing as an unwinnable case. You can think what you want about me, but I'm on your side with this one."

I laughed louder than I wanted to. "My side? Jesus, Liam. You are so far from anything to do with my side."

He took a step toward me. "I'm trying to help. That's why I came here."

"You're a sociopath," I said. "A month ago you got your people doing surveillance on my family. You put my niece— my teenage niece—in the crosshairs of your twisted bullshit. Those pictures? What you did? It's a crime, Liam."

"It was a serious lapse in judgment, I'll admit it," he said.

"Bullshit!" It was too late, he'd lit my fuse. "You're back-tracking now because Killian stepped in. You're nothing without his support."

"I've saved his ass more than you know," Liam spat. I'd lit his fuse too, it seemed. "You think he's blameless? You think he's your white knight?"

I took a step toward him and jabbed a finger in his chest. Liam's nostrils flared. He could go off. Would he? Some sick part of me wanted to test him. He had no idea what I was capable of now or what I'd survived. I was afraid of him before, but in that brief second, I wasn't. I was just furious.

"Get the hell out of here," I said.

"You need help, whether you want to admit it or not."

"Not from you," I said. "I never want anything from you again."

"How hard is Richards pushing you to put him on the stand?" he said.

"Goodbye, Liam," I said.

"I know he is. He's not taking this seriously enough."

"You're coaching him? Please do not stand there and tell me you're still in communication with him. I thought I made it clear I won't put up with that."

"He's scared," Liam said. "Whether he wants to admit it or not, he's afraid this one's going to stick. It'll make him his own worst enemy. But he's a smart man. Frighteningly so. He might actually be able to do himself some good if you let him testify."

Unbelievable. This wasn't about Liam checking up on me at all. Richards had reached out to him.

"If it matters to you so much," I said. "then you go in there and defend him. Oh wait ... that's right ... you can't. You're a disaster in the courtroom. I've seen it."

His eyes flashed. "And you'd be nothing if I hadn't plucked you out of this hell hole of a town."

"Fuck you, Liam. You've made a career out of riding on everyone else's coattails. The only reason you're not back in

Belfast shoveling horse shit is because of some promise
Killian made to your daddy to keep you busy."

He snapped. Liam's lips curled into a snarl. He grabbed
my arm.

Then the shadows came to life. I hadn't heard anything.
Never saw him coming. But Killian appeared out of
nowhere, thundering down the dock like a freight train.

With one swift movement, he had Liam by the throat,
shoving him backward. Liam took a swing at him. Killian
neatly ducked it. Liam lunged at him, catching him in the
midsection. The two of them tumbled back toward the boat.

Liam landed a hard blow across Killian's jaw. He hissed
and doubled over. Then Killian was on the balls of his feet
charging forward.

Lights came on up and down the shore. This was Delphi.
The east side of Finn Lake. To most of my neighbors, this
was just another Friday night at the Leary house. For me, I
wanted to throw up.

I knew better than to try to intervene. I ran a hand over
my face and went to a safe distance up in the yard.

Killian and Liam spat insults at each other, both of their
voices dropping low, their accents thick.

They seemed well matched at first. Liam was bigger,
broader around the middle. But Killian was the true brawler
between them. Lean and lithe, he absorbed every blow Liam
landed and answered it with a punishing strike of his own.

Killian was toying with him. This was sport for him. Joey
and Matty didn't go at each other like this much. Growing
up, Joe had always been so much older. But I'd seen both of
my brothers defend what was left of the family honor down
at Mickey's more times than I could count.

Then Killian grew weary of the game. As Liam charged
him, Killian sidestepped. He caught Liam in the shoulder,
shoving him back. He landed a solid blow across the bridge

of Liam's nose, sending him reeling backward. Liam lost his balance and fell sideways off the dock, right at the drop-off. He landed in a great splash, disturbing the geese bedded down a few yards to the south.

Killian spat blood, shook his fist, then walked back up the dock toward me.

Liam emerged from the water. He climbed back on the dock, shaking his hair like a dog. But the fight was out of him for now. He knew when to retreat.

"Don't ever come back here," Killian said.

Liam paused. His lips were still curled in a snarl as he looked from me to Killian. Whatever retort he had in mind died on his lips. He sulked past us and went up to his car. His driver stood with his arms folded, waiting. He was Liam's bodyguard too, no doubt. Whoever he was, the man knew better than to get in the middle of Killian Thorne's wrath. There was never any real doubt about who held the power in the Thorne family.

Liam slid into the back seat and slammed the door before his driver could.

"You should have called," I said, turning to Killian. He was still panting hard, his adrenaline racing.

"I can go," he said. "I just ... I knew you've had a long week."

I should have told him to go. But seeing him here stirred something in me. He was like a drug to me. And I knew exactly how dangerous that was. But for now, I was just too damned tired to fight it.

"Your hand," I said. I reached for him. Killian had broken the skin over his knuckles.

"I've done worse," he said.

"Come on," I said. "You need some ice on that."

"That was ..." He looked back toward the dock. "I didn't mean to bring trouble here."

"Right."

"With brothers, it's complicated, Cass."

I smiled up at him. "Right." I said again. "I know a thing or two about brothers. Come on. Let's see about that ice. The neighbors have had enough of a show."

Smiling, Killian followed me up to the house.

Chapter 26

I woke again to the delicious aroma of fresh coffee and cooking bacon. Killian moved through the kitchen, singing a hymn he loved in a clear tenor voice. I showered, slipped into a pair of shorts and a tee shirt and stood in front of my bathroom mirror.

I'd let my hair grow longer than I normally wore it. Only the very ends still held the platinum blonde I favored when I lived in Chicago. I still hadn't found a salon I liked as well since I came back to Delphi. I twisted it up and secured it with a clip.

Dogs barked down the shore. From the window, I watched the geese glide across the water. They were headed to the neighbor's house for their morning bread.

"Son of a bitch," I muttered.

Killian appeared, holding a steaming mug of coffee. Smiling, he handed it to me.

"I like your hair like that," he said. "I never cared much for it when you fussed with it."

He came behind me, slipping his arms around my waist. He felt strong and solid at my back.

"Plans for the day?" he asked.

"You already know. As much as I'd love to hang out on the water, I need to go to the office. I'm still in the middle of trial."

He nodded, kissed the back of my neck, and let go of me. "I have to get back too," he said. "I don't suppose you have a toothbrush I could use in one of these drawers."

"Third one on the left," I said. "I keep a pack. Holdover habit from my grandmother. She always wanted people to have hotel amenities when they stayed here. She said you never know who's going to show up. The truth was, it was more likely my dad or uncles would be too drunk to drive home."

Killian opened the drawer. He found the toothbrushes and something else. He pulled out a worn leather shaving kit. His brow furrowed as he opened it. He set the gleaming straight razor and boar bristle brush on the counter. His expression turned hard as he looked at them.

Part of me resented the accusation in his eyes. A deeper, pettier part of me didn't mind that he was jealous.

"Grandpa Leary's," I said.

Killian's eyes flashed, as if he were considering whether to believe me. I knew his mind as well as he knew mine. A tiny smile played at the corner of his mouth.

"Sure they don't belong to a certain local detective?"

I reared back, not expecting that. "Where did that come from? You mean Wray?"

He put the items back in the leather case.

"I'm sorry," he quickly said. "Rough attempt at a joke. It's none of my business."

"You're right. It isn't. But no, Eric's a friend. Nothing more. I keep that stuff because it reminds me of my grandfather. Never in my life did I see him without a clean shave. And he taught me how. When he got older, his hands shook.

Grandma Leary's eyes were too bad. And he knew my father was more likely to slit his throat with that thing than shave him. So I did it."

I slid the kit back into the drawer. Killian caught my arm and turned me to face him.

"I'm sorry," he said. "Truly."

I hesitated. I knew every second Killian stayed here with me or that we spent together made things that much more confusing. I knew in my heart what I had to do. I just wasn't ready to do it yet.

"Come on," he said. "Let's go downstairs before your breakfast gets cold. Then I have to head back home and you have work to do."

He made things so easy and yet impossible all at once.

Chapter 27

KILLIAN WENT BACK TO CHICAGO, and Monday morning, I faced the worst day of Ted Richards's trial.

"The state calls Sally Ann Richards to the stand, Your Honor," Abbato said. My heart froze. Jeanie muttered an obscenity under her breath and started shuffling through papers. Beside me, Ted started to rise out of his seat. His skin turned a mottled purple and he clenched his jaw so hard I was certain the jury heard it.

"Do something," Ted said, his voice a deep monotone.

"Sit tight," I said through gritted teeth.

The bailiff led Sally Richards through the gallery. She was perhaps once a pretty woman, but she had a haggard, spent appearance. She shuffled her feet as she walked and trembled her way past Ted. He was making a noise. It almost sounded like a growl.

"Do something," he whispered again.

"Shut up," I said.

Sally was sworn in. Abbato waited at the lectern. Pure theater. He wanted to make sure the jury saw Ted Richards grow increasingly more uncomfortable. For once, I wished he'd just keep doodling.

"Ms. Richards," Abbato finally said. "Can you tell us how you know the defendant?"

She swallowed. Her eyes darted back and forth. Sally's hair was steel gray and stringy. She pulled her pink cardigan around her as if it were a shield.

"I'm ... Ted is my husband. We're married."

Ted was still making that low, vibrating sound. He reminded me of a dog about to snap. He wasn't helping himself one bit. No matter what else happened, Sally Richards was clearly terrified of him. She hardly needed to say a word to do damage.

"She can't do this," Ted said. "She's my wife."

I wrote an answer on the pad of paper between us. "It doesn't matter if she's choosing to testify. Stay calm."

"Mrs. Richards, how long have you been married to the defendant?"

"Almost thirty years," she said, stumbling over her words. She cleared her throat and sat a little straighter.

"When was the last time you saw Mr. Richards?"

She looked down, pulling at a thread on her sleeve.

"We haven't lived together for almost two years. I live ... do I have to tell you where I live?"

"No, ma'am," Abbato said. "I didn't ask you that. Do you still communicate with Mr. Richards?"

She shook her head. "He's called me a few times. I changed my number. I don't ... I don't want contact."

"Mrs. Richards, can you tell us why you no longer have contact with the defendant?"

"Objection," I said. "Your Honor, this witness has pretty much just said she's had no contact with the defendant in nearly two years. I fail to see how ..."

"Overruled," Judge Benitez said. "I'd like to hear what

she has to say."

"I'll bet you do," Ted muttered. Good lord, he was going to sink his own case before his wife had a chance to do it for him. And I had no earthly clue what she was going to say. Up until five minutes ago, she had vanished into thin air. But she was on Abbato's witness list.

"Your Honor," I said. "May we approach the bench?"

Benitez expressed his displeasure with a sigh, but motioned for both Tony and me to a sidebar.

"Make it quick," he said to me.

"My predecessor filed discovery on every person listed on the state's witness list. She failed to answer our subpoena. She disconnected her phone number."

"How hard did you try to find her after that?" Benitez said.

"Your Honor," Tony said. "As Ms. Leary has pointed out, Mrs. Richards was disclosed as a possible witness for the state months ago. There's no surprise here. She called my office late last week."

"And you didn't deem it necessary to update your discovery?"

"I haven't …"

"Save it," Benitez cut in. "She's on his list. She's here voluntarily. I'm satisfied. Let's proceed."

"Your Honor …"

"I've made my ruling," Benitez said. "Just because you may not like what this woman has to say, you've got no grounds to keep her from saying it. Next time do your own due diligence, Counselor."

I gave the judge a tight-lipped nod. I knew I was grasping at straws keeping her out, but I had no choice but to try. If I tried any harder, it would only make the jury that much more interested in her testimony. All I could hope for now was some level of damage control.

"Thank you for your patience, Mrs. Richards. Let me read back my last question. Why is it you've had no contact with the defendant in all this time?"

"I'm afraid of him," she said. "He's ... things didn't end well."

"Didn't end well," he said. "Can you be more specific?"

Ted sat with his fists clenched on the table. I put a hand on his upper arm. He let out a breath and relaxed a little.

"Mrs. Richards," Abbato said. "I know this must be difficult for you. But have you had a chance to review the charges against your husband?"

She looked at the judge and back at Abbato. "I know ... they say he murdered that lawyer. It's been on the news."

"Yes," Abbato said. "And did my office reach out to you in preparation for this trial?"

She nodded. "I ... I know you tried to call. Yes."

"Did you answer that call?"

"I ... no. Not at first. I didn't want to be involved."

"But you're here. Do you want to tell me why?"

She shrugged one shoulder and kept pulling at the thread on her sleeve. "Since the trial started. I ... things came out in the paper. I still read one. Isn't that funny? I know most people like their phones for that. I still like the newspaper. They say they're going to switch to an internet one soon. Anyway ... I saw in the paper last week about what happened to that poor man. And I couldn't ... I just couldn't live with myself if I didn't say something."

"Mrs. Richards, what about what you read made you think you'd have something relevant to add to these proceedings?"

Tears rolled down Sally Richards's face. She wouldn't look at Ted. For his part, he hadn't taken his cold eyes off her.

"They said he was strangled," Sally said in a voice so quiet the judge had to ask her to speak up.

"They said it was a wire. A piano wire. I hadn't heard that before. I didn't know."

"Why is that significant, Mrs. Richards?"

"He's got a temper," Sally said. "Ted's got a temper."

"Objection," I said.

"Sustained," Judge Benitez said.

"Mrs. Richards, I just have one question. Once you answer it, then I suspect Ms. Leary over there will have a few for you as well. But let's try to get through this. Why did you call my office after reading about Mr. Channing's manner of death?"

Sally Richards loosened the collar of her blouse. She slipped her arms out of the pink cardigan. Her skin was smooth and pale. But she had a scar across her neck in a distinct U shape.

I heard Jeanie behind me whisper, "Son of a bitch."

"The last fight we had," Sally said. "Ted gave me this."

"Mrs. Richards, you have to verbalize what you're referring to."

"Objection," I said. "Your Honor, counsel knows prior …"

"Save it. Overruled," Benitez said.

"Go ahead, Mrs. Richards," Tony said.

"Ted choked me," she said. "He choked me with the wire he took from my grand piano."

I was still on my feet. Juror number seven's expression turned to ice as he looked at Ted.

Before I could stop him, Ted was on his feet beside me. The deputies behind him moved. Jeanie moved. Sally Richards shrank further into her seat.

"You lying little bitch!" Ted yelled. He pounded his fists against the table and Sally Richards screamed.

Chapter 28

I PACED in the conference room next to Judge Benitez's chambers. He'd called a recess after Ted's outburst and I waited for the deputies to bring Ted in. It took three of them to subdue him.

It was bad enough the jury had seen Ted's reaction to his wife's testimony. Now Benitez refused to let me cross-examine her until the next day. The jury's impressions would harden overnight. It was a disaster upon a disaster.

They led Ted into the conference room in belly chains. As one last parting gift, Judge Benitez ruled from the bench that Ted would stay in them throughout the rest of the trial.

It was over. We were sunk. Nothing else would matter to the jury after what they heard. I wasn't sure it mattered to me anymore either.

He came in, shuffled to the table, and sat.

"You sure about this?" the deputy said to me.

"I'm sure," I said. "He's in chains now, what can he do?"

"I'll be right outside," he said, then left me in the room alone with Ted.

I couldn't sit. I was too damn angry.

"You fucked yourself," I said after the deputy closed the door. He could see through the window in the door, but he couldn't hear us.

"You fucked me," Ted said. "I told you to put me on the stand."

"And what? Were you going to tell the jury you only make a habit of garroting women with piano wire? Why the hell didn't you tell me about this?"

"She's lying," Ted said, shrugging. As enraged as he'd been in the courtroom, he was strangely calm now.

"She's got the scar to prove it, Ted."

"It's her word against mine. Ask her if she ever filed a police report. Ask her if she ever even went to the doctor. She's on the take or something. That Abbato asshole probably promised her a payday. Those marks look new. Tell the jury she did it after she read about Channing in the paper. She admitted that much herself."

I put both hands on top of my head. "Is that really the story you're sticking to? Your bullshit might work on everyone else, but it doesn't work on me."

He raised a brow and smirked at me. Then he lifted his shoulder and popped his neck. The crack of it echoed. It felt like a "fuck you."

"I've seen the file, Ted. I know who you are."

"You don't know shit," he said.

"Haggerty? Walter Dunham? How many others, Ted?"

He shook his head. "It's all bullshit. If the feds had something on me about that other crap they would have charged. They didn't because they can't."

"You're going down for this," I said. "You get that, right? The jury believes that kid saw you parked in front of Channing's house."

"That is the biggest crock of shit and you know it. You did a good job showing what a fucking liar he is."

I threw up my hands. "The jury will believe him if they have a reason to. Sally just gave them a reason. You make me sick. If she files charges, you'll have to answer to them. I ought to let you hang just for what you did to her alone. "

He was smiling. "But you can't. You know that's not how it works. And I know just how good you are."

"Now, you listen to me," I said. I finally took the seat in front of him. "I've poked some holes in the state's case. It's true. But that jury knows you tried to kill your wife. They know you wrapped piano wire around her neck and tried to strangle her."

Ted had a grin on his face. He closed his eyes slowly and took a breath. As he exhaled, he opened them.

"If I wanted Sally dead, she'd be dead."

At that moment, I knew with cold clarity he was telling the truth. And God help me, I knew the next thing he said was also true.

"I didn't kill Mark Channing. You said you read the file. If you believe all of that shit about me, then you know it wouldn't have gone down like that. I've been set up. So you go out there and you do your job."

"My job is to provide you with the best defense I can. Right now, I think the best you can do is plead this out."

He laughed. "To what? You just said you think I'm sunk. Why the hell would Abbato offer anything? Plus, I told you, I didn't kill that fucker. I will not stand in front of a judge and admit to shit I didn't do. Not for you, not for Liam Thorne, not for anyone."

"But there's plenty you would do for Liam Thorne. Fuck you, Ted."

"Be careful," he said, letting his tone drop. It was a

threat. There was something about it that sent ice through me. I hadn't let myself be afraid of him, no matter what I believed about him.

He started smiling again. Then he leaned far forward and spoke in a whisper.

"Dunham was a screamer," he said. "Haggerty was just for fun. And you? Well ... I can make it go quick or I can make it go slow. Call it a gift. One turn of the knife, or I could have just let you fall over the side."

I couldn't breathe. Black spots swam in front of my eyes. My wrists ached where the zip ties had dug in. *One turn of the knife, or I could have just let you fall over the side.*

I wasn't here anymore. I was back on the deck of the *Crown of Thorne.* Why hadn't I realized it before? That voice. It was Ted. He'd been there. He'd held me against the railing, ready to carry out Liam's orders to throw me over and let me drown.

I remembered something else he said. He said it again now. "Ah darlin', don't you know? I'm already a ghost."

Ghost man.

This wasn't happening. In spite of myself, I flinched. I rose from the table and turned my back on him.

Again, Ted spoke the words of my nightmares. *I'm already a ghost.*

"Nice night for a boat ride, don't you think?" Ted said, laughing. He cracked his neck.

For over a year, I'd tried to block it out of my mind. But now there was no way to escape the truth. Ted Richards had been there on the deck of the *Crown of Thorne.* He was everything the FBI said he was. And fourteen months ago, Liam Thorne had hired him to kill me.

I felt the zip ties on my wrists. I smelled his breath as he slipped a sheet over my head. And I heard those words over and over as he promised to throw me over the side to drown.

My hand shaking, I tapped on the door. The deputy opened it and gave me a polite smile.

"We're done here," I said, refusing to look back and give Ghost Man the satisfaction of seeing my fear.

Chapter 29

I FOUND Jeanie buried in the case file as I made my slow, trudging way up the stairs into the conference room. It was dark out. A low, yellow moon glowed in the window. Jeanie was drinking coffee at ten o'clock at night.

"That's not good for you," I said, lifting her cup to smell it. She made it Irish. She kept a bottle of whiskey hidden behind one of the tort law books I kept on the shelf.

"You know we're fucked, right?"

I sat down heavily in the chair across from her. I was just tired now. The adrenaline rush from my last few minutes with Ted Richards had worn off. I had three missed calls from my brothers. One from my sister in Florida. A single text from Killian that just read, "call me."

"We are," I said.

Jeanie finished her coffee and set the mug down hard enough I thought it would crack.

She flipped through the police report on Channing's murder. We both knew every line by heart.

"He's a monster," she said.

"I can't argue that," I said. My heart felt hollow. I

couldn't tell her what happened. Not yet. Maybe not ever. And I couldn't do a damn thing about it for now.

"The fucker perfected one of his techniques on his own wife." She threw a copy of Channing's autopsy photos across the table. It was one where the ligature marks were in close-up. Purple, angry, deadly.

She grabbed another photo from the FBI case file. Jerome Haggerty. The same wound cut through his neck. I felt sick.

"Benitez though ..." I said.

Jeanie sat back, her eyes flicking over the photo array she made. "Oh, he's out for blood. You had a good argument for keeping Sally's testimony out. He wouldn't even hear it. If they send him up for this, he's got a good decade worth of appeals ahead of him."

"Not with me," I said.

Jeanie sat with her hands folded. "Is this the last one?" she asked.

I stopped myself from giving her an automatic answer. Jeanie knew what she was asking and so did I.

"Do you love him? Killian Thorne?" she asked. I jerked my head around. That hidden bottle of whiskey called to me.

"I don't know how to answer that," I said.

"Sure you do. It's yes or no. Don't feed me your usual line of bull that it's complicated. It's not. It's really not."

"I owe him," I said. I still couldn't tell Jeanie or anyone else about what really happened when I left Chicago. She couldn't know that I'd barely escaped with my life. And now, I couldn't tell her it was Ted Richards—Liam's Ghost Man —who held me over the side of the Thorne family yacht, my wrists and ankles bound, the fathomless waters of Lake Michigan churning below me.

"You owe him for your sister," she said.

"Yes," I answered. "Killian found Vangie for me. You know what could have happened if she hadn't come forward in the Ames trial. She's back in our lives now. She's safe. That was worth whatever price I had to pay."

"And you still haven't answered my first question. Do you love him?"

I smiled. "It *is* complicated, okay?"

"Stop it."

"Yes!" I raised my voice. "Okay? Yes. I do still love him. Killian's not his brother. God. He's torn his family apart trying to pull the business out of the mess his father left for him."

Jeanie inhaled. "He's trying to go legit. Is that what you're telling me? Jesus, Cass. Then he's fooling himself. And he's putting you at risk."

"He's just ... Killian ..."

"Oh I get it," Jeanie said. "He's sure as hell not like the guys around here. Rich. Gorgeous. Sophisticated, but he earned that. I can tell. The accent doesn't hurt. Hell, I can see how he revs your engine."

"It's not about that," I said. "I mean ... sure ... but ... he handles things. Do you know? With every other thing, it's always fallen to me. Matty's issues. Joe's family drama. Vangie. My father even, when he was around. I'm the one left cleaning up after everyone. With Killian ... I never needed to. He's the first guy ... pretty much the only guy ... I've ever known that I could truly rely on. When I needed something, he was always there. Most of the time before I even knew what it was I needed."

"Like with Josie," she said.

"Yes. Shit. Yes."

Jeanie nodded. "Joe's amended custody order came through this morning. She signed off on everything. That was Thorne? He paid her off?"

My head pounded inside my skull.

"It's okay," she said. "I get it. Doesn't mean I don't worry about you. But this …" She spread her hands, gesturing to the massive Richards case file.

"This is the price you're paying," she said.

I couldn't answer. There was no need.

"You going to tell me this is positively the last thing you're going to do for Thorne?"

I steepled my fingers beneath my chin. "Yes."

She raised a skeptical brow. "You know what the bitch of it is, don't you?"

This got a laugh out of me. "I can't even …"

She picked up one of the stapled sections of the report. I was looking at it upside down, but still recognized it as the initial search warrant for Richards's car.

Jeanie waved the papers in the air. "The bitch of it is, this whole thing has smelled wrong from the very beginning. Ted Richards is a fucking demon. I'd like to wrap piano wire around his balls. As a start. But … dammit all to hell. I know it in my gut. He didn't kill Mark Channing."

"So how the hell do we prove it?" I said. God. I couldn't believe I was still in this hell. It felt like there was no way to go but down. "Forget about the damage Sally Richards did for now. We're sunk because of Patrick Johnson's testimony and the forensics on that car."

"The jury has no reason to believe anybody other than our guy did this. So the real question is, how do we get 'em to start thinking about somebody else?"

I crashed my head to the table. "I've been over this a million times. So have you. Channing had no other enemies outside the people he put behind bars. He got along with his colleagues. His superiors. Perfect life. Perfect wife."

"Trophy wife," Jeanie said. She slid Richards's doodle pad out of her briefcase. I left it to her to take care of it after every trial day. She stared at the drawing of Catherine Channing. Below it, Ted had written those words along with an outline of an actual trophy.

"It's weird she never called the cops when he didn't come home for dinner," Jeanie said. "He went somewhere. Unless he was drinking in the office before he left. The man was drunk when he died. And nobody claims to have seen him. Not at a bar, nowhere. And he's found with a shoe missing."

"That doesn't mean anything," I said.

"Sure, Catherine's the grieving, pregnant widow, but she also came off a little like a spoiled brat. You scored some points with her in spite of it."

"Which were all but obliterated when Sally Richards loosened her collar and Ted scared the hell out of everyone in that courtroom."

She nodded. "I just ... even the way these two met gives me the creeps. Catherine Channing is the daughter of the best friend of Jordan Elliot. Former Lieutenant Governor. He's now considered a kingmaker in state politics, for sure. But with Channing he was branching out."

"So, he handpicks Catherine to marry Channing because she checks all the boxes Elliot thinks a political wife needs."

Jeanie flipped the page on Ted's notebook. He'd drawn a shockingly good copy of Mark Channing's photo ID, complete with the American flag in the background.

"Between Fitzgerald and us," Jeanie said. "We've interviewed everybody. I didn't get so much as a weird vibe from anybody connected to Channing, did you?"

"No. Dammit, no."

"It just doesn't track though. If Ted Richards is the guy in this file"—she held up the Ghost Man folder—"Channing makes no damn sense. He sits outside his house for three nights in a row. In the car he later uses to transport the body. It's too neat."

"It's too sloppy," I said. "Even the FBI thinks so."

She gave me a wry smirk.

I held a hand up. "I've got a friend. An agent I've had some dealings with in the past. He met me for drinks the other night. He's not directly involved in either the Kinsell investigation or this dossier on Richards, but he let me pick his brain. Reluctantly."

"He?" Jeanie smiled.

"Stop it. Anyway, he wouldn't come out and say it, but the Bureau knows there are issues with the way Channing's murder went down."

"Issues ... hmmm. But they're not willing to go to the mat on that. They figure he's guilty of all the rest of these. So what if he gets convicted of one he didn't do? A collar is a collar."

"Maybe," I said. It seemed too harsh an assessment. But nobody, least of all me, could deny that Richards was better off behind bars. And yet, here I was strategizing about how to keep him from that when I knew he had orders to kill me last year.

"My life is messed up," I said. Though I couldn't tell Jeanie everything I knew about Ted, she knew me well enough to sense something.

"It's something, all right," she agreed. "But let me tell you something. I'm proud of you. I don't like how you got dragged into this case. I sure as hell don't give a damn what happens to Ted Richards. If I could kill him myself for what he did to Sally, I would. But this case? It stinks."

"It does. I'm just afraid I'm running out of time to prove it."

"Your FBI friend have anything else useful to impart?" she asked. She knew I was being cagey about Lee Cannon. I could never tell her that I met with him last year on my suspicions about Liam Thorne and a jury-tampering scheme.

"You're full of surprises and secrets, Cass," she said.
Jeanie wasn't stupid. I didn't have to say a word for her to put two and two together.

"Are you safe?" she asked.

"I'm safe," I answered.

"Good. So let's call it a night. Tomorrow's a big day. I'm pretty sure Abbato is going to rest."

I grabbed my keys off the table. "I'll drive you home. How many of those have you had?" I pointed to her coffee mug.

"Well, I was just planning on crashing here," she said.

"No. Warm bed. Quiet. You need it. I'll pick you up on the way to court in the morning."

Jeanie gave me a salute. I was just about to give one back when my phone rang. My stomach clenched, thinking about all the missed calls and texts I'd ignored. But as I glanced at my phone, new fear flared. Detective Eric Wray's number came up. Jeanie saw it too.

"Shit," I said. There was no good reason for him to be calling me this late in the day.

"Hey, Eric," I said, holding Jeanie's gaze as I answered. She was bracing herself for my reaction.

"Cass, I'm sorry to have to call. I know your plate's been pretty full. But uh ... I've got your niece, Emma, with me. She's okay. Don't worry. It's just, uh ... she was at a party tonight. One of her friends. A few of them got popped for M.I.P.s."

My stomach dropped. "Minor in Possession," I mouthed to Jeanie. From her expression, I gathered she could hear Eric's end well enough even though I hadn't put him on speaker.

"Christ," I muttered.

"She hasn't been charged," he said. "Responding officers

didn't catch her with anything. I got to her before anybody could run a breathalyzer but …"

"No. I get it," I said.

"What do you want me to do?" he asked.

"Where are you now?"

"On Fletcher Road. I was going to drive her home but I figured you'd want to know."

"Thank you," I said. I could hear Emma crying in the background.

"It's no problem. I know you've all been through a lot. With Josie and … everything."

"I've got this," I said. "I'll meet you over at my brother's house. And just … Eric. I owe you. I know that."

He grew silent on the other end of the phone. Then finally, "I'll see you in a few, Cass." He hung up.

"Shit," Jeanie said. I was right. She'd heard enough.

"Come on," I said, sighing. "Your place is on the way. I'll still drop you off."

She grabbed her purse. "Well," she said. "One thing's pretty clear, Cass."

I paused at the stairs. She gave me a thin smile.

"Killian Thorne's not the only guy who looks out for you, honey."

I shook my head and gently pushed her toward the stairs. "Go," I said. She was already laughing as she made her way down.

Chapter 30

To his credit, my brother kept his temper when Detective Wray pulled up with Emma. She'd stopped crying, but kept her head down as she sat in the back of his unmarked cruiser.

I beat him to the house by a few minutes. I half figured Eric had done a few circles before getting here just to make sure I would. One more thing I owed him for.

"It's been a rough couple of months for her," I said to Joe. Katy hung back. My sister-in-law looked weary as she stood in the kitchen, watching. I knew she had to feel like her whole life had been sucked up by Leary drama lately. It had. But she loved my brother and Emma like her own. It's why she fought so hard to protect her, even against her own mother. Emma was lucky to have her. At the moment, my niece didn't appear to understand that.

"Looks like one of her friend's parents is out of town for the week," Eric said. "One of our guys got a tip from a neighbor. By the time we got there, things were getting out of hand."

"Thank you," Joe said. I knew he hated having to.

Growing up, both of my brothers had their wild days. Matty still didn't trust the cops. For Joe's part, like me, he always associated them with awful news. It was a hard thing to shake. But Eric was a friend. "No problem," Eric said. "I trust you can handle all of this within your family."

"We can," Joe said, his voice more clipped than Eric deserved. I forced a smile and put a hand on my brother's chest.

"Come on," I said. "I'll walk you out." Joe went to the car and opened the back seat. Through gritted teeth, he muttered something to Emma. She flew out of the car and threw her arms around her father. He stayed still as a stone mountain. But he seemed calmer. Emma let go and ran to me.

"Thank you. Aunt Cass, it's not what you think." Eric wasn't even back in his car yet.

"Stop," I said. "I think you've probably said enough."

"Don't be mad. It wasn't my fault!"

I could smell the alcohol on her breath from here. So could Joe. But this was one family mess he would have to clean up without me. At least for now.

"I love you, kiddo," I said, pulling her into a hug. "But this can't be the story you want to write for yourself."

I was tired. Hungry. Feeling defeated.

Joe caught my eye over Emma's shoulder. I turned her, giving her back to her dad.

"We'll talk later," I said.

"Thanks," he answered.

Eric slid into the driver's seat. I went over to him and leaned in the window.

"I know you went out on a limb for this. And I also know you won't be able to the next time."

"I don't know," he said. "It just seemed like maybe the

kid needed a break this one time. Make sure your brother knows I don't want to live to regret that."

"Understood."

"How are you?" he asked.

I couldn't help it. I laughed.

"Ah," Eric said. "That bad, is it?"

"It's been worse," I said. And that was true. Eric more than anyone knew that.

His expression darkened. He was so much different than Killian and I don't know why that occurred to me just then. Killian wore a sly smile most of the time. His eyes carried a devilish twinkle. Eric Wray could be like that too. But his looks were hardened, more rugged. He carried the weight of his job in every line on his face.

"Well," he said, turning his engine. "Let me know if I can help you out at all."

"You already have. I meant what I said. I owe you one."

"I thought I owed you one," he said.

I straightened. "You know? I'm starting to lose track."

This got the first genuine laugh out of both of us. Joe was still watching from the porch. He'd sent Emma into the house. I raised my hand to wave goodbye to him. Eric turned to look. I stepped away from his window and he slowly made his way down the driveway. Joe went back inside.

It was nearly midnight. I was due back in court in eight hours. I was exhausted, but I knew I'd never sleep. I thought about calling Eric back. He was good company, and a beer or two at Mickey's sounded like heaven. But he was another one who would start asking questions. For now, I was out of answers.

Ten minutes later, I pulled into my own driveway. I sat behind the wheel for a moment, looking out at the lake. It was the first moment of silence I'd had all day. It should have calmed me. Instead, I could only hear the echo of Ted Richards's whispering voice.

Ah darlin'. Don't you know. I'm already a ghost.

He was a killer. If it weren't for Killian intervening, he would have killed me. He brutalized Sally Richards. And those were just the things I knew for sure. The Ghost Man file sat beside me on the passenger seat.

There was something I had overlooked. I felt it in my bones. Exhausted as I was, there would be no sleep for me tonight. I tucked the file under my arm and headed inside.

The house was quiet. Empty. I couldn't remember the last time that was true. Killian had gone back to Chicago for the week. I owed him a call, but I couldn't bring myself to do it. He would sense something in my voice. I didn't know if I had the courage to tell him Ted Richards had been the man on the yacht last year. Part of me wondered if he already knew and the reality of that would gut me. It would be the final straw and one I wasn't yet ready to face.

So I went to the kitchen and made myself a cup of coffee. No whiskey. I wanted my head.

I spread the file out on the kitchen table. Witness statements. Photographs. The federal task force's written report. The Kinsell operation would face trial later this year. The case against them appeared solid. I looked over the redacted pages of the report. The FBI had contact with mainly four people during the investigation. The one identified as Witness X met with a special agent at least six times, giving information on wire transactions between Kinsell and top officials in the government contract scheme for the parking garage. They met in different cities over a two-year period. Channing had notes from a telephone conversation a few weeks before the trial, but they never met in person.

He worked out immunity deals with two other informants, all related to the money Kinsell apparently laundered for other crime families over the last decade. Those families weren't mentioned by name, but the Thornes had to be one of them. Another witness by the name of Chip Edgar was granted immunity, but the heaviest redactions surrounded whatever Edgar would testify about.

Then there was the informant named Loomis. He'd been the one to provide most of the details on Ghost Man. But the investigation ultimately went nowhere. A rabbit hole. No concrete connection to Kinsell. Channing couldn't even take it to a grand jury. There wasn't enough here to convict Ted Richards of any of the dozens of murders profiled. There was only suspicion.

Until Mark Channing was murdered.

Names, dates, transactions. It was all here. I'd seen this kind of thing a million times before working for the Thorne Law Group.

My eyes started to bleed as I pored over the reports for at least the hundredth time since getting them. There was just nothing in here that had much, if anything, to do with Mark Channing's murder.

"Why him?" I said aloud. Great. I had resorted to talking to myself. "Killing Channing wasn't going to make the RICO case against Kinsell go away."

To the contrary, now Andy Tate was lead counsel. And if he for some reason couldn't try the case, Laura Wyler or Ryan McGuinness would. The FBI investigation was complete as far as Kinsell was concerned. Why in the hell would the organization think killing Channing would torpedo it? If anything, the government was even more committed to going after them now. It made more sense for Ted to go after this Loomis, or Witness X, or even this Chip Edgar.

I'd stared at the documents so long, the sun started to rise. I was due in court in less than three hours. Yawning, I started to fold up the paperwork. Staring at it a second longer would do me no good. A shower, however, might.

I stayed under the spray so long, the water turned cold. That helped me too. I let it sluice down my face until my fingers became mottled and pruned.

Finally, I felt awake enough to get dressed. My brain buzzed in the way it does from lack of sleep. But it was time to leave.

Killian's text still blinked at me when I checked my phone on the charger. I picked it up.

"Heading to court now," I texted. "I'll try you this evening. Long night."

The cursor blinked. Then he responded. "Sounds good. I'm still sorry about the other night. L won't be coming back to Delphi again. Promise."

Another promise. I prayed he would keep it. I went to put the phone back on the charger. It rang, startling me. It came up as "no caller ID."

I hesitated. Probably a telemarketer or a wrong number. But something made me answer anyway.

"Cass Leary," I said.

There was silence on the other end for a beat. Then I heard the caller take a deep, unsettling breath.

"You have to keep asking questions," a female voice said.

"I'm sorry? Who is this?"

"They're not telling you everything," she said. "But nobody will listen to me."

"I'm listening," I said. My skin crawled. The caller had a familiar voice, but I couldn't place it.

"I shouldn't have called," she said.

"But you did. Do you want to tell me what this is about?"

She paused again. "Channing," she finally said, though in my bones I already knew it. My mind raced.

"What is it you want me to know? What questions haven't I asked?"

"If they find out I called, they'll fire me. Or worse."

Fire her. "Who's they?" I asked. "Listen, you're wasting both of our time. I'm due in court in a couple of hours. If you have information that bears on the Channing trial, tell it. Or better yet, why haven't you told it to the police?"

"You don't understand," she said.

"So make me."

"Your client ... he's a seriously bad guy. He shouldn't ever be allowed out of jail. It's just ..."

"It's just, he didn't kill Mark Channing, did he? Do you know who did?"

"I can't ... he wasn't. Mark Channing isn't who everyone thought he was. That's all. Everyone just assumes."

"But you know different," I said. I fished for a pen. I kept a pad of paper in the drawer of my nightstand. It wasn't uncommon for me to wake from a dead sleep with a thought or idea when I was working on a case. I started to jot down my observations about the caller.

Possibly young. Claims to know Mark Channing. Mistress?

I took a shot.

"You loved him," I said.

"What? No. Gross."

Okay, so she *was* young probably.

"Did he do something to you? Look, you called me."

"I shouldn't have. I'm sorry."

"No, wait. It's okay. I understand." Instinct told me I had to keep her talking. It could be nothing. Just some crackpot. High-profile cases like this tended to draw them. And yet ...

"It doesn't matter, maybe. Your client should go to jail for what he did to his wife anyway."

"He just might," I said. "If she chooses to press charges."

"I'm sorry," she said. "I can't talk about this anymore."

I heard laughter in the background. She wasn't alone.

"What's your name?"

She hung up. My phone beeped as the call disconnected.

"What the actual hell?" I was talking to myself again.

I looked at my notepad. Young. Mistress? I wrote, "thinks Richards should pay for the attack on Sally."

That's when my hand froze. I hadn't checked the news yet this morning. I swiped my phone screen and went straight to MLive.

Nothing. There was nothing. Judge Benitez's gag order was still holding. It wouldn't forever, but the events from yesterday hadn't hit the internet yet.

My caller had just said she wanted Richards to pay for what he did to his wife. She intimated she knew Mark Channing personally. At least, enough to form an opinion as to what kind of man he was. And the only way she knew about what happened to Sally Richards was if she had been in the courtroom during her testimony.

It was the thinnest of threads. I punched in Jeanie's number. I had a pretty good hunch who my mystery caller was.

Chapter 31

I EXPLAINED my theory to Jeanie on our morning ride to the courthouse.

"Yeah," she said. "I've seen the girl you mean. Pretty, but mousey. She sits in the back row every day taking notes. You're sure she's with Channing's office?"

"One hundred percent. She was with McGuinness, Wyler, and Tate the day I tried to meet with them. She seemed kind of skittish that day too but I didn't think much of it."

"Hmm," Jeanie said. "You think she had a crush on the guy? That's where I'd put my money."

"Maybe," I said. "I just want to talk to her alone."

"Well, that's the trick," Jeanie said. "She sits in the courtroom, but every time she leaves, Wyler, McGuinness, or Tate meet her outside. Abbato's been careful not letting them in the gallery. Doesn't want to taint their testimony if they take the stand."

"Well, she's scared of something. And she doesn't think Richards killed Channing. If she knows something, I need to know it too."

"I'll keep an eye on her if she shows up today," Jeanie promised.

"Follow her if you see her head to the bathroom or something. It's not the smoothest play, but it might be all we get."

"Sure," she said. "And I'll call my investigator and see if he can dig anything up. Stockton. Victoria?"

"Right."

We'd arrived. I found a decent parking spot and hoped it was a good omen for the rest of the day. I would need it. After my cross-examination of Sally Richards, I expected Tony Abbato to rest his case. For the moment, I had no star witness to call, no dazzling trick up my sleeve. Ted's entire defense rested on his thin excuse for an uncorroborated alibi and a leap of logic that a professional hit man, if the jury believed he was, would be better at it. And that was *if* the jury could get past the idea that he'd also tried to kill his wife.

Late yesterday, Tony got a motion granted to keep Ted out of the courtroom for Sally's cross-examination. He was watching from another room in the courthouse on closed-circuit television. I'd fought it, but only just. It wasn't the worst thing to keep the jury from seeing his hard face as his terrified wife tried to tell her story.

My best strategy was to keep this short and to the point.

"Good morning, Mrs. Richards," I said. "Thanks for coming back today. I can only imagine how difficult this is for you."

In an odd way, as I spoke to her, I realized Sally and I had a strange bond. I didn't believe Ted killed Mark Channing. But I knew in my heart he put his hands on Sally. Those same hands had held me over the deck of the *Crown of Thorne*.

Sometimes, I really hated this fucking job.

"Mrs. Richards, before yesterday, when was the last time you had contact with Ted Richards?"

"It's been almost two years," she said. "It was a phone call. He asked me to come back home and he said he wouldn't give me a divorce. I changed my number after that."

"Two years," I said. "So you have no direct knowledge of Ted's comings and goings over the last two years."

"No."

"Haven't spoken. Haven't texted. Nothing."

"No," she said.

"You have no earthly clue whether Ted committed the crime for which he's now charged."

She shook her head. "Mrs. Richards?"

"No," she said. "I don't know."

Now came the question I hated but had to ask.

"Mrs. Richards, have you ever lied under oath before?"

She looked at Abbato, then she looked at the judge.

"Please answer, Mrs. Richards," Benitez said, but he was staring hard at me.

"I ..."

"You were charged with filing a false police report in 1986, were you not?"

I went to the table and picked up the charging document. Jeanie's investigator had come through after a tip from Ted, of all people.

"That was Ted's idea," she said.

"What was Ted's idea? Mrs. Richards, I'm going to hand you what's been marked as defense exhibit number twenty-one. Can you tell me what it is?"

With shaking hands, she took the document. "It's a police report. I ... I had an ex-boyfriend. He wasn't very nice to me. He wasn't taking the break-up well. Brad, my ex. He and my brother Ronny, the two of them got into an argument. It got physical. They charged Brad for assault after I told them ..."

"What did you tell them?"

239

She let out a sigh. "I told them Brad started the fight."

"Did he?" I asked.

"No," she said.

"So you lied to the police," I said.

"I didn't want Ronny to get in trouble."

"Is that a yes?"

"Yes. I lied. I was young and stupid and I thought it was the right thing to do. Brad wasn't a good guy. I thought ... even if he didn't do this, he deserved to get in trouble for all the other things he'd done. So Ted encouraged me to lie so I could keep Ronny from getting arrested too."

I couldn't believe she said it. Behind me, I knew Tony couldn't believe she said it.

"Thank you," I said. "I've got nothing further."

"Mr. Abbato?" the judge asked.

"Mrs. Richards." Tony rose. "Have you been truthful with your testimony in this trial?"

She was crying. Her lips quivered. "Yes," she said. "And Ted deserves to be held accountable."

"Objection," I said.

"Sustained. The jury should disregard everything the witness just said after the word 'yes.'"

"Thank you," Tony said. "At this time, Your Honor, the prosecution rests."

"All right," Judge Benitez said. "We'll do our procedural housekeeping after a short recess. Ms. Leary, I assume you have some motions you'd like to file?"

"Yes, Your Honor," I said.

Benitez gave the nod to the bailiff. He started clearing the jury.

"I need a few," Judge Benitez said. "We're back in twenty minutes. Not a second longer, counsel."

He rose; his robe swirled behind him. On my feet with him, my phone vibrated from inside my messenger bag. I turned back to Jeanie but she wasn't there. What the hell? I looked back toward the gallery. Victoria Stockton wasn't in her usual spot against the wall either.

My phone buzzed again. I grabbed it. The one line text from Jeanie read simply, "north stairwell."

Shit.

Abbato was watching me. I had no time for pleasantries. I had nineteen minutes.

I tossed my papers into my bag and walked out. Andy Tate and Laura Wyler stood near the elevators. They each gave me a hard stare as I passed them. They could hate me all they wanted, I just hoped to God neither of them followed me.

As soon as I rounded the corner, I nearly broke into a run. I pushed through the stairwell door and nearly tripped over Jeanie's foot. She had an aggressive stance. Victoria Stockton looked scared as hell, her back pressed up against the wall.

"Victoria," I said, putting a hand on Jeanie's arm. "Thanks for meeting me."

"I'm not ... I can't do this."

"But you did," I said. "You called me last night. I know it was you. I recognized your voice and you tipped your hand talking about Sally Richards's testimony. You're a smart girl, Victoria. It's not easy to land the job you have with the U.S. Attorney's office. I know how competitive it is."

"I can't talk to you," she said. "I don't have anything else to say."

It wasn't a denial, so I took it as an admission.

"You need to tell me what you know," I said. "You said Mark Channing wasn't who people thought he was. I believe that. His wife? His life? It was orchestrated. Built for how it would play to voters. I know that."

She cast a nervous glance toward Jeanie and then the door.

"I have to go," she said. "They're going to figure out I'm gone."

"They," I said. "You mean Tate and Wyler? Victoria, cut the crap. If you know something, it's past time to tell it."

I'd done it on a whim just before driving in this morning. I produced a subpoena and handed it to her. Victoria recognized the document right away and her color drained.

"You can't call me."

"That's a court order, Victoria. I can and I will. Are you planning to subject yourself to contempt of court over this?"

She shook her head. "You don't get it. They'll fire me. They'll do more than that. They'll tank any chance I have of a decent career after this."

I crossed my arms. "That's what you're worried about? Your job? Victoria, you're a law student. Right?"

She nodded.

"And you know in about a year and a half you're going to have to pass a character and fitness exam if you ever want to practice. How do you think subpoena dodging will look on your resume?"

"Or perjury," Jeanie said. She was pissed and impatient. So was I. I had maybe ten minutes to get back to the courtroom. Less if anyone else opened that stairwell door.

"You called me because you want to do the right thing," I said. "So do it. Tell me what you know. I'll find out anyway. You can either be the hero or the villain in this."

"Villain?" she said. "Ted Richards is the villain. Don't kid yourself about that. He's a murderer. Everything you read in that FBI file? It's true. And that's just the tip of it. You know it. And yet you're in there defending him anyway."

"And you're out here withholding evidence," I said.

Her eyelids flickered as she held back tears.

"He was a good guy," she said. "Mark was trying."

I dropped my shoulders, taking a softer tone.

"He was good to you," I said.

She nodded.

Jeanie shot me a look.

"Did he promise to leave her for you?" Jeanie asked, her tone bordering on sarcasm. I gave her elbow a light pinch.

Victoria's eyes snapped wide. "What? Are you kidding? You think I was ... ugh. No. I wasn't in love with the guy. Not me."

Not her. It was a strange way to put it.

"You found something out though," I said.

She nodded. "You have to look harder," she said.

"And I don't have any time for games or parsed breadcrumbs, Victoria. Say what you know or quit wasting my time. You can do it here or you can do it on the witness stand. Your choice."

She bit her lip. "I wrote up the immunity deals. Subpoenas. Orders. I drafted all of it. Mark would review them. Sign off."

"Of course," I said. "That shows he thought you were a good writer."

"Except for one," she said. "Chip Edgar."

Jeanie and I passed a look. He was the witness whose potential testimony was the most redacted in the file I had. At best, I guessed he was a low-level courier for the Kinsell organization. He had no connection to the Richards file though, as far as I could tell.

"She got angry when I asked about it. Told me to mind my own business. And she told me to quit meeting with Mark for lunch. I only did that maybe twice."

"She," I said, my heart tripping. "You mean Laura Wyler. She's the one who wrote Chip Edgar's deal?"

Victoria nodded. "She didn't want me to run it by Mark.

I had it in a stack of things I meant to go over with him, about two weeks before ..."

"Before the murder," Jeanie finished for her.

"You saw them together," I said on a hunch. Mark and Laura.

She cast her eyes downward. Slowly, she lifted them and nodded.

Of course. Still, it was hardly a smoking gun. But it gave me plenty to look into. Only we had precious little time. If I was lucky, I could tie the judge up with my directed verdict motion for the rest of the day But then I had to call my first witness.

The stairwell door opened. Victoria took the opening. She brushed past Jeanie and charged through the door. She was still holding my subpoena in her hand.

Jeanie stared at me.

"Well, I'll be goddamned," she said. "I can't believe I missed it. Channing and Wyler."

"It's the longest of shots," I said. "I need you to get a hold of your investigator again. Have him find out anything he can about Chip Edgar. For all we know, it's an alias. And tell him we need it yesterday."

I patted her arm and raced through the door. I had a tiny ray of hope, but zero time.

Chapter 32

TED RICHARDS WAS LED into the courtroom in chains. Subdued, slouching, I started to suspect if he was on something. He sat beside me with a thud and gave me a glassy-eyed smile that made me think my first guess was accurate.

"He stays in those," the deputy said. He was a big, burly guy with a rosy-cheeked baby face. His name was Nick Pauley.

"Are you serious?" I had hoped the judge would reconsider.

Pauley nodded. "Take it up with Judge Beni. His orders."

I let out a sigh. As if the jury needed a further reminder of how dangerous Ted Richards was. But today, more than any other day, I knew I needed to pick my battles.

Ted blew Pauley a kiss and got a middle finger in response. Their shenanigans were one thing, Jeanie's absence was another. She pulled an all-nighter with her investigator. I got a text from her at four in the morning saying she was onto something, but needed a little more time. She assured me she'd be at my side by the time Benitez took the bench.

"All rise!"

"Shit," I muttered under my breath. As I rose, I leaned toward Pauley.

"Is Laura Wyler still out there?" I asked.

Pauley took his position right behind Ted. "The DOJ lawyer?"

"Yes."

"Think so. She and her buddies have been keeping vigil outside the coffee shop."

I looked back. Jeanie was still gone, but so was Victoria Stockton. Double shit. If she went south on me ... if she changed her mind and warned the others ...

"You ready to proceed, Ms. Leary?" Benitez asked.

I took a breath. The next hour could win my case or detonate it. It felt a little like trying to manage a freeway on-ramp with my eyes closed. Nothing to do but accelerate ... and pray.

"Yes, Your Honor," I said. The jury filed in.

"The defense calls Laura Wyler to the stand."

"Your Honor?" Tony said. "I don't believe Ms. Wyler is under subpoena."

"She's on your witness list as well as mine," I said. "And she's in the courtroom."

I turned back to Pauley. He gave me an angry stare in return. He didn't want even the remote suggestion that he'd done anything to help a defense attorney. Certainly not one attached to Ted Richards.

"She is here, Your Honor," Pauley said. He spoke into the radio at his shoulder as Benitez gave him a nod. My heart thundered behind my ribcage as we waited. A full minute later, another deputy opened the doors and ushered a white-faced Laura Wyler up to the stand.

She gave me a hard stare as she took her oath and climbed into the witness box.

"Ms. Wyler," I said. "Can you tell the jury what you do for a living?"

Laura Wyler had cold, gray eyes framed with long, dark lashes. She wore her brown hair in a severe bun, not a drop of makeup on her porcelain skin. She didn't need it. She was stunning but with a hard beauty.

"I'm a federal prosecutor," she said. "I work in the U.S. Attorney's office. Violent and organized crime. Detroit Field Office."

"Thank you. How long have you held that position?"

She settled a little. Some of the fire went out of her eyes. I knew it would soon return. "Twelve years," she said. "Before that, I clerked for a federal judge."

"Can you tell me how you knew Mark Channing?"

A shudder went through her. "Mark was my colleague in the unit. As is Ryan McGuinness and Andrew Tate."

"How long did you work with Mark Channing?"

She looked down. Her words faltered a bit. "I was hired on just a few months after Mark. So, it was a little over eleven years."

"Are you familiar with the case Mark Channing was preparing to take to trial against the Kinsell organization?"

"Yes," she said.

"Did you work on it with him?"

"Mark was lead counsel. Andy Tate was going to serve second chair. I wasn't going to participate in the trial phase of that litigation."

"But you were familiar with it. You were involved in strategy sessions. You all—Mark, Tate, McGuinness—you discussed the case frequently, isn't that right?"

Tony scooted his chair back. From the corner of my eye, I saw him lean over to confer with his paralegal.

"That's fair," Laura said. "But Kinsell was Mark's case."

"Ms. Wyler, part of the prosecution of this case, of any

criminal prosecution really, did it become necessary to proffer immunity deals with any witnesses?"

She gave me a scowl. "Are you asking generally or specific to this case? The form of your question is vague, Counselor."

I smiled. "Let's talk the Kinsell case. Are you aware of any immunity deals that might have been struck with testifying witnesses?"

"Objection," Tony said. "The contents of any such deals are not relevant."

"I'm not asking about the contents," I said. "I'm just asking if there were any."

"You can answer, Ms. Wyler," Judge Benitez said. His posture changed. He leaned forward toward Laura Wyler. Judge Benitez was paying attention.

"Yes," she said. "I believe there were immunity deals offered as part of the prosecution of the Kinsell case."

"Isn't it true that there were actually four such deals made with potential witnesses in preparation for the Kinsell trial?"

Laura looked at Tony. He was furiously scribbling notes.

"Objection," he popped up. "Relevance. Again."

"I'll allow it," the judge said. "But let's not get too far afield here."

"Of course," I said. "Do you need me to repeat?"

"No," Laura said. "I don't know the number of deals. But yes, that would have been within Mark's authority. He handled that."

"Except for one," I said. I had a copy of the signature page for the immunity deal of a single witness.

"Excuse me?"

"Except for one. Mark Channing signed off on all immunity deals proffered in the Kinsell litigation except for one. Do you know which?"

"Objection," Tony said. "Counsel is assuming facts not in evidence."

Benitez gave me a scowl.

"Your Honor, if I may, I'd like to mark defense exhibit twenty-seven for identification."

I handed the page to Tony. He'd of course seen it before.

"May I approach the witness?" Benitez assented. I handed Laura Wyler the pages.

Her lips pursed as she flipped to the signature page. Slowly, her cold stare returned. She was beginning to catch on.

Where the hell was Jeanie? I cast a furtive glance over at the defense table. Ted was back to doodling. Even in cuffs, he managed to wield his pencil.

"Do you recognize this document?" I asked.

Laura calmly flipped the pages. "Yes," she said.

"Can you tell me what it is?"

"It's an immunity agreement regarding the testimony of a potential witness in the Kinsell matter."

"What is the name of the witness?"

"Objection!"

"Save it," Judge Benitez said. "Not yet, anyway."

"Ms. Wyler?" I asked.

"The witness's name is Charles Edgar."

"Charles Edgar," I said. "Chip. He went by Chip? Is that right?"

"I have no idea," Laura said.

"Who signed the agreement, Ms. Wyler? Is that Mark Channing's signature?"

"Objection," Tony said. "This witness hasn't established that she's qualified to identify Channing's signature."

I couldn't believe what I was hearing. In his haste, Tony hadn't even bothered to read the last page.

"I believe the witness can answer that question for herself," I said.

"Ms. Wyler?" the judge said.

"No," Laura answered. "This isn't Mark's signature. It's mine."

"Your signature," I said. "So you signed this particular immunity deal with Mr. Edgar. Not Mark. Is that correct?"

"Yes," she said.

I moved to have the agreement admitted into evidence.

"Ms. Wyler, you drafted this agreement yourself, isn't that true?"

"What?"

"You drafted it. You didn't farm it off to a paralegal or other associate. Correct?"

"I don't recall," she said.

"But isn't it the customary practice in your office for the document's drafter to put his or her initials in the bottom left corner of the signature page?"

"Objection," Tony said. "Again ... she's assuming ..."

"It's no assumption," I said. "I'm asking the question if it's customary. The witness can answer."

"Agreed. Overruled," Benitez said.

"Yes," Laura hissed. "Generally, yes."

"But there's no initialing on this document. Correct?"

"No, there isn't," she said.

"You drafted it yourself?"

"I said, I don't recall."

"But you likely did."

"Objection!"

Benitez sighed. "Move on, Ms. Leary."

I was stalling and all of them knew it. I needed Jeanie. Now. I was running out of road.

I paused, walked around the lectern then back behind it. All the while, I tried to will those courtroom doors open with my mind. It was almost ten o'clock. Jeanie was supposed to have been back hours ago.

"Ms. Leary?" the judge said, growing irritated.

"Ms. Wyler, you had access to the Kinsell file, correct?"

"What do you mean by access?"

I tapped my pen on the lectern. "All the discovery materials. The FBI reports, witness statements, deposition transcripts. You had access to it, correct?"

"Access," she said. "As I said, I wasn't lead counsel on this case."

"That isn't what I asked you. Let me give you a scenario. If you wanted to walk over to the trial book and read any of those discovery materials, you could, correct?"

"Objection," Tony said. "This is not relevant. Counsel is fishing and she's wasting precious time."

"Get to your point, Ms. Leary," Judge Benitez said.

"Your answer, Ms. Wyler?"

She shifted in her seat. "We all had access to the file, yes. But as I've indicated no less than three times now, this was Mark's case. Not mine."

"And yet, you wrote up an immunity deal for Chip Edgar on your own," I said.

"Is there a question in there?"

"When was the last time you saw Mark Channing alive?" I asked. I had Laura's statement to the police in front of me. "I don't know the exact time," she said. Her voice dropped. "And I didn't know it would be the last time. But we were in the office the afternoon of October eighteenth."

"Did you leave the office with him that day?"

"I don't know what you mean."

"I'll clarify. Did you walk out of the office at the same time he did?"

"Roughly, yes," she said.

"In fact, records show your key card was swiped at 5:02 p.m. Exactly thirty seconds after Mark's. Isn't that right?"

"We left the building together," she said. "It was Friday afternoon."

"And he was going to meet his new wife for dinner," I said.

Laura flapped her hands. "I guess."

"Security cameras don't show Mark's vehicle exiting the structure until fourteen minutes past five. You drove out two minutes after that," I said.

"If that's what it says," she said. "I have no independent recollection."

"What did you and Mark talk about for the intervening twelve minutes, Ms. Wyler?"

She narrowed her eyes at me. "I don't recall."

"Did you talk about the Kinsell case?"

"I don't recall."

"Did you talk about your weekend plans?"

"I don't recall."

"Did you have an argument?"

"Objection," Tony said. "This has been asked and answered three separate ways now."

"Sustained."

"Ms. Wyler," I said. "You were the last person to see Mark Channing alive. You had more than a ten-minute conversation with him, and then he vanished. And you're telling me you have no recollection of what you spoke about?"

"That's what I'm telling you," she said. "It was a normal day. Mundane. I had no reason to think there was anything remarkable about it until after the fact."

"You were close though," I said.

"Is that a question?"

"You were more than friends?" I asked.

"We were colleagues," she said, tight-lipped.

I was so far out of road now. I was jumping off the damn cliff Thelma and Louise-style. Sweat poured down the back of my neck. Ted Richards stared at me. Even he knew this particular train was about to wreck.

"The immunity deal you prepared for Charles Edgar," I said. "Can you tell me the date of it?"

Laura flipped the stapled papers open again, licking her finger. Her cold stare firmly in place, she fed off the growing irritation of the judge and now the jury. Juror number seven dusted lint off his sleeve. When I made eye contact with him, he actually rolled his eyes.

"January twentieth," she said. "Last year."

"Interesting," I said. "Was that before or after Mark Channing married Catherine Channing?"

"Your Honor," Tony said.

Laura Wyler made her first tell. Her nostrils flared. "I wouldn't know," she snapped.

"Were you friendly with Catherine Channing?" I asked.

"I've met her," Laura said.

"Did Mark tell you when he started dating her?"

"I don't recall."

"But the marriage ... did you think it was sudden?"

"I wouldn't know," she said.

"Well, you said you and Mark had been working together for over a decade. Did he date a lot during that time?"

She lifted a hand and smoothed her hair against the side of her head.

"He didn't date," she said.

No more road. Not even any more air. All I had left was gravity and the big drop. Then ... splat.

"Ms. Wyler, you were in love with Mark Channing, isn't that true?"

Abbato threw his pen. Ted Richards slammed his fist to

the table. Juror number seven sat up a little straighter. The courtroom doors stayed shut.

"You're not doing this," Laura Wyler hissed.

"Were you in love with Mark Channing?" I asked.

"Objection!" Tony said. "There is no probative value whatsoever to this question. There is no …"

Judge Benitez folded his arms. "You can answer, Ms. Wyler."

She looked away from him. Her cheeks went crimson. Behind me, I heard murmuring and then someone shuffling in their seat. McGuinness and Tate had come in just after Laura did. It looked like literal steam coming out of Andy Tate's ears.

"No," she said. "There's no story here, Ms. Leary. We were colleagues."

I could see the ground coming up at me fast.

"You had to have been shocked when he married Catherine, weren't you?"

"It was sudden," she said. "Yes."

My stomach lurched. A sound echoed across the marble floors. The courtroom doors opened. With them, I prayed to God so had my parachute.

Jeanie hustled up the aisle. She had two pieces of paper in her hand. Her suit was crumpled, her hair matted. She was sweating. Judge Benitez sat straighter and raised a brow as Jeanie pushed through the partition and practically leaped over the defense table to hand me the paper in her hand.

I had no time to ask her about them. No time to call for a recess or gather my thoughts. All I could do was mouth three words.

"Are you sure?"

She answered with a smirk and a nod. My heart dropped. My breath came up short. The ground beneath me felt a little more solid.

I scanned the paper. A memo in Jeanie's scrawling short-hand. The contents of it made my stomach drop once again. The air went out of my lungs, but I found a way to speak.

"Ms. Wyler," I said. "Who is Charles Edgar?"

"Objection," Tony said. "This ground has already been fully covered."

"Ms. Leary, have you got anything new to add?"

"I'll rephrase," I said. "Ms. Wyler, who is Patrick Johnson to Charles Edgar?"

Laura Wyler's face froze. Her chute wasn't going to open. "This is insane."

"Ms. Wyler, you're aware that Patrick Johnson sat in that very chair and testified he saw a silver Jaguar parked in front of Mark Channing's home for three nights before he went missing?"

"Yes," she said.

"And did you know that Patrick Johnson also testified he moved into the neighborhood near Hickory Circle roughly three months before the murder?"

"If you say so," she said, all confidence draining from her voice.

"Charles Edgar was facing a ten-year sentence for drug possession, isn't that right?" I had Edgar's charging document stapled to Jeanie's note.

"Yes," she said.

"And you knocked it down to time served, correct?"

She looked away.

"Ms. Wyler?"

"I don't recall."

"Ms. Wyler, where is Charles Edgar now?"

"Objection," Tony said. "The whereabouts of a material witness in a pending RICO case aren't relevant. Even if they were, in the interest of ..."

I put up a hand. "Let me rephrase. Ms. Wyler? Mr.

Edgar is no longer incarcerated, isn't that true? He's a free man today as a result of this deal you cut."

"Yes," she said, her lip quivering.

"Have witness lists been filed in the upcoming Kinsell trial?"

She smoothed the other side of her hair. "Yes."

"You're familiar with the names on them?"

"Yes."

"Is Charles Edgar one of them?"

She couldn't lie. This might be the biggest gamble I took. I didn't have access to that witness list but I'd bet my life ... no ... I was betting Ted Richards's that Charles Edgar was nowhere to be found.

"No," she said. "He's not on the list."

"So Edgar gets a walk for ... nothing?"

"I'm not going to sit here and explain the ins and outs of our trial strategy, Ms. Leary. Though clearly you could use a few pointers."

"I'm sure I could," I smiled. "So, if Mr. Edgar didn't have to do anything in return for his freedom, I sure hope someone did. His brother, perhaps."

"Objection. Is Ms. Leary testifying now?"

"Ask a question, or dismiss the witness," Judge Benitez said.

"Isn't it true that Charles Edgar and Patrick are half-brothers on their mother's side?"

"You fucking bitch!" Ted yelled from behind me.

"Jesus Christ," Tony Abbato muttered.

"I wouldn't know," Laura Wyler said.

I walked over to Tony's table, tore off the back sheet of paper and handed it to him. Tony glared at me. He put on his reading glasses and scanned the paper.

"You've gotta be kidding me," he muttered. The paper

had copies of Johnson and Edgar's birth certificates. Their mother was the same.

"I am not," I said. "If you want a minute …"

"Something you'd like to share with the class?" Judge Benitez said.

"Ms. Wyler," I said. Now came the biggest leap I might take. I had nothing more than Jeanie's quickly scribbled note about a phone call her investigator had less than an hour ago and a prayer. "Isn't it true that you purchased a silver Jaguar in Nashville, Tennessee on August seventh of last year?"

The courtroom doors opened again. A heavy-set bald man with squeaky shoes walked in. He sat down directly behind Jeanie and she let out a sigh. I tried to question her with my eyes. She grabbed Ted's doodle pad and wrote two words in bold letters. She flashed it, shielding it so the jury couldn't see, but Laura Wyler and I both did.

"Car dealer." She drew an arrow pointing to the man behind her.

"Your answer, Ms. Wyler," I said.

She was shaking. Andy Tate leaped to his feet and ran out the back of the courtroom. Ryan McGuinness sat there, dumbfounded.

"I didn't … you can't …"

"Did you or did you not purchase a silver F-Type Jaguar from Cafferty Jaguar in Nashville?"

The bald guy in the ill-fitting suit had a folder of papers in front of him. He shuffled through them as if he were preparing to have to explain it all.

"No," Laura Wyler said. "I don't own a Jaguar."

It wasn't what I asked. But until I had a chance to talk to Jeanie, I'd ridden this particular train as far as it would take me.

For now …

Chapter 33

JUDGE BENITEZ CALLED a thirty-minute recess after Tony finished his fumbling two-question cross of Laura Wyler. Ted Richards straight up growled at her as she walked by him on the way out of the courtroom.

"We need to talk," I said to Tony as soon as the jury was out of the room.

"Judge says to take his conference room." Benitez's bailiff overheard us. I took it as the first positive sign Benitez might finally believe there was more to this case than met the eye.

"Find Victoria Stockton," I quickly said to Jeanie. "I'm going to need her."

Jeanie nodded, but her eyes said something else. I was afraid to ask. Plus, I had no time.

I grabbed my messenger bag. Ted caught my wrist. His strong, heated grip made my skin crawl.

"You better fix this," he said.

I jerked my arm away. "Your job is to sit there and not make things worse. So far you're failing."

I pushed through the gate and followed Abbato into the

adjoining conference room. Judge Benitez was in his office, one closed door away.

"What the fuck is this?" Tony said. He was fuming, his skin blotchy.

I crossed my arms and stood near the door. "You took my line, Tony. Why the hell didn't you disclose the connection between Chip Edgar and Patrick Johnson? That's grounds for a mistrial right there."

He gestured toward Judge Beni's door. "Be my guest."

"Sure. You already want a do-over. Jesus, Tony. Even you have to see what's going on."

"You keep going down this road, it'll kill your career," he said.

"My career? Is that a threat? You should be looking at Laura Wyler. Do you want to stand there and tell me you didn't know Edgar and Johnson were brothers?"

He blinked.

"My God," I said. "You really didn't know."

He didn't answer. He started pacing, hands on hips.

"Ted Richards killed Channing. Nobody else. That shit you pulled was nothing but a cheap stunt. I'm telling you, this won't go well for you. You're going to bring the Justice Department and the FBI down on your head."

"Only if I'm wrong," I said. "I'm not."

"You know what people say about you, don't you?"

"Save it."

"Words I won't repeat, Cass. I know about your stint in Chicago. Everyone knows who you keep company with. You stand there pretending you're just some aw-shucks small-town lawyer. You're not though," he said.

"You think I'm pretending? Look, I don't give two shits what you or anyone else thinks of me. If all you've got left is deflection, then you know I've already won. Do the right thing. Call your people and get Patrick Johnson back here.

He needs to tell the jury the truth about whatever deal he cut to save his brother. I want to put him back on the stand. I know you've got a deputy sitting on him. Make the call."

"Now you want me to do your job for you?" he asked.

"Make the call," I said. I was done talking. I needed a few minutes with Jeanie. Hopefully she'd made headway with Victoria Stockton. After everything, I still felt like I was trying this case by the seat of my pants.

I left Tony Abbato staring after me as I exited the door to the hallway. I nearly tripped over Jeanie. She was right outside with her ear pressed against the door. She was alone.

"Come on," she said, leading me back to the stairwell.

Chapter 34

My heart lifted when I saw Victoria Stockton sitting on the landing. Tears streamed down her face.

"It's gonna be okay, honey," Jeanie said.

"Jeanie, the car dealer? How in the hell did you pull that off?" If he was ready to testify the way I thought, I might even be able to wrap this up without poor Victoria.

Jeanie bit her bottom lip. She gestured with her chin toward Victoria. Whatever she had to say, she didn't want the girl to hear. Jeanie leaned in and whispered in my ear.

"He's not a car dealer. He's my lawn guy."

I reared back. What the hell did her lawn guy have to do with ...

"You're kidding me," I said.

"I stalled for time," she said. "My investigator is on his way to Nashville as we speak, trying to pin down the real car dealer. I just have Laura Wyler's credit report. The dealership down there ran a check on Wyler two months before Channing showed up dead. I just figured if Wyler *thought* I had the dealer here ... she'd let something slip."

My head was spinning. "But you don't really have proof she bought a car matching Richards's?"

"Not yet. I need a day. Tops."

"Shit," I said. "I don't know if we have it."

I turned to Victoria. She sat with her arms around her knees.

"Victoria," I said. "I'm sorry it has to be like this, but I need to put you on the stand. You need to tell the jury what you know about Laura Wyler and Mark Channing."

"You said I wouldn't have to testify," Victoria said.

"I never said that. You came to me, Victoria. I didn't seek you out. If you hadn't, I'd never know about Chip Edgar and Patrick Johnson. No one did. Not even the prosecutor. But you did. Didn't you?"

"No," she said. "Not for sure. I just knew there was something. Edgar wasn't even going to testify at the Kinsell trial. And Laura didn't want anyone else talking to him."

"I need you to say that. I need you to tell the truth up there. That's all I'm asking. If you don't, an innocent man might go down for a murder he didn't commit."

Fury came into Victoria Stockton's eyes. "Ted Richards isn't innocent. He's a monster. You've seen the file. You know who he is."

I let out a breath. "Yeah. I do. But not Channing. He didn't do this one. And no matter how much I want to see him pay for everything he's done—and I know more than you think—letting him go down for this doesn't bring justice to Mark Channing. It's wrong. You know it is. It's why you reached out to me. So now, you have to be brave enough to stand up for Mark Channing, even if it means helping Ted Richards. He's innocent of this. Putting him away for life for this ... it's wrong. I hate that it is. But it is."

She closed her eyes and exhaled. When she opened them again, they were filled with tears.

"I hate this."

"So do I."

Victoria gave a nod to Jeanie. I offered Victoria a hand. She rose to her feet and followed me up the stairs.

———

SOMETHING CHANGED in Victoria as she took the stand. Her back straightened and the fear left her eyes. She wouldn't look at Ted Richards.

"Ms. Stockton," I said. "Please tell the jury how you knew the victim, Mark Channing."

"He was my boss," she said. "I'm a paralegal for the U.S. Attorney's office in Detroit. I've worked there since March of last year."

"Did you work on the Kinsell litigation?"

"I did."

"And can you refresh my memory, which attorneys were assigned to that case?"

"Mark and Andy Tate, primarily. But Ryan McGuinness and Laura Wyler were also pulled in from time to time to handle pretrial motions and they both came to strategy sessions."

"So, is it fair to say that those four people had equal access to the litigation materials on the Kinsell matter?"

Victoria picked at her nail. "That's fair," she said.

"When was the last time you saw Mark Channing, if you recall?" I asked.

"I saw him the day he died. Or at least, I mean, it was Friday the eighteenth at the office. I don't know for sure exactly when he was killed."

"Did you see him leave the office?"

"I did," she said. "I worked a little later than the attorneys did that day. I stayed to reorganize parts of the file.

Mark was going to come back to the office on Saturday afternoon. He asked me to pull a few things so they would be ready when he got there."

"Did you see him leave with anyone?"

Victoria Stockton had a deep dimple in her right cheek when she frowned.

"He left with Laura. Laura Wyler. They went to the stairwell. I know that because I had a question for Mark and I ran down to see if I could catch him. I didn't realize he was with Laura, but I came up on them in the stairway. Or rather ... I heard them talking."

"Did you hear what they said?"

She nodded. "Yes. They were arguing."

"Did you go talk to them?"

"No," she said. "I opened the door, but I didn't go down as soon as I heard them. It was mostly Laura yelling. Mark was ... he was trying to get her to calm down."

"What did he say?"

"Objection," Abbato said. "We're getting into hearsay here."

"It goes to state of mind of the victim," I said. "Not to the truth of whatever Mr. Channing may have said."

Benitez let out a hard sigh. "Overruled. The witness may answer."

"I don't know what they were arguing about specifically that time. She was calling him a liar. That's what I heard."

"That time," I said. "So you heard Wyler and Channing have arguments prior to that day? In the office?"

"Yes," she said. "A few times. The stairwell is where they usually had them."

"Do you know what they generally fought about?"

Victoria folded her hands. "Mark Channing and Laura Wyler were having an affair."

"Objection! Calls for speculation," Tony said.

"How do you know Wyler and Channing were having an affair?" It was Judge Benitez who asked the question.

Victoria practically chewed through the inside of her mouth. She knew there was no walking any of this back.

"Because I saw them. At the Christmas party the year before. So, nine months before he died."

"You saw what, Ms. Stockton?" I asked.

"We had an office party at one of the restaurants in Greektown. I left early. I wasn't feeling well. I saw Mark and Laura in Mark's car. They were ... they were having sex."

"Did they see you?"

"I didn't think so at the time. But after that, Laura was different toward me. She stopped talking to me. Once I tried to take her aside and try to reassure her that I wasn't planning on making trouble for her. It was none of my business."

"So this tryst you describe happened in December the year before last?"

"Yes."

"And were you aware that Mark Channing got married just a few weeks after that?"

"Yes," she said.

"Do you know whether this affair continued after he married Catherine Channing?"

"I don't know for sure. But it was after that I started to hear them arguing with each other. That's what I heard him say. He told Laura to just be patient. She told him she knew he was lying."

"Objection," Tony said.

"Sustained," Benitez said. "The jury will disregard what the witness stated about the substance of those arguments."

"Thank you, Your Honor," I said. "I have nothing further at this time."

Tony charged the lectern, buttoning his suit coat as he went.

"Ms. Stockton, isn't it true you were the one in love with Mark Channing?"

"What?"

"You asked for a transfer early last year to the civil division, correct?"

"Yes," she said.

"And it was Laura Wyler who got in your way. She recommended against it to H.R. Isn't that true?"

It was a hit, but hopefully not a fatal one.

"I don't know about that."

"But you don't like Laura Wyler, that's true?"

Victoria took a moment. "I don't respect her very much. That's true."

"She was in your way," Tony said.

"That's not true."

"Did you ever tell anyone what you saw or suspected about Mark Channing and Laura Wyler?"

"It wasn't a suspicion. I saw them together."

"Did you report it to H.R.?"

"No, I did not."

"Did you confront Channing or Wyler about it?"

"Not Mr. Channing. I already said, I tried to tell Laura it was none of my business."

"You never said anything to Andrew Tate or Ryan McGuinness?"

"No, of course not."

"And you never gossiped about it with the support staff?"

"No," she said. "I meant what I said to Laura. I wasn't trying to make trouble for either of them."

"So, there's no one who can corroborate your sordid story. We are just supposed to take your word for it."

"I have no reason to lie," she said. "Just by coming here, I know what's going to happen. I probably won't have a job after this. My name will be in the papers. Do you think any other firm will hire me?"

"You said it yourself," Tony said. "Your name will be in the papers."

"Your Honor," I started to object.

"No more questions," Tony said.

I chose not to redirect. Victoria Stockton left the witness stand. She still refused to look at Ted Richards.

Chapter 35

"WHERE ARE WE, COUNSEL?" Judge Benitez said. He called Tony and me into his chambers.

"I need half a day," I said, lying. Jeanie hadn't heard back from her guy in Nashville. I knew in my gut Laura Wyler was behind the physical evidence in this case. But without the dealer's testimony or some other concrete evidentiary path tying her to the purchase of an identical Jaguar, there was just too much left to chance.

"Half day? We've been at this going on two weeks. When I asked you if you were ready to present your case, you said yes."

"There has been new evidence that came to light at the eleventh hour, Your Honor. The state should have disclosed the familial relationship between their star witness and Mark Channing's office. It's not a coincidence. I need to recall Patrick Johnson to the stand. Mr. Abbato has agreed to produce him. My understanding is he's in protective custody."

"That true?" the judge asked.

"Not exactly," Abbato said. "We've had a deputy on Mr.

Johnson at his request. As of last night, I've been informed he withdrew that request. Mr. Johnson is currently ... um ... we don't know where he is just at the moment."

You could have heard a pin drop, or at least the furious thump of my pulse.

"He's in the wind? You've got to be kidding me. He's still under subpoena," I said. "Your Honor."

"We're willing to stipulate to the relationship between this Edgar and Johnson. It's not in dispute. Ms. Leary is free to make whatever argument she'd like in closing."

Judge Benitez raised a brow. I felt certain he'd at least give me the half a day I asked for. I was wrong.

"Fair enough," Benitez said. "Enter your stipulation. We'll put it to the jury."

I couldn't believe what I was hearing. "Your Honor, my client has a right to confront this witness. At the very least, Chip Edgar needs to be called."

"He on your witness list?" Benitez said.

"He is not. Again, the relationship was withheld from me to the extreme prejudice of my client's defense. The remedy has to be ..."

"The remedy is what I say it is. He's not fighting you on the relationship. Argue it to your heart's content. If you have no other witnesses to call, then prepare for closing arguments and let's wrap this up."

"I have one more witness to call," I said. "My associate is in the middle of arranging for a car dealer from Nashville to testify ..."

"You mean he's not already here?" Benitez asked.

"No, Your Honor. Again, these are unusual circumstances. Had the disclosure about Edgar been made in a timely manner, I would have had the benefit of discovery. My client shouldn't be penalized for ..."

"Your client has had eight months to mount a defense. I

don't want to hear one word about his previous lawyer. Nobody forced you to take this case. If you've got another witness, go out there and call him. If you don't, we're moving on. What's it going to be?"

This was insanity. I think even Tony Abbato knew it. Judge Benitez wanted a conviction, pure and simple.

"Reversible error," I said, blurting it before I really thought it through.

Benitez fumed. His eyes narrowed and he pointed a finger at me.

"You're not fooling me or anyone else," he said. "I know your kind. I know who pays your bills. You might get away with shady shit in someone else's courtroom. It won't happen in mine. If your witness isn't here, we're done."

He stopped just short of saying he knew Ted Richards was guilty or that he didn't care.

To his credit, Tony looked embarrassed. But there was nothing either of us could do. Benitez dismissed ... no ... he practically threw us out of his chambers.

"I'll write up the stipulation," Tony said. He brushed past me, almost as if he were afraid to look me in the eye another second. He would take this gift from Judge Benitez. And to both of them, I was the bad guy.

I met Jeanie at the defense table. The deputy left to retrieve Ted.

"Where are we?" I asked.

"I was about to ask you the same thing," she said.

"No dice," I said. "He wants me to call the dealer if he's here but that's it. Please tell me you have something."

Jeanie put a hand to her face. "Shit. We're fucked. The guy's gone for the week. Barbados or somewhere. Shut the whole office down. We can't confirm Laura purchased the Jag. They've got eyes on her house, but there's nothing there."

"She wouldn't be dumb enough to park the thing in her garage, Jeanie. It's probably long gone by now. Son of a bitch. As it stands now, the jury will never hear it. Shit. I should have seen this. She had access to that file on Ghost Man. She knew his M.O. She knew what he drove. She was planning this for months. Pretty much as soon as Channing married that girl, he was a marked man."

"There may be another way," she said.

I was about to ask her what she meant, but I saw the answer in her eyes. Killian. She meant Killian.

"Jeanie."

"I don't like it," she said. "And I'm sure I don't want to know the details. But if your guy has any ability to make this happen, now is the time."

I closed my eyes. There was nothing Killian Thorne could do at this late stage of the game that wouldn't be at least borderline illegal. I just didn't know how far down that path I was willing to go again.

"All rise!"

Ted shuffled up the aisle, still cuffed.

"No," I whispered to Jeanie. "Even if he could ... we're out of time."

Chapter 36

I HAD NO MORE witnesses I could produce. I had a judge
unwilling to see reason. He could only see a murderer
standing in front of him. For now, I had no other choice but
to rest my defense. Even Tony looked embarrassed. But he
did nothing to intervene. I supposed he had plenty of outside
pressure on him too besides just the judge. So he stepped to
the lectern and faced the jury.

In his closing, Tony said all the noble things about the
gravity of the jury's civic duty. They listened. Juror number
seven sat straighter in his chair. He was a military man. He
understood.

Tony presented a methodical summation of all the key
pieces of evidence. He was calm, compelling, weaving a dark
story with a deliberate cadence. All of it leading up to the
crescendo of Mark Channing's brutal last few moments.

"Ladies and gentlemen of the jury, it's your job to seek
the truth. It's been presented to you. No amount of smoke
and mirrors on the defense counsel's part should sway you
from it. They want to discredit the testimony of Patrick
Johnson. Perhaps they have cause, perhaps Mr. Johnson is a

liar. But even if you completely discounted what he had to say, we cannot forget what we know to be true. Carpet fibers matching Ted Richards's car were found on Mark Channing's body. He was in that trunk. The blood found matched Channing's type. And we know Ted Richards is capable of murder. We know he has been driven to at least the brink of it before. Piano wire was found in his garage matching the type used to kill Mark Channing. He has no alibi. He is a killer. He must be brought to justice. Thank you."

It sounded so perfect. So neat and clean. He stopped just short of implying that even if Ted wasn't guilty of killing Channing, we all knew he was guilty of so much more. What's the harm in putting him away for life?

I waited for a moment. Part of me hoped by some miracle, I'd get the movie ending and Jeanie's investigator would burst through the doors bearing indisputable proof of what I already knew. Laura Wyler likely killed Mark Channing.

But this wasn't the movies. This was just me. A killer at my side. And I had to stand up and claim he was innocent.

"I have more questions than answers with this case," I started. "So should you."

"Mr. Abbato wants you to think Patrick Johnson's testimony didn't matter. Ted Richards is a bad enough man. He deserves what's coming to him. Mark Channing didn't deserve what happened to him. Someone should pay."

"He's right. Someone should pay. Mark Channing could have been a champion for all of us. I know I've stopped myself so many times throughout this case and wondered what if. What might have been. It's not fair. We want to make sense of it.

"And then, there's Ted Richards. He seems a likely villain. He may not even be a good man. The prosecution wants you to hate him. They want you to think he's a monster. If Mark Channing is the perfect hero, then Ted Richards is the perfect villain.

"But this isn't a fairytale. We deal in facts here. The state can't convict someone of murder based on feelings. They have the highest burden of proof under the law. Reasonable doubt.

"Mr. Johnson was lying. He didn't tell you about his brother. He cut a deal. Tell a lie about what he saw in front of Mark Channing's house. Put a monster away. Seems perfect. That's because it was.

"Patrick Johnson moved into that neighborhood a short time after his brother got his immunity deal. It was on purpose. Patrick Johnson worked nowhere near Hickory Circle. It makes no sense for him to live there. Now we know the lie and Mr. Johnson is nowhere to be found. He skipped town before he could answer for these lies to you. That's not a coincidence. That's a setup.

"Laura Wyler had access to the intel on Ted Richards. And you can't convict a man based on innuendo and suspicion of unrelated acts. No charges were ever brought against him because the evidence wasn't there. What *was* there was enough detail about Ted Richards's personal life to make him the fall guy for the perfect crime. Laura Wyler knew what kind of car he drove. She knew where Ted Richards lived. And she had shady people in her back pocket tripping over themselves to do her dirty work. Laura Wyler had the motive. When Mark married Catherine Channing, she made up her mind to do something about it. If she couldn't have him, no one would.

"The only credible witness in this entire case was Victoria Stockton. She had no reason to come forward. She more than anyone knows the price she might pay for doing it. But she also knows what justice—true justice—means.

"Mark Channing needs us now. You have to be his voice.

Ted Richards is the wrong man to punish for his death. You know it. Victoria Stockton knows it.

"You have more than reasonable doubt. There is no doubt that Ted Richards is innocent of this crime. He was set up. If you convict him because it plays into some story the prosecution wants to tell, then you let his real killer go free. Mark Channing deserves better than that. He was brave. He fought for his country. In a very big way, I think he died for it. Please don't let that sacrifice be in vain. You must return a not guilty verdict. You must let justice prevail. For Mark. For all of us. Thank you."

Ted Richards gave me his stone-cold stare as I made my way back to the table and took my seat beside him. Bile rose in my throat.

Later that afternoon, Judge Benitez turned the case over to the jury. Now there was nothing left to do but wait.

Chapter 37

"A whole day, you're sure that doesn't mean anything?" Matty asked. He sat in the captain's chair of my pontoon boat, sipping pop from a plastic cup. I know he longed for a beer. He'd been so good though. I was proud of him. One day at a time and all.

"No," I said. "It just means the jury's carefully reviewing everything."

When I said carefully, I knew it was juror number seven. And I knew it meant I had no slam dunk.

Joe started down the dock. Emma was inside. I'd hired her to clean my house for the week while I was in trial. Joe had a worried look on his face. The boat rocked as he stepped on the platform.

"Everything okay in there?" I asked.

"You shouldn't be paying her," he said. "It should be part of her punishment."

Joe had taken her phone and grounded her for the upcoming summer except to go to and from school and work when she started her gig at the local ice cream parlor in a few weeks.

"She's a good kid, Joe," I said. "Better than we were, that's for sure."

He nodded. "I know. But she could have really fucked herself over. If it weren't for your friend Wray ... she'd have already blown her chances of getting into Michigan."

"Wow," Matty said. "Didn't know that's where she wanted to go."

"Well, she does," Joe said. "She's smart enough. She could be anything. She could get the hell out of here."

"Just like me," I said, giving him a wry smile.

He scowled. "You know that's not what I meant."

"I know."

Things had been tense between us. I was getting damn tired of the reason why. The trial had worn me out. If it weren't for that, maybe I would have held my tongue. Or not.

"Just come out and say what's on your mind," I said.

"Leave it alone," Joe said.

I sat with my bare feet curled beneath me. Out of respect for Matty, I'd foregone a glass of wine for the afternoon. I sorely needed it.

"It's been coming on a long time, big brother," I said. "But do us both a favor and get it out. I'm tired of the looks you keep giving me."

My brother's fuse blew. He kept his voice down though. It was less about the neighbors and more about Emma. I could see her from the living room window, running the vacuum.

"I just don't ... I'm tired of worrying about you."

"Me? You're worried about me?"

"Yes!" Both Matty and Joe spoke in unison.

"This case," Joe said. "Win or lose, it's messed with your head. I know you. You're not sleeping. You're barely eating. And ... this ...

"Killian," I said. "His name is Killian."

"I don't want to owe the bastard, okay? That might be fine for you, but not for me. I know he paid Josie and her douchebag of the month off. I'm grateful. But I sure as hell don't want to be. Not to him."

"I know," I said. I was so tired of fighting.

"We can take care of ourselves," Matty chimed in. It dawned on me then they had planned this. This was a family intervention.

"Wow," I said. "I'm surprised you didn't wait for Vangie to get back in a couple of weeks."

"I wanted to keep her out of this," Joe said. "She's been through enough. Sometimes ... I wonder if it's better if she just stays down in Florida."

"Do you also wonder if it would be better if I just stayed in Chicago? Is that what you're trying to tell me?"

Joe, to his credit, looked gut-punched when I said it. I hadn't realized until that very moment that I worried about his answer.

"You're leaving again," he said. It was a statement, not a question. "I know you."

It was my turn to feel gut-punched. "I never said that."

"But he makes you happy. You're in love with him," Matty said. "Cass, don't deny it. And we want you to be happy. It's just ..."

"Ah," I said, not liking the defensive anger rolling inside of me. It was too much. This case. My life. "That would be convenient for you, wouldn't it? You're still pissed at me Grandpa left me the lake house instead of you."

Matty actually laughed. When I heard my words back in my head, I did the same.

"Shit," I muttered. "I'm sorry."

We were silent for a few minutes. From the house, Emma

started singing along to some song on my streaming service. She sounded better than the recording.

"What is it?" I said. "I mean, really."

Joe sat at the back of the boat. He put his foot up on the seat.

"I don't want him around," he said. "Not here. He doesn't belong in Delphi. I don't want Emma to know him. Do you understand that? I don't want that world touching her. I'm fighting for her life in a way. And I don't know what the hell I'm doing half the time."

"I get it," I said.

"No," Joe said. "I don't think you do. I need you, Cass. If I haven't made that clear, let me do it now. I'm sorry as shit if that's selfish. But Emma, she's on the brink of something. It could go either way. I'm terrified. And I need your help. Both of your help."

"You have it," I said. "I promise."

"But not his," Joe said. "Not Thorne's."

I let out a sigh. "I get it. I do. But you need to trust me that I know what I'm doing. I've got a handle on it."

Joe smiled. He could always see straight through my bull-shit. He knew I was shoveling it now. Only it was the first time I'd admitted it to myself.

I looked at my brother. Really looked at him. The lines in his face seemed to have deepened in the last few weeks. I hated that I was in any way the cause of it.

"Things are better now," I said. "The stuff with Emma is out in the open. I know you hate that Killian had any part in it, but even Katy has to be relieved that ..."

"Katy wants me to move out," Joe said abruptly. It felt like a knife blow.

"Shit," Matty said. Even he didn't know.

"But ..." I started.

"The stuff with Josie this time, it was the last straw for

her, she said. She skipped town even. Josie. I don't know if
you knew that. I didn't want to tell you. But whatever your
friend gave her to shut her up, she used it to take off. I'm
worried she's going to get herself into even more trouble
now. And that's what's got Katy so upset. She thinks ... she
accused me of ..."

My heart ached. "She thinks you've still got feelings for
her," I answered for him.

Joe nodded. The hard part was, he didn't immediately
deny it. I figured he must have done the same thing in his
fight with Katy.

"You're a dumbass," I said.

Joe's eyes widened. His face flushed red with anger.

"No, I mean it," I said. "If you gave Katy even a flavor
of the look you just gave me, you screwed yourself over with
her. If you *do* still have even an inkling of a feeling for Josie,
you need to do a better job of faking it. Katy's the best thing
that ever happened to you. Don't you dare blame me for
screwing this up for you. You did it all by yourself, big
brother. And you're going to fix it or I'm going to kick your
ass."

I caught Matty's eyes. He tried to look innocent and
chugged the last of his pop. But I could tell he agreed with
me. That was something, at least.

"I'm right about Emma though," Joe said. "This stuff
with Katy ... yeah. I know I need to work harder on it. I will.
But it's you, Cass. I mean it when I say I need you. Josie is
Josie. Katy's amazing, but she's not Emma's mom. As much
as Josie and Emma go at it, Emma looks to her. But she looks
to you more. Don't you see it? I need you to be worthy of it.
And you are, don't get me wrong. It's just ... this guy you're
with scares me for you and I'm not going to pretend he
doesn't. Something happened back in Chicago. I saw it in
your eyes when you came home last year. I see it now every

once in a while. More so since you took this Richards case. I can't help but figure he had something to do with it. I know you'll never tell us what it was. I hope to God it's not worse than what I imagine. I know you think you're protecting me by not telling me. That's fine. I'm asking you to be honest with yourself about it. I'm asking you to take care of yourself. Not just for me, but for Emma."

I both hated and loved that my brother could read me that way. I wanted to hug him and throttle him all at once. I didn't get the chance to do either.

"Aunt Cass?" Emma called from the house. She had my phone in her hand as she walked down the paving stones toward the dock.

I sat up.

"It's Jeanie," she said. "She said they called from the court. She said your jury is back."

My brothers rose beside me. The pair of them made a formidable wall of muscle between me and the lake beyond. The Leary brothers took care of their own.

"Coming," I said.

Chapter 38

THEY LED Ted into the courtroom, still in chains. He still managed his swagger, but his eyes had darkened. For the first time since I met him, he seemed a little scared. I was terrified.

"What happens now?" Ted asked. He stood beside me, still cuffed.

It had been four hours since Jeanie called. It took that long to get everyone back to the courthouse.

"They'll read the verdict," I said. "If it goes your way, they'll still take you back for processing. If it doesn't ..."

"Then I'm fucked," he said. "And you'll appeal. That bitch lawyer set me up and everybody knows it."

Not everyone. So far, Jeanie's investigator still hadn't tracked down the purchase of the Jaguar in Laura Wyler's name. Patrick Johnson and Chip Edgar had pretty much vanished into thin air. And here we were, about to get the answer to Ted Richards's next step.

Joe's words hung heavy in my heart. He'd given voice to my own conscience. He always did that. I thought of Emma. The truth was, she could go either way right now. She was enough like her mother to scare me to the bone. But she was also enough like me. At the moment, I didn't know if that was good or bad.

I turned to Ted. I honestly didn't know what to hope for when the jury came back. I had given a part of my soul to this case. I couldn't deny it. I wasn't sure if I would ever get it back.

"My representation ends today," I finally said to him. "For better or worse, Ted. That was the deal."

"I'd say the deal is whatever Thorne wants it to be," he said, leaning down so his breath brushed my ear. "He owns you. You can try and pretend you're better than me. But you do what he hires you for. Just like me. We're about to find out if you're as good at your job as I am at mine, sweetheart. For your sake, I hope you are."

"Don't you ever threaten me again," I said through clenched teeth. No one but Ted could hear my words, but my anger had to be obvious. It even caught Tony's attention. He stopped mid-sentence as he whispered to his paralegal. His face went white and he swallowed hard.

"It doesn't matter what happens here today. It will be my pleasure to watch them charge you for attempted murder based on what Sally did. You're done, Ted. It's over for you either way."

He kept on smiling. No matter what happened, Sally Richards would need to be in protective custody. I said a quick prayer for her safety.

Once again, I realized I had no idea what I wanted this jury to say.

If Ted was found guilty, he'd never get out of prison. Even with an appeal, I had a hunch too many people would worry about what he'd do on the inside. He knew things about powerful people. Someday, he might decide to try and cut himself a deal. I knew in my heart that's what Liam

Thorne was so afraid of. I'd bet money Ted threatened him with exactly that when he asked him for my help. There was no death penalty in Michigan, but I didn't think Ted would survive in prison for long. There was justice in that.

But Laura Wyler was guilty. I believed it in my heart. If they put Ted behind bars, she'd get away with it. Everything Victoria Stockton risked would be for nothing.

And if he were found innocent ... Ted Richards would walk out of this courtroom a free man. I shuddered in true fear at the thought of it.

The door to Benitez's chambers opened and his bailiff stepped out. My heart fell to the floor. This train was moving. I had done everything I could do.

Judge Benitez took the bench. He wore reading glasses this time, perched at the end of his nose.

They brought the jury in. One by one, they stepped into the box. They each looked straight ahead, unreadable. Only juror number seven looked at Ted Richards as he took his place at the end of the jury box. His eyes were cold, his posture stiff.

"Mr. Foreman," Judge Benitez said to him. "Have you reached a verdict?"

"We have, Your Honor," juror number seven said.

He handed the verdict form to the bailiff. He slowly walked it over to the judge, his footsteps echoing on the marble floor.

Judge Benitez took the form and read it. He stole a quick glance at Ted over his glasses. Then he handed the form back to the bailiff. He began the slow, maddening few steps back to juror number seven.

"You may read your verdict," Judge Beni said.

Juror number seven cleared his throat. He didn't look down at the form. He spoke in a clear, deep voice. He already knew the words by heart.

"We the jury in the above-entitled action on the count of murder in the first degree find the defendant, Theodore Richards ... not guilty."

A rush of air hit me from behind. It was the collective gasp and exhale from the crowd gathered in the gallery. Jeanie swore something under her breath.

My ears rang. My heart turned to ash.

Ted Richards cracked his neck beside me. Then he leaned down and whispered in my ear.

"Nice job, sweetheart. Turns out you *are* as good at your job as I am at mine. And don't worry. It was never anything personal."

Then he lifted his wrists and waited for the bailiff to come and take him away.

Chapter 39

THE SUN DIPPED, turning the outer bands of the sky purple and pink. Two ski boats whipped by, churning the otherwise placid water as I stood at the end of the dock. It would be busy on the lake, Memorial Day weekend. Tomorrow, I would see four times as many boats and jet skis. We weren't busy here on Finn Lake like the bigger Devil's and Vineyard Lakes. Still, now would be the best and only time for a leisurely cruise for days.

The pontoon boat idled beside me. My phone rang. I had it charging on the console next to the captain's chair. I leaned into the boat and grabbed it. I paused for a moment, not sure I wanted to answer once I saw the caller ID. I did anyway though, staring out at the sunset.

"Hello, Tony," I said.

Tony Abbato answered by way of a sigh. "Cass, I just wanted you to hear everything from me."

"I appreciate that," I said. In the week since the Richards verdict, I wondered if this call would ever come.

"They're charging Laura Wyler. She's already in custody."

"Good," I said. "I'm glad."

"Your lead about the car came through. Took some doing, but a Jag matching Richards's was purchased for cash down in Nashville. Just like you said. She used an alias for the title work. Still sorting through how she pulled that off. We found the car in a storage unit. She didn't use an alias for that. Channing's DNA was all over it. We're pretty sure she had an accomplice. Probably Chip Edgar. He's being taken into custody as well."

I exhaled. "You think she was the one who actually killed Channing?"

"Yeah," he said. "They had a motel off the Lodge where they would meet. The desk clerk came forward once the Richards verdict hit the news. She killed him there. We've got them both on security tape going in. Working theory is they met up there after the fight in the stairwell. Had a few drinks. He's sitting on the bed putting his shoes on with his back to her and ... well ..."

"God," I whispered.

"Then she calls Edgar to help her get the body over to the Gross Pointe Farms house."

"She was planning it for months," I said. "As soon as she realized Channing wasn't going to leave his wife for her."

"Looks that way," he said. "You were right. She had everything she needed in that book on Ghost Man. It was a solid plan, actually."

"Except for Victoria Stockton," I said.

Tony got quiet. "Yeah. Brave kid. She's ... uh ... she left the U.S. Attorney's office."

"They fired her?" I said.

"Don't know. Doubtful. Maybe she just figured she didn't want to be in that environment anymore. Anyway, she left a forwarding number. We'll still need her testimony if Laura Wyler doesn't plead out."

"Thanks for letting me know," I said. "You didn't have to."

Tony chuckled. "You're good, Cass. If you ever want to come over from the dark side, we could use you. You'd make a hell of a prosecutor."

"Thanks," I said. "I mean that. But I think I'm going to stay down here in Woodbridge County for now. I like my little corner of nowhere."

"Sure," he said. "It's just ... Cass ... Ted Richards ... you know what he is. He was working for Saul Kinsell, but also for a few other mob bosses. He was hedging his bets. One family goes down, he's got contract work all over to cover it. The feds just can't prove it. They will. He might not have killed Channing, but a lot of the agents are taking this shit personally. They feel like the man died because of Richards, even if he didn't actually carry out the hit."

Our group of mallards skimmed the water right in front of the dock. They were looking for a handout. I held out my empty hand. The lead female gave an indignant quack and led her brothers further down the shore.

"I appreciate the heads-up," I said. Footsteps behind me shook the dock. "And you know I can't discuss my client with you."

"Yeah," he said. "I know. Just ... take care, Cass. I wouldn't mind squaring off with you again."

"Enjoy the holiday," I said. Tony said goodbye and I tossed my phone into the boat.

Strong arms encircled my waist. Killian rested his chin on my shoulder and looked out at the water.

"It's beautiful," he said.

"It really is."

"You ready? I've wanted to see this lake for weeks."

I reached up and touched his cheek. As Killian stepped into the boat, I tossed off the ropes. I shoved the boat away from the dock giving Killian a head start as he took the wheel, then hopped on.

I came behind him, pointing out the shallows as Killian headed to the center of the lake.

We found a spot to drop anchor, just past the stretch of luxury homes that had cropped up in the last decade. One sat high on a hill on the largest peninsula of the lake, a majestically restored Victorian home with a slate roof and two spires poking above the tree line. You couldn't get to it from the main road. It had a winding, private drive that only the locals knew how to find.

"That one," he said. "That's the one I'd pick."

"That's what my gramps would always say. Grandma said it reminded her of Cinderella's castle. He used to say he'd buy it for her and they'd live happily ever after. It never went up for sale though. Of course, he couldn't afford it even if it had. It sold a few years ago for almost a million."

"Everything's for sale if the price is right," he said. He meant it as a throwaway comment. My response died on my lips.

I took a seat across from him and opened the hidden cooler beneath the bench. I poured myself a glass of wine and tossed him a bottle of craft beer.

We had things to talk about today. Killian's visit was coming to an end. It would have been easier for both of us to just leave things unsaid. No promises. No heartache.

"Do you really like it here?" he asked.

I sipped my wine. "I really do."

"You're different. This place ... you seem ... settled."

"I am," I said, smiling. "I spent so many years running from it. But Delphi is my home. It's where I belong."

He nodded but he was unable to hide the tinge of sadness that came into his eyes.

"Kinsell," I said. Just that one word had the power to

pierce through some of the magic of the lake. Out of respect for Tony, I had no intention of telling Killian a word of our conversation. But there was something that had been nagging me since the moment I opened the FBI case file. I debated how much I would tell Killian.

"You know it's just the beginning. I believe the government is going to win that case. And when they do ..."

"You worry too much, Cass."

I set my glass down and leaned forward. "Richards is going down. They'll get him on the attempted murder of his wife. It doesn't matter he didn't kill Mark Channing. The feds are taking this one personally. They won't stop. And that makes me glad."

"As well he should go down," Killian said.

"But they're never going to stop coming for you. Everything you've done to try and legitimize the business, it won't be enough."

The fading sun lit his eyes, making them shine like sapphires. "I never hired Ted Richards. I never hired this Ghost Man."

"You've heard of him though. You know who and what he is. Can you sit there and tell me Liam never used him? You don't know because you never asked him. Richards went to him to get to me. It was Richards who told me that. My representing him wasn't Liam's idea. It was Ted's. And I know the position it put you in. Your associates were nervous about what he'd say if he ever went to prison for this. They've been nervous about me too ever since I left. I know you didn't initiate it, but once it was set in motion, you couldn't stop it. You say you want to protect me. We both know you can't. Not really. The only real way you could protect me this time was by showing your associates I'd still jump when you called."

Killian stared out at the lake.

"And I can't jump for you again," I said. "Not anymore. My debt is paid, Killian. You need to make sure that message gets across. I'm out. For real this time."

I was telling him two things at once. I hadn't meant to do that yet. But the moment the words were in the air, I knew they had to be true.

A muscle jumped in his jaw. "I'll protect my own, Cass. I said you worry too much."

"You'll have to," I said. "That's what I need you to hear, Killian. There are things …"

"Don't," he said. "Don't break your sacred attorney-client trust on my account."

"Listen to me," I said. I touched Killian's knee. I waited until his eyes locked with mine.

"I know you'll do what you have to to protect your family. It's what you've always done. But I'm going to have to do the same for mine now. I'll say it again. You can't really protect me. I can only protect myself. And I'm going to. You need to know that. No matter what. No matter who else gets hurt."

It was as close to a warning as I could give him.

"And I suppose that starts here," he said.

I nodded. He knew what was coming. We both did.

He didn't say anything for a long while. Not until after the sun finally dipped below the horizon.

"I need you to know," he said. "If you ever need anything …"

I put a hand up. "No. I won't."

He smiled, reaching for me. I went to him. This time, when Killian kissed me, we both knew it was a goodbye.

A moment later, I pulled up the anchor as Killian started the engine. We headed back to shore under the light of a new moon.

Chapter 40

WE SAID our goodbye in another way after we got back to the house. Afterward, I lay there in the quiet, listening to his slow, rhythmic breathing. He would be gone before morning, I knew.

Part of me wanted to stop time. I wished I could exist in some bubble. A place I could return to and Killian would be there. No commitments. No judgment. No debts to be paid. But as the stars came out, I knew life just didn't work like that.

I left him there, sleeping. I went to the bathroom to splash some cold water on my face. I passed by the balcony window. The lake was still as glass. It was going to be a beautiful weekend.

I quietly shut the bathroom door and looked at myself in the mirror. For the first time in a long time, I liked what I saw. Saying goodbye would always hurt, but this felt like the closure I missed when I left Chicago a year ago. Then my life had been ripped out from under me. Now the choice was mine.

I took a washcloth from the basket and ran it under the water. I smoothed it over my neck. I brushed my teeth.

As I shut off the faucet, silence set in again. Killian made a small noise from the other room. I hoped I hadn't woke him. I thought about leaving before he woke. I could steal away in the quiet of the morning. It would be simpler. When I came back, he would just be gone.

I put the towel in the hamper and started for the door. The neighbor's dog barked. His name was Beasley. He was a beagle mix and he spent his days chasing after those mallards but never catching them. Beasley was half blind. A good dog. Long ago, my grandparents had a beagle that looked just like him. This house, this land was built for one with the long dock to run and ducks to chase. I peered out the window, trying to see Beasley as he made his morning patrol up and down the shore.

Maybe it was time for me to get a dog of my own. Emma would love that. So would my other little niece when Vangie finally came back home with her. I moved away from the window as Beasley finally quieted down, called back to his porch.

I heard the next sound first on some preternatural level. A crack. An echo.

My hand froze on the doorknob.

A thump. Again, that snapping sound. Subtle. Innocuous really. Except I knew with cold clarity what it was.

A bad habit. A tell. He cracked his neck as he took another step.

I'd heard that sound dozens of times as he sat with a table between us at the Wayne County Jail. I'd heard it a dozen more as he listened to the testimony in the trial of both of our lives. In the dark stillness, I think I'd heard it as the churning waters of Lake Michigan waited to swallow me whole.

My heart pounded. I pressed my back against the wall next to the door. Sweat broke out on my forehead. I couldn't breathe. I couldn't move.

Light flickered in the crack at the bottom of the door.

He was coming. I had nowhere to run.

He was quiet. It was as if he already knew where the floorboards would creak. I was frozen. Trapped. And he was coming toward the door. If I moved, he would hear. He could anticipate. *He was the ghost and he was made for this.*

I felt along the vanity, my mind racing. I needed a weapon. I thought about the lid on the back of the toilet. It was heavy enough to knock him out. But he would have to be all the way through the door before I could swing. Too late.

He paused. I could sense him on the other side of the door. Waiting. Calculating.

I crawled my fingers down the vanity, opening the third drawer.

Grandpa Leary's leather shaving kit was unzipped. Trembling, I slid my hand inside.

The doorknob turned.

I closed my fingers around the handle of the razor. Praying. Sweating. Choking on my own breath.

The door moved inward. He was coming.

I don't remember exactly how it happened. I would play it in my mind over and over on an endless loop.

Ted took a step. He was a shadow. Dressed in black. One gloved hand slid around the door.

I waited. Then I saw my target as the first morning light came through the window and cast him in shadows.

Two-handed, I slashed the straight razor across his neck.

He kept coming. His eyes beneath a dark knit cap made contact with mine. He smiled. No. It was impossible. I felt the blade go in.

I staggered backward. He came forward.

Then a line of red opened on his neck and his blood began to flow.

He still took one last step, before crumpling to the ground at my feet.

Blood poured out, filling the cracks in the tiles as I found my voice to scream.

Chapter 41

THE LIGHTS STILL FLASHED, blinding me. Suited men charged in and out of my house while I sat sideways in the back of Eric Wray's sedan, my slippered feet rolling the gravel beneath them.

Someone had wrapped a thin blanket around my shoulders. It was still warm, over seventy degrees as the sun came up. But I was shivering.

"Here." Wray appeared, his expression grave, filled with concern. He handed me a cup of coffee from a Styrofoam cup.

"Thanks," I said, managing a smile. My hands were still shaking. I wondered if they'd ever stop.

I gave my statement over an hour ago. Eric had wanted to take me down to the station with him, out of the glare of the patrol car lights and gawking neighbors. But I wanted to get it over with. At a certain point in the near future, I was fairly sure I'd collapse. Not yet, though.

"You sure he didn't hurt you?" Eric asked for at least the tenth time.

"He never laid a finger on me," I said. A few minutes

ago, the crime scene detectives came out bearing a zippered bag with my grandfather's straight razor in it.

"Well, score one for Grandpa Leary," Eric said. He had stood with his jaw on the ground as I recounted that part of the story. "I remember him on Sundays, you know. Crisp blue suit, yellow tie."

"He was a Wolverine fan," I said, sipping the coffee. It was black and bitter, but it felt good going down.

"Clean shaven," Eric said. I narrowed my eyes.

"Not funny. Not yet." Then. "Will I get it back?" I don't know why it was important to me. But at that moment, it was.

He squinted toward the sun. "No, I suppose that wasn't funny at all. But what you did ... you never stop impressing me, Cass. I'll make sure you get your things back. That's a promise."

"Thanks," I said.

"I just wish you could convince your ... friend to go to the hospital."

Killian sat in the back of the ambulance, giving his own statement. He held an ice pack to his head but had refused any other treatment.

I found him on the floor, unconscious, his hands bound with zip ties. Richards had pistol-whipped him. Dried blood still caked the side of his head.

Killian sensed me looking. He caught my eye across the yard. He was stoic. His rage and fear for me subsided some. In those few, desperate moments after I cut him loose, he had held me, shaking in the dark. He was safe. We both were. For now.

"I've never been able to convince him to do anything he didn't want to do," I said to Eric, smiling. "But I'll try one more time."

"We'll be finished here soon," he said. Matty's truck pulled up, kicking gravel.

"Shit," I said. "Did you call them?"

Eric shrugged. "Actually, no. But this is Delphi, Cass. How long did you think it would take before someone else did?"

Matty and Joe tumbled out of the truck. Joe's eyes were wild. Then they settled on me and his shoulders dropped. He doubled over as if he forgot how to breathe. I knew the feeling.

Eric stepped aside. He put a hand on my shoulder. "You may not want to stay here today," he said as Matty and Joe got to me.

Somehow, I managed to get to my feet. Joe grabbed me, pulling me into a bone-crushing bear hug. His body shuddered. He was holding back tears.

"Jesus," he muttered.

"I'm okay," I said. "Promise."

"And I'm getting really tired of getting these kinds of phone calls," he said.

I hugged Matty next.

"Part of my charm, brother," I teased. Joe was my touchstone. Just hearing his voice quieted the noise in my head. He was real. This was home. Everything would somehow be okay.

"My guys will need a few hours to process everything," Eric said. The moment he did, the back door opened and two men came out, rolling a stretcher between them. They brought Ted Richards, Ghost Man, out in a body bag.

Killian rose, his face hard as stone. He stood over the body as they passed him on the way to the second ambulance. Killian said something low under his breath. A vile word in Gaelic. A curse. I said my own. I hoped it took.

Then he walked over to me. Joe and Matty moved, forming a wall in front of me.

I put a hand on Joe's shoulder, gently pushing him aside.

"You sure you're okay?" I said to Killian. "You've probably got a concussion, at the least."

"Got granite for a head," he said, his accent thick. He was smiling, but the pain made his eyes hard.

"Thank God for that," I said. There was more I wanted to say, but not in front of my brothers and Eric Wray.

"I have to go now," Killian said. "There are some things …"

I stepped away from the rest of them and pulled Killian with me.

"Killian …"

"It's all right, a rúnsearc," he said, sending a shiver through me at the word. He hadn't used it in months. It was a term of endearment his grandfather used to use for his grandmother.

"You'll be all right?" he asked.

I let out a breath. "I'll be all right," I answered.

A black Lexus pulled up behind him. The tinted window slowly lowered. Killian's driver was here.

Killian paused, looking from me to my brothers. Some unspoken, male message passed between them. I read it in their postures, their hard stares. If testosterone had a smell, they were all reeking from it.

"Take care of your family, Cass," Killian said.

I dipped my chin. "Always. And you take care of yours. Remember what I said. I think we both know who sent Richards here."

"We don't know that," he said.

"Yes, we do."

"I owe you my life," he said.

"No. We're done owing each other," I said.

"Things may get ... difficult for a while. I don't know where all this is going to lead. It's better if ..."

"It's better if you don't call me. It's better if you go back to your world and I stay in mine. Promise me you'll be careful. Don't underestimate Liam. And don't ... don't underestimate me."

"I'm sorry," he said.

"I know. But I'm not."

A muscle jumped in his jaw. Killian touched my arm. Then there was nothing more to say.

"We'll be in touch," Eric said to Killian, coming closer. "If I call, I expect you to answer."

Killian's charming, lethal smirk came back. "It'll be my pleasure, Detective."

Killian Thorne shook Eric's hand then slid into the back of the Lexus. He gave me a last glance before closing the door. He was hidden behind the dark tint of the window. The sun flashed across them, as Killian's driver made a U-turn and headed away from the lake.

I pulled the ends of the blanket tighter around my shoulders and squinted against the sun.

Chapter 42

ONE WEEK LATER ...

My key card still worked at the parking garage gate. That surprised me. It was one more loose end Liam Thorne had failed to tie. I don't even know why I kept the card. I got a friendly wave from the attendant as I pulled in. He recognized me, but he didn't seem to know from where.

I drove up to the fourth floor of the Thorne Building and found a spot near the elevators. I wondered if my reserved space was still open. I decided not to check. Instead, I sat for a moment, mustering up the courage to do what I came here for.

I killed the engine. A thin red folder sat on the passenger seat beside me. I grabbed it.

My heels clicked across the cement as I made my way to the elevator. While waiting for the car to reach this level, I looked up, giving the security camera an unobstructed view of my face. He would know I was coming from the second I entered the garage anyway.

I took the elevator to the top floor. It felt like a million years since I'd been here. It felt like just yesterday.

The doors opened to the grand, marble-tiled lobby with the shimmering chandelier. Gold letters spelled out *Thorne Law Group* on the massive reception desk.

The girl behind it was new. Pretty. Young. She smiled and tapped her headset as I approached. I wasn't doing this dance. Not for her. Not for the man I came to see. Not for anyone.

"May I help you?" she said cheerily.

"I doubt it," I said. "I already know the way."

I went past the desk, heading down the hallway to the right.

"Ma'am, you can't just ..." But her voice died down. She heard something in that headset that made her stop, no doubt.

The sounds. The smells. The air itself was so familiar. Maroon-plush carpet. Shiny, reflective black-paneled walls. I had to pass by my old office to get to his. I swore I wasn't going to, but I stopped.

The door was open. They hadn't changed the furniture. I had a cherry wood desk with gold handles. Cream-colored leather furniture, and the best view in the building. Floor-to-ceiling windows gave a stunning, unobstructed view of Lake Michigan. The Gold Coast. The top of the world, it seemed.

"Can I help you?" The man sitting at my old desk had a phone to his ear. I recognized him. A year ago, he was one of the new clerks. Ken Girard.

"Congratulations, Ken," I said, smiling. I supposed it was fitting they'd given him my office. He was hungry. Ambitious. Oblivious.

"Cass," Ken said. "I'm sorry ... did we have an appointment?"

"Not today," I said. I stole one last quick look out the window then headed back down the hall.

Liam was waiting for me. He stood in the doorway to his

office. His secretary stood off to the side. By her flushed face, I guessed they might have argued about my presence. Liam likely had appointments back to back today.

"Come in," he said. "I would have appreciated a heads-up though. I only have a few minutes for you."

"That's all you'll need," I said.

He ushered me into his office. His was the second-best view in the office, in my opinion. Liam liked the street view, overlooking Grant Park.

I took a seat in the black leather chair. He moved behind his desk. He opened a drawer and took out a long manila envelope.

"I was planning to mail this, Cass. There was no need for you to come all this way."

He tossed the envelope to the desk in front of me. I didn't touch it.

"We're all really impressed with your work," he said. "Again."

"I'm not here for that," I said. "And I have no intention of staying here a second longer than I need to."

"I understand. You've earned some time off, for sure."

I couldn't believe it. Was he just going to sit there and pretend nothing had happened?

I put the red file on top of the envelope. Liam looked at it, but made no move to open it. I saw a tiny nerve twitch near the corner of his eye. Good. He was starting to catch on, perhaps.

"You sent that monster after me," I said.

He raised a brow. "Are you kidding?"

"What was the order? Were you going to have him kill your own brother too? Or was Richards just supposed to leave him alive so he could watch me die? That's what you wanted, isn't it? Send a message to Killian. Take away the thing he cares about and make sure he knows he's the reason why."

Liam's face changed, dropping all pretense. His eyes were hard and cold. I realized with bone-chilling clarity that Liam Thorne had maybe even more evil in him than Ted Richards did.

"You overplayed your hand," I said. "I want you to know that."

I picked up the red file and opened it. "I wondered why you never bothered to ask me what the FBI had on Kinsell. At first, I thought that's why you really wanted me on the Richards case."

"I wanted you on the case because I knew you were the only person smart enough to win it."

I smiled. "You know? I actually believe that. I suppose I should be flattered. But here's the thing. The case against Kinsell? It really is somewhat of a house of cards. It was hard to see at first. So much of what I got in discovery was redacted."

I pointed to the thick black bars obscuring line after line of text in the section of the report I brought.

"I know the truth, Liam. All of it. Richards was smarter than you gave him credit for. He told me hiring me was his idea, not yours. You didn't see that coming, did you? You never would have brought me into this otherwise. You knew it might put me too close to your truth. But, you had to keep Ted happy. He knew too much about you."

Liam stayed silent. Only the slight glint in his eye betrayed his thoughts.

"Alan Fitzgerald was on to something. If he'd have lived, I wouldn't be sitting here. He never would have been able to understand what he was looking at in that FBI report. I don't even think Ted understood. Not completely."

"Enlighten me," Liam said. He was still trying to play it

cool. He was scared though. A tiny bead of sweat broke out on his upper lip.

"Saul Kinsell's a made man. He's got important contacts. But he's just the tip of the iceberg. He's facing life. Mob bosses all over the country have to be squirming, waiting for how his case shakes out. None of them can risk doing anything now because of what happened to Mark Channing. Too much heat. Too much attention. You know, that's the first thing that got me thinking his death wasn't a paid hit. It never made any sense."

"You were the right lawyer for the job. I don't think Alan Fitzgerald, may he rest in peace, had that broad of an imagination. It's lucky you do," he said.

"He'll flip," I said. "There's no way Saul Kinsell is going down for the rest of his life. That's what you were counting on, isn't it? Kinsell starts talking. He takes down anyone he can to save his own skin. Including your own brother. And if *that* happens, well, that's just a bonus for you. You get what you want."

He ground his teeth.

"You're right," I said. "Fitzgerald suffered from a lack of imagination. But do you want to know what? So did I. At least, at first. I mean, as much as you and Killian have your differences, he's your brother. I know how sacred family is to him. And to you. Ted could have killed him the other night. But he didn't. Because that's not what he was there for. You though ... I get it now."

His nostrils flared. "You're full of shit."

"No," I said. "It took me a while. But now I know you're willing to burn the whole house down around Killian to get rid of him. Then you get to rise from the ashes. Take over the business. Run it the way your Da and Grandda always intended. You gave the feds Saul Kinsell, so he'd flip on

Killian. Only it didn't work out quite how you imagined, did it?"

Liam regarded me with cold contempt.

"I'm curious," I said. "Did you even ask Alan Fitzgerald to bring you in on this case before he died? I wonder what would have happened if you had. You had no idea he'd go after the FBI files. You screwed up, Liam. You should have asked for what was in them."

I picked up the red file and tossed it closer to him. He kept his eyes cold as stone and slowly opened the file. It took him a moment. At first, all he could see were the heavy black redacted lines of text. I decided to make it easy for him.

"There were four main informants. Chip Edgar was a wash. A front, really. He ended up being useful to Laura Wyler, but he had nothing real to offer on the Kinsell case. The others were almost useless. But the gold mine came from the one they identified as Witness X."

His eyes darted over the file. "Cass …"

"It was you," I said. "You're Witness X. You were smart, Liam. Not smart enough. You see, some of the bank transactions you gave them. Some of the players. I recognized the names. And the meetings? Different cities. Hotels. I was with you on those trips for some of them. I kept my own travel records for the firm, Liam. I cross-checked the dates. I found a match. You fed information to the FBI about the Kinsell organization. It was your way of making a problem for your brother without getting your hands too dirty."

He stayed silent, his eyes flicking over me.

"I figured something else out," I said, leaning forward. I rested my hands on his desk. "Last year, on the *Crown of Thorne*, you sent that monster to deal with me. You never wanted me dead because I took a meeting with the FBI. You wanted me dead because you were afraid I'd find out *you* did. Now I have. What do you suppose would happen if the heads of the other families find out you're the rat, Liam? How long do you think you'll last?"

There it was. My heart raced. The cold look in Liam's eyes confirmed the truth. He was a liar. A killer. And he'd been pedaling information to the F.B.I. But I held the keys to making sure he never hurt me again.

"What do you want?" he said, flinching.

"Nothing," I answered. "Not a damn thing. But you need to know this. If you ever come near me again ... if you ever come near my family ... this goes public. I've left instructions with people I trust. Law enforcement, the press. Encrypted files. If anything happens to the people I love or me, it gets decoded. You're exposed. You'll be eaten alive."

His eyes narrowed with rage. "You come after me like that, what do you think happens to my brother? Huh? You can't take me down without taking him down."

I waited for a beat, my heart pounding. Then I slipped the manila envelope out from under the red file.

"I take care of my own family first, Liam. Always. Don't ever forget it."

With that, I ripped the manila envelope in half and tossed it at him. It was my payment for handling the Richards case.

"Are we clear?" I said.

Liam looked straight ahead. He curled his lips back. "We're clear," he said. I knew him well enough to recognize the tremor in his hand. I had him scared. Terrified.

"Keep your money," I said, putting a finger on one half of the torn check. "I never want anything from you again."

I stole a glance at the torn corner of the check and somehow managed to keep my expression neutral as I counted the zeroes. Miranda would send her own hit out on me if she ever found out.

"Cass ..."

"We're done talking," I said. "You're beaten. All you have to do is forget you know me. It's a simple request. Or ... maybe you should ask Ted Richards what happens to people who underestimate me."

I left him fuming as I walked out of his office, the red file still spread out in front of him.

I kept my back straight, my eyes forward as I walked with purpose out of the Thorne Building for the very last time. I got as far as my car door and away from the security cameras before I doubled over and threw up.

Then I stood up, smoothed my hair back, and slid into the driver's seat. My hands were steady as I turned the key.

I got another friendly wave from the oblivious parking attendant as I made my way out of the structure. I waved back, opened my window, and tossed my key card into the street.

It was a gorgeous day. The sun nearly blinded me as I made the turn onto Lakeshore Drive. Ahead of me, the sign for I-94 gleamed. I merged into traffic as my phone rang. It was Joe. I punched the Bluetooth speaker.

"Hey," he said. "I'm at your place. I think you've got a bad spark plug on the pontoon."

I turned toward the on-ramp and picked up speed. "Matty said he put some in the shed."

"Shit," Joe said. "Did he say where?"

"Um ... he did not."

"I swear I'm gonna put a damn lock on that thing. He fucks shit up every time he goes in there. You'd think he could figure out how to put a fishing pole away without tangling the hell out of it. I spent about an hour unfucking those this morning."

I accelerated to seventy-five as my brother bitched in an unbroken stream of obscenities. Matty had just arrived. In the background, I could hear him putting up a fight about the fishing poles. Behind that, even Beasley, the neighbor's beagle, joined in the ruckus. His howl came through clear and sharp.

I had the Chicago skyline, the Willis Tower, rising high in my rearview as I hit the freeway. Joe was still bitching as I rounded the next curve. It made me smile. I opened my window to let the fresh air in and the warm sun blasted my face. Summer was almost here and they were predicting a scorcher out on Finn Lake.

THE END

Up Next for Cass Leary

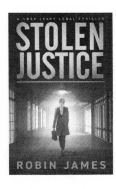

Click to Learn More

Cass takes the case that could bring down the whole town.
Twenty-four years ago, Delphi experienced what will forever be known as "That Awful Summer." During the hottest summer on record a young, popular nursing student went missing. After a two-week search, she was found brutally raped and murdered in the woods. Now, Cass's new paralegal, Tori Stockton enlists the firm's help to prove the wrong man, Tori's very own father, went to jail for it.

Now, that same oppressive heat has returned to Delphi, and Cass will have to take on the town if she wants to clear Tori's father's name. Along the way, she'll discover some secrets are best left buried.

Don't Miss Stolen Justice -Available Now!

Keep reading for details on how to grab an exclusive

ebook copy of *Crown of Thorne*, the bonus prologue to the Cass Leary Legal Thriller Series.

Newsletter Sign Up

Sign up to get notified about Robin James's latest book releases, discounts, and author news. You'll also get *Crown of Thorne* an exclusive FREE ebook bonus prologue to the Cass Leary Legal Thriller Series just for joining. Find out what really happened on Cass Leary's last day in Chicago.

Click to Sign Up

http://www.robinjamesbooks.com/newsletter/

About the Author

Robin James is an attorney and former law professor. She's worked on a wide range of civil, criminal and family law cases in her twenty-year legal career. She also spent over a decade as supervising attorney for a Michigan legal clinic assisting thousands of people who could not otherwise afford access to justice.

Robin now lives on a lake in southern Michigan with her husband, two children, and one lazy dog. Her favorite, pure Michigan writing spot is stretched out on the back of a pontoon watching the faster boats go by.

Sign up for Robin James's Legal Thriller Newsletter to get all the latest updates on her new releases and get a free digital bonus scene from Burden of Truth featuring Cass Leary's last day in Chicago. http://www.robinjamesbooks.com/newsletter/

f

Also by Robin James

Cass Leary Legal Thriller Series

Burden of Truth

Silent Witness

Devil's Bargain

Stolen Justice

Blood Evidence

With more to come…

Mara Brent Legal Thriller Series

Time of Justice